T0267272

Acclaim for

COLOR THEORY

"Compelling magical fare for early teens. Innocent romance . . . and the hint of a battle to come will hook readers . . ."

— KIRKUS REVIEWS

"The sequel I've been waiting all year for did not disappoint! It's simply magical!"

— S.D. GRIMM, author of the Children of the Blood Moon series and *A Dragon by Any Other Name*

"*Vivid* first captured my attention with an original, fascinating premise: a young girl coming of age in a world divided into different colors of magic: Augmentor Red, Shaper Blue, and Mentalist Yellow. But it was Bustamante's brilliant cast of characters—led by the determined Ava Locke and the unforgettable, charming Elm Ridley—as well as her exquisite worldbuilding, snappy dialogue, and fast-moving plot, which sucked me into the story and wouldn't let go. With echoes of *Divergent, Inception,* and *The Story Peddler,* this first installment of The Color Theory series is sure to leave readers begging for more!"

— J.J. FISCHER, author of The Nightingale Trilogy

"This rich fantasy is bursting with romance, mystery, and characters both dark and delightful."

— JESSICA ARNOLD, author of *The Looking Glass* and *The Lingering Grace*

"As rich and colorful as its title suggests. The land of Magus blooms to life from page one, drawing you into an addictive world of irresistible—and forbidden—magic. I simply couldn't put it down. Readers will swoon over this fantastical debut."

— SARA ELLA, award-winning author of the Unblemished trilogy, *Coral,* and *The Wonderland Trials*

"*Vivid* truly lives up to its name! With some of the most vivid imagery and heart-racing tension, Ashley has written a story that kept me turning pages till I had finished the entire thing! This book will take you on an incredible, twisting, driving plot with some of the most unique and clear world-building that will leave you begging for the second installment!"

— VICTORIA LYNN, author of the Chronicles of Elira

"Captivating. Ashley Bustamante expertly draws the reader into the Magus world where Red and Blue magic thrive and Yellow magic is outlawed . . . If that isn't enough, the relationship between Ava and Elm kept me flipping pages for more."

— CANDICE PEDRAZA YAMNITZ, author of *Unbetrothed*

RADIANT

ASHLEY BUSTAMANTE

COLOR THEORY | BOOK TWO

To Mom and Dad—

you have given so much

to help me create these stories.

Thank you.

1

"THEY'RE LIKE LOCUSTS, AREN'T THEY?"

I elbow Blake's side and hold a finger to my lips. There could be other Mentalists working for the Benefactors besides Jace. I'm not willing to take the chance of someone hearing us, even if we are using Elm's invisibility devices. Supposedly we're the only ones who can hear and see each other while we're invisible, but how infallible is this illusion?

Blake is right, though. Compared to last time, there must be at least twice as many Benefactors around Prism's grounds, and they're certainly plaguing us. How many of them are aware of what they're doing?

A chilled breeze breathes down my arms and stirs the dead leaves at our feet. Every move we make could be betrayed by the crunching of those leaves. Thanks to Jace's cowardice, the Benefactors still don't know about the secret entrance to the school through the oak tree—the last thing Jace would want is to reveal his one escape route if things went south. But getting to it unnoticed with so many Benefactors is another story. We weren't prepared to circumvent this many people.

I scan the area, knowing I'm looking out not just for myself, but also for those with me. Besides Blake, our group has four other former Prism students present: Blanca Valencia, Kaito Hayashi, Sarah Fischer, and Jazz Robinson. This visit is especially important to Jazz—we're here to get his little sister. He twitches and fidgets, eyes darting in every direction. I haven't ever seen him this jittery. Bringing him might have been a mistake.

Then again, we all look pretty bad, resembling wide-eyed statues as we strive to remain undetected. Nobody questions the importance of getting Jazz's sister out of Prism, but we all wonder when our luck will run out. When we might trust the wrong person. When somebody won't come home.

No time for wondering about that right now, though. Right now the only thing we need is a diversion. Something to clear the area around the oak.

In the fading light, a squirrel scratches its way up a tree a few yards to my left. Would an erratic woodland creature catch their attention? Maybe not, since the animals have been a bit jumpy lately anyway, but it's worth a shot. I focus on the squirrel, remembering what Elm taught me. I imagine myself flowing into the mind of the squirrel. Merging our wills together . . .

The eyes of my companions turn to me, darting between me and the squirrel and waiting for some kind of direction or clue as to what I'm doing next. But the squirrel continues to make its way up the tree and out onto a limb, its mind still its own. Shoot. I don't have that skill down yet.

CRACK.

The squirrel goes flying—branch and all—right over the heads of a cluster of Benefactors. That wasn't me, was it? I make eye contact with Kaito, whose face relaxes out of his state of concentration from moving the branch. He gives a sheepish smirk and shrugs. Well, I guess there's more than one way to move a squirrel. Nice job, Shaper.

The Benefactors jump, eyes wide and fearful, then rib each other and laugh with relief when they see the squirrel, now grounded and scrambling wildly away. They are human, after all, some of them not much older than we are. It must feel good to have a moment to laugh about something ridiculous.

I motion everyone forward as the Benefactors wave their friends over to share their hilarious squirrel anecdote. One crank of the right branch on the oak tree opens the secret entrance, and I wait, allowing everyone else to slide in before me. I pause as a stunning red butterfly lands on the bark of the tree, hesitantly fluttering its wings.

What are you doing out so late, little butterfly? I wonder as I follow my friends inside. It's as out of place as we are.

Being inside the chamber doesn't placate me at all. The air is cold and musty, and my eyes fixate on the device that held Elm captive for so many years. The unforgiving gurney with yellow stone shackles. I'm glad he isn't here now for the painful reminder. How did he survive this place? Thankfully, one of my fears hasn't been realized, at least for now. Selene hasn't restrained a new prisoner in Elm's place, and if I have any say in the matter, she never will.

"You okay?" Blake asks quietly. As always, he notices everything I'm feeling.

"I'll be better once we get out of here."

"Well, let's get to it, then."

I amplify my voice just enough to make sure everyone can hear. "Jazz, Kaito, and Sarah will go get Brie. Blake and Blanca will come with me to the cafeteria storage." While getting Brie is our main purpose, there are now 37 of us living in the cave—38 once we rescue Brie. It's getting harder to feed everyone. Elm has been working on maximizing his garden space, but of course that takes time.

We huddle around the door that leads into the main corridor. Kaito pulls out a flat, circular piece of brassy metal with a blue stone in the center and a tiny lens just above the stone. He presses the device against the door. We wait. A projection flits to life, showing various blue and red dots, some still, some moving. There are far more of them than I would like. There is also one orange dot.

"Guess you and Elm have been busy," Blanca says to Kaito. "What's all this stuff?"

"It detects people by sensing their magic," Kaito says. "The dot projections represent people within a 30-yard radius." In the hallway on the other side of the door, five dots—most likely Benefactors—keep a close eye on the faculty hallways.

"How do we know where everyone is?" asks Sarah.

Kaito produces a sketch pad and pencil from the bag he wears over his shoulder, and we huddle around him, the dots in the projection moving as we do.

"This weird little orange dot is Ava," he says, giving me a slight grin. "So here's where we are." He holds the paper beneath the projection and sketches out an approximation of the room. He glances at the door and holds up two fingers on either side of it, then scales them down and starts sketching on the paper again. He scribbles out a map of the L-shaped faculty hallways and holds it so that all the dots lie on top of it.

"This should be about where everyone is."

Nobody has to say it—we all know it's going to be impossible to open the door of this room without those Benefactors noticing.

"There has to be a way to do this," Jazz's anxious voice breaks through the heavy silence. "We have to get my sister out of this place."

"We'll get Brie. Don't panic." I speak with confidence, though it's all bluffing. I'm not sure how we can pull this off. But we can't have come this far just to get set back by something as minor as opening a door.

We stare at the dots, as though watching them long enough will make our options clear. Odd, though . . . the room to the left of us currently has no dots inside.

"Does anyone know whose office that is?" I ask.

Kaito's eyes widen. "Oh, actually, I do. That's my mentor's office. Well, former mentor."

"Students move in and out of this area all the time," Blake muses.

"And," Jazz adds, "the Benefactors probably don't know who everyone mentors. So if we can get into that office from here . . ."

"How would we get in there without going through the door?" Sarah wants to know.

Blanca grins and grabs Kaito's pencil. She smashes it down into the sketch of the wall between our room and the office next door.

Kaito sighs. "Please stop breaking my pencils." He pulls a spare from his bag.

"Relax. I'll swipe you another one." Blanca laughs, tossing back her dark ringlets.

I redirect to the task at hand. "Okay, we break through the wall. But how do we do that without alerting every Benefactor in the area?"

"I don't think we can," Sarah says with a frown. "It would just be too loud."

Blanca is noticeably disappointed. The pencil remnants in her hand take the weight of her frustration and are now merely dust.

"Could we cut into it?" asks Jazz. "It would take longer, but wouldn't be as loud as breaking through."

Blake shakes his head. "Getting the tool through the wall to start with would still require a pretty loud hit."

We fall silent once again. We should have come in the daytime. We thought it might be easier to get around in the evening with fewer students wandering about, but it also means unusual noises are a lot more noticeable.

"If we just had one loud moment to get a good hit in . . ." I murmur.

Jazz suddenly perks up. "I have an idea. The last time we were here scoping things out, we noticed a bell signaling the Benefactors' shift change. If we can get a hit on the wall right during the signal, it might go unnoticed."

"When does the shift change?" I ask.

"Seven p.m."

I check my watch. "So we have around 20 minutes."

"Can I be the one to hit the wall? Please?" Blanca begs.

Everyone looks to me, waiting for an affirmation. "It's risky," I say finally, "but it's the only chance we have right now. Blanca, make sure you're ready to go so you can land that hit exactly when the bell goes off."

"Piece of cake!" She grins.

Every ounce of her is Red to the core. "Everyone else, be on alert. Watch those dots on Kaito's map. We need to scramble if they start moving this way."

Kaito closes his eyes for a moment, visualizing. He points to his diagram again. "If I'm remembering correctly, I think there's a rolling bookcase right here. If we make the hole there, we can keep the case in front to cover our tracks."

"I'm still not exactly sure what we're doing once we're in there," Sarah says hesitantly.

"If Kaito pretends he's meeting with his mentor, he can open the door while the rest of us sneak by invisible."

"Won't they recognize him?"

"I doubt every single Benefactor is keeping track of each student that left," Kaito tells her.

"We should disguise you a little," Blanca announces. "Ooo! There's something I've always wanted to do to you. Come here!" She yanks Kaito over forcefully, spits in her hand, and ruffles his mop of dark hair, attempting to spike it in the front.

"Gross," he sputters.

We spend the remaining time before the shift change going over the specifics of our plan and nervously watching the dots to be sure nobody approaches our room. I twist Elm's silver locket around in my hands, grateful for the modifications he made. Now it simply cloaks me, as everyone else's devices do. This mission would be a lot more difficult if I was still running around in that ridiculous yellow dress. Today I'm wearing a much more practical green button-up shirt and black jeans. It still feels odd to wear my favorite color instead of the red that would be expected from an Augmentor. Strange that such a small thing would feel so rebellious.

"Thirty seconds," Sarah says.

Blanca positions herself, and we all brace in case something goes wrong. Beads of sweat shimmer on Jazz's brow.

"It's for Brie," he says to himself over and over. "For Brie." He's definitely not the combative type.

"This is it," says Blake, and Blanca pulls her fist back. "Three, two, on—"

The bell shrieks through the air, making us all jump, except for Blanca, who delivers a punch to the X Kaito drew on the wall. Her fist goes through the drywall as easily as if it were an eggshell. Her aim and force were perfect, making a hole straight through without going too far.

"All yours, Blakey Boo," she says, batting her brown eyes at Blake and stepping aside.

Blake smiles nervously and steadies himself in front of the hole. He concentrates, and we all watch in awe as the hole expands, bits of drywall crumbling and flaking off in the process. Now, the hole is plenty big enough for a person to crawl through.

Kaito was right about the rolling bookcase. Jazz pushes it aside, and one by one, we work our way into the office. We do some quick cleanup and move the bookcase back where it belongs.

"Go-time, Kaito," says Blanca. "I hope you're a good actor."

"Remember," I warn, "we only have 25 minutes of invisibility left. Get Brie and go. If we're cutting it close on time, just leave, even if we're not all back." *Please, let everyone make it back.*

We use our devices, and Kaito approaches the door. He takes a deep breath, then opens it and steps out. We quickly follow. Once in the hallway, he turns back and says loudly, "Thank you, Mr. Miley. I promise I'll submit the makeup work on time." He closes the door and moves down the hallway as we tiptoe behind. So far, so good. The Benefactors look bored.

"Hey," one of the Benefactors says suddenly. We freeze, but Kaito manages to maintain his composure.

He looks at the Benefactor squarely. "Yes?"

To my surprise, the Benefactor smiles. "I just wanted to say hang in there. I struggled, too, but I made it."

Kaito flashes a wide, appreciative smile. "Thanks. I'm working hard!"

As soon as we hit a gap in Benefactors, Kaito becomes invisible. We split up from there, Jazz, Sarah, and Kaito going to get Brie, and Blake, Blanca, and me in charge of food. We each came armed with two large duffle bags, waiting to be stuffed with pilfered goods.

The cafeteria seems eerie now that the lights are off and the people are gone. This used to be a spot students gathered to unwind after classes. A place to laugh and socialize. But everything at Prism has been altered in my eyes. Colored ugly with secrets and deception. Now, it feels more like a haunted house with the potential of a new horror hiding in every shadow. Except anyone that finds us in *this* haunted house could actually do us harm.

We listen to the bouncing echo of our footsteps as we make our way to the back of the room, where large double doors lead to the storage area. The doors screech like crows as we open them, and we collectively wince at the sound. Fortunately the area is empty, dinner preparation having ended hours ago.

"Probably okay to turn invisibility off," Blake says. "We should save it in case we need it to get away."

I don't fully trust my Mentalist abilities enough to recharge my locket on command yet, so I go visible along with everyone else. Now is not the time to be overconfident.

Blanca quickly identifies large sacks of dried essentials—beans, rice, and lentils—stacked against one of the walls. She hefts two of them on her back and one in each of her arms, using a strengthening spell to help with the weight. "These should last us awhile."

We stuff our duffel bags with anything that looks like it could feed a large group without spoiling: pasta, dried fruit, oatmeal, flour. My mouth waters at the sight of a crate full of fresh strawberries, but we need things we can store at length.

Blanca and I are burdened by our bags while Blake uses a spell to float his. I frown, noting Blanca carries a much heavier load than me, with two bags of grain on her back in addition to the duffel bags.

I could carry more. I *should* carry more. "You guys go ahead."

"What's wrong?" Blake asks.

"I want to go back for a couple more things. I can lift more, and we should get as much as we can while we're here."

"We'll all go," Blanca says, taking a step that way, but I quickly stop her.

"No, we risk drawing more attention if we all go. I'll just be a minute."

I return with haste and sling a few more bags on my back. I test the weight. Still doing fine. This is probably enough.

By the time I hear the noise, it's already too late.

Someone moves in front of me, blocking my exit. In the dim light my eyes register a long dark braid and glasses. Dr. Iris? I step to the side to try and dodge around her, but she moves with me. Drat! I never reactivated my invisibility. How could I make such a careless mistake? A sharp pain slashes across my left upper arm, and I gasp. Everything I'm carrying falls to the ground as blood rushes from the wound.

What? Dr. Iris knows the body tearing spell? How can someone who spent her whole life healing others—including me—use a spell that can do so much damage? Dr. Iris, who showed me such kindness on so many occasions, especially when Selene took my magic.

She moves close to me as blood continues gushing from my arm. As I strengthen myself in preparation to fight, she presses her hand into the injury. Hard. I scream, and my spell cuts off as I lose focus.

"I'm sorry," she says. I feel a flash of heat through my arm, and she retreats, the double doors flapping from her rapid exit.

I lay stunned for a moment on the ground. She healed my arm. What just happened? Did she have an immediate change of heart when she hurt me? I shake away my muddled thoughts and quickly load up the supplies again, turn invisible, and move as fast as I can back to our meeting spot.

The alarms are sounding.

2

WHEN I ENTER THE HALLWAY, IT'S
immediately obvious what gave us away: giant sacks of floating
food. We may be invisible, but anything we aren't touching
isn't. Blake may not even realize it.

Blanca must have escaped, because I don't see her, but
Blake is surrounded with Benefactors darting wildly about
to try and find the invisible intruders. A few of the Shaper
Benefactors use their powers to send chains through the air,
ready to wrap around anything in their path. It's only a matter
of time before one of them finds their mark.

"Leave the food!" I scream.

Blake turns and sees me, relief in his eyes, but Benefactors
are running toward us, eyes fierce and feet flying. Blake sends
sacks of food plowing into them, and I force my way past.
Even using a strengthening spell, I can't move easily under the
burden of what I'm carrying. Reluctantly I fling another bag
into an oncoming Benefactor to lighten my load.

Blake looks over his shoulder as we run. "I could probably
carry—"

"Forget it!" I breathe quickly. "We just need to get out."

We retreat back to Kaito's mentor's office. The bookshelf
has already been moved to uncover the hole in the wall, which

I hope means our friends are there. I shove my remaining duffel bags through and hoist myself in after. Blake follows.

Once in the room, my heart stops. Blanca's sacks of food are there, but no Blanca.

"Do you think she got out?" Blake asks.

"I don't know. I don't know!" My frustration spills over. In spite of telling everyone else to go ahead no matter what, it feels impossible to leave her behind. But there's no way of knowing if she's even still in the school.

"We can't let the Benefactors find this spot," Blake reminds me.

I know he's right. Everyone who came knew this was a risk. If our entrance is discovered, we lose our most accessible way into Prism, not to mention the danger we could be in if discovered. We'll lose a lot more people than Blanca. I know she would hate me for that.

"Close it off," I relent.

Blake uses a movement spell to slide the bookcase into its original place, and we scramble back up the tunnel of the tree. Blake is cursing softly, and angry tears sting my eyes.

Our one saving grace is that there are fewer Benefactors in the woods outside the school now since many of them went toward Prism when the alarms sounded. Blake uses a spell to take on one of my bags since he had to abandon his. We then run wildly.

We make it hardly a hundred yards into the forest when I feel warm arms enclose me. In the height of fearful adrenaline, I almost shove them away, but when I catch the familiar scent, I lean into the embrace.

"Thank goodness you're alright," Elm says.

"Keep moving, please!" Blake growls. "Some of us have to worry about our visibility."

Elm grabs my free hand as we hurry on.

"I told you not to come this close to the school," I scold, panting from constant running. "I didn't expect to see you here."

I see the twinkle in his sideways glance. "Apparently you don't know me very well, Miss Ava."

"Have you seen anyone else?" Blake asks him.

"Kaito, Jazz, and his sister passed me."

"And Blanca? Sarah?" I think I already know the answer, but I have to ask anyway.

Elm slows his pace for a split second. "I haven't seen them."

We run in silence the rest of the way.

Blake and I exhale as we let our stash of food fall to the ground. The sound of the bags hitting unforgiving stone echoes through the cave.

"You should have let me take one," Elm chides.

I heave in a few breaths of cool air before responding. "You know it's easier for me."

"Could have used Shaper abilities, though, right?" Blake says. "Oh wait," he holds up a hand, "I forgot. You don't know how yet."

The hand suddenly raises higher and flicks Blake on the nose. "Ow!"

"Whoopsie," Elm says. I glare at him, and his smug look dissolves. "Apologies, Miss Ava."

"Don't apologize to *me*."

He gives a dramatic eye roll. "My apologies, Blake, that you lack the power to resist my control."

Elm is spared from Blake's retort by a relieved shout.

"You made it back!" Nikki rushes toward us, accompanied by Kaito. "I'm so glad you're safe." She hugs me, then glances at Blake, who shrinks a bit under her pretty smile. "Thanks for looking out for her."

Nikki and I had bonded quickly, largely due to the fact that she's the vivacious type who makes friends easily. I'm still trying to take her lead on forming friendships, though I'm not sure I'll ever reach her level.

Kaito scans the space behind Elm, Blake, and me. His face falls as the realization hits. "Blanca and Sarah weren't with you?"

Well, there goes the shred of hope I had that they somehow got back unseen before us. "I really hoped they would be with you." My voice cracks. I shouldn't have left. I should have sent Blake back here and stayed at the oak until I knew everyone had made it.

"I'm going back." Kaito pushes past us, but Blake grabs his arm. Kaito shoves him away and stares at him, challenging. He's two years younger than Blake and not usually hot-headed, so this has us all staring.

"I get how you feel," Blake says, remaining calm. "But we can't just charge right in without a plan. We didn't expect so many Benefactors this time, and there are probably even more after what we just did. We can't lose anyone else."

Kaito tightens his fists. "Who knows what could happen to them while we wait."

"Probably nothing, because those Benefactors are nitwits."

We whirl toward the voice. A smug-faced Blanca and a sheepish-looking Sarah enter the cave.

"What happened?" I ask after we happily greet each other. "We saw you left your food bundles behind but couldn't find you."

Blanca tips her head toward Sarah with a grin. "That's because she had an idea for something even better."

Blanca and Sarah step aside, and I notice for the first time an object on the ground behind them: Prism's copy machine.

We won't have to worry about food anymore.

3

THE ATMOSPHERE IN THE CAVE IS MUCH
lighter with Sarah and Blanca's return, or perhaps it's just that
my own mind is now at ease. As we head deeper into the cave
to find Jazz, we listen as the pair (well, mostly Blanca) recounts
their tale of going back for the copy machine.

"Sarah was waiting in the tree room when I got there. I was
pretty proud of the food I had secured, but thinking of all the
people we needed to feed, it suddenly didn't feel like enough.
The alarms were going off, and it was kind of chaotic."

Sarah nods. "I thought since they already knew we were
here, we might as well make the most out of the visit. It made
more sense to get something we could create more food with
so we wouldn't have to keep putting ourselves in danger."

"So then," Blanca says, "Sarah made a bunch of noise
down one hallway while I busted into the supply room to grab
the copier. She freaked me out, though, getting back to the
room almost five minutes later than I did. I almost had to
book it."

"Navigating the hall with all those Benefactors was a lot
harder than I expected," Sarah admits with a short laugh.

We approach the small group gathered around Brie and
Jazz. It's easy to pick Jazz's sister out of the bunch. She and
Jazz share the exact same shade of dark-brown skin and black

hair. However, whereas Jazz's eyes are gray and thoughtful, Brie's brown eyes are bright and full of mischief.

Jazz's face washes with relief as he sees us nearing. "You made it! I was starting to worry."

"And we're glad you made it here together." I share in his relief and smile at his sister. "Nice to finally meet you, Brie. Your big brother obviously loves you."

"Hey, why isn't she in quarantine yet?" Blanca interrupts before Brie replies.

"I was just getting to that." Jazz's discomfort is obvious, and I wonder if he's concerned about how his sister will respond.

When someone new comes to the cave, we take them to one of the caverns. There, they remain under round-the-clock surveillance for 72 hours to make sure the effects of the Benefactor's mind control have worn completely off. We can't risk bringing someone here only to have them turn on us.

"We do it to everyone," Jazz tells Brie. "It's for the good of—"

"I get it," Brie stops him, rolling her eyes. "It's no big deal. Let's just get this isolation stuff over with."

She and Jazz are definitely different from each other, I think, bemused.

The isolation chamber is a pit about fifteen feet deep into the floor of the cave. It's not meant to be a prison, so we've done what we could to make it more tolerable. Furniture, courtesy of Elm, books for entertainment, and of course, one of Elm's light spheres. Already waiting is Garren, who will be taking first watch. Garren is only a first-year student, but he's massive. His size combined with his Augmentor capabilities make him a natural choice for guard work, although his mellow personality makes me think he'd rather make friends than be a watchdog.

He brushes his mop of blond hair out of his eyes, then extends a mighty hand to Brie as we approach. "I'm Garren. I'll be looking after you for now."

"Cool. Thanks, Garren."

Jazz looks first at Brie, then down into the pit. "Does she really have to go in there?"

"You know she does. It's only three days. She'll be safe, I promise. And it's not like you won't be able to see her. You can come and talk to her as often as you want."

"Can't I just go with her?"

"No, because if I'm corrupted, I might hurt you." Brie rolls her eyes. "What are you thinking? It's all right."

We unroll the rope ladder that's secured at the top of the pit and throw it down. If I'm being honest, it does feel wrong putting people there, but fortunately everyone understands the reasons for it. Nobody wants to put our little pack in jeopardy.

"See you in three days!" Brie gives a jaunty salute and climbs down the ladder, the rope swinging with her weight. She immediately checks out her new surroundings and sorts through the books, examining the covers with curious interest. I know she's going to be fine.

"What a day," I sigh, picking up a watering can to help Elm with his garden. After all the fuss, all I want now is to relax, but my mind can't stop spinning. "So we'll need to find a place for Brie. I guess that won't be hard because she'll want to be with Jazz. But we'll need you to make another bed for her. I hope that's okay. I feel bad that you're the only one who can—"

Elm clasps his hands over mine and gently tilts the watering can up so I won't drown the carrots. "Breathe."

I inhale. Exhale. Then I turn around to face him.

He smiles and runs his fingertips up my shoulders and neck until he holds my face in his hands. "I am so glad you made it back safely, Miss Ava."

"Me too." My cheeks warm against his touch, and I lean into his hands, inhaling his familiar cedarwood and orange-blossom scent. A heaviness descends on my mood. Some of us almost didn't make it back today. And I still haven't mentioned my odd encounter with Dr. Iris.

I stand on my tiptoes and kiss him. He seems surprised at first, but quickly reciprocates. A sudden sense of urgency sets in—how much time do any of us really have? What if I didn't make it back? What if something happened to Elm while he came to look for me? We were safe today, but what happens tomorrow?

I pull away and stare into Elm's eyes, a question breaking free from my lips before I can stop it. "Do you love me?"

He furrows his brow. "What is this about all of a sudden?"

"Do you?"

"I would have thought the answer to that was obvious . . ."

"I just need to hear it."

He opens his mouth but then stops himself. He's choosing his next words carefully. "I think perhaps . . . now isn't the best time for this. When emotions are so high."

I gaze at him, perplexed. "Did . . . did I do something wrong?"

"Oh, no." He smiles warmly. "You do everything exceptionally well, Miss Ava."

"Then why are you . . . rejecting me?" I blurt, suddenly embarrassed.

He shakes his head. "Not rejecting. I simply think this

specific moment is likely not the best time for . . . well, it's complicated, I suppose."

I set the watering can down, not looking him in the eye. "Oh. Well, goodnight, then." I hurry away from the garden, a jumble of emotions. Mortified. Hurt. A little angry. Back in the chamber I share with Nikki, I'm grateful she hasn't yet returned for the evening. I inhale the cool, damp cavern air, but it doesn't clear my mind the way it usually does. The stony cave walls seem especially frigid and the *drip, drip, drip* of water in one corner of the room grates against my ears like the buzz of an insect.

Why did he have to put me off like that? How hard is it to just say, "I love you"? I know he does. The things he's risked for me . . . who does that if they don't care about someone?

So then why do I need him to say it? Why are the actual words so important?

They're not, are they?

Demanding that he say it, when he's demonstrated it so fully must have been . . . insulting. And besides, I haven't said it to him yet either. So what right do I have to be mad?

Stupid Ava! The anger abates and shame pummels me full force. How could I not even consider how Elm might feel? Flustered, I hide my face in my pillow. I hear Nikki come inside a moment later, and I pretend I'm already asleep.

4

THE AIR IS DELICIOUS. I NEVER KNEW
anything could feel so wonderful. The first time Elm brought
me to this clearing with the horses felt like my first taste of
freedom, but somehow this is a thousand times sweeter. The
sun cascades over my skin, warming every part of me. The
sharp scent of pine trees invites me to take another breath.
This is different from lifeless cavern walls. This is refreshing.
Renewing.

I know even while I'm invisible it's dangerous to be out here
in the open, but I had to get away. I spent all night stewing in
my thoughts and wishing I had played things out differently.
What was I thinking trying to force a verbal confession out
of him after a dangerous mission in which he was obviously
concerned about me?

Practicing illusions is a good diversion. I'm still shaky in my
Yellow magic use, and it's harder to practice in the cave with
everyone else around. I feel self-conscious and trapped there,
and I'm always worried about something going wrong. I know
I should feel more concerned about the eyes that might find
me here, but I'm not.

Another one of those stunning crimson butterflies drifts
lazily overhead, and I watch it disappear on the breeze before
returning to my task. My Mentalist work is still sloppy, and I

can only do the basics, but I'm improving little by little. I focus on the grass in front of me, staring hard and imagining the vision: a perfect white daisy.

Slowly, a shape forms in the green blades, soft petals growing steadily whiter and blooming into floral perfection. I can't suppress the feeling of pride as I inspect my creation. It's too bad nobody else is here to witness it. I'm only recently learning to create illusions that others can see, and the novelty hasn't worn off.

"I had a feeling I would find you here."

I jump, and then mutter as I turn to find Elm standing right beside me. "You're way too good at sneaking up on people."

"And you're far too skilled at sneaking out." He nudges me lightly, wearing a slight frown.

"Sorry," I turn from him, rubbing my arm. "I needed some air."

"A fair enough desire," he agrees. "But I really wish you would let me accompany you. Nobody is safe out here alone."

He doesn't seem mad or uncomfortable. I, on the other hand, can't even look him in the eye.

"Practicing?" He gestures toward the daisy.

I nod. Are we not going to talk about this? Maybe I prefer it that way.

"Hey," he says, gently tipping my chin and enticing me to look at him. He gives a wry smile. "I could possibly control your thoughts if I wanted to, Miss Ava, but I certainly can't read them."

I avoid his eyes. "It's just . . . last night. I shouldn't have pressured you. I'm sorry."

He pulls me close. "So am I. It wasn't my intention to hurt you."

"Mine either." Some stupid part of me still hopes that now that he isn't surprised, he'll say the words I want him to say.

"Well, let's pretend it never happened," he says,

simultaneously dashing my hopes and bringing relief. "Now, why don't you show me another illusion? Something moving, perhaps?"

If he's not worried about it, I'll try not to worry either. I know he's attempting to take my mind off it.

"Okay," I say. "Watch this."

I turn toward the forest and concentrate on the image I want to project, outlining the details in my mind. Elm waits patiently, observing the direction I'm facing. Finally, a slight movement stirs in the forest, and a creature emerges. Bloated and disproportionate, it floats eerily out of the cover of the trees. It has three legs that stretch too long and one that is far too short. Its color is a strange brownish mauve.

Elm raises his eyebrows at the deformed creature. "What is *that*?"

A flustered heat rises to my cheeks. Ducking my head slightly, I mumble, "It was supposed to be a horse."

His mouth twitches. "Oh . . . it's . . . it's a very good effort." His voice strains as he attempts to keep his composure.

"Oh, hush." I grimace as the creature's head flops back and forth lazily. It looks boneless and unsettling.

"What?" Elm grins. "I didn't say anything bad."

Just then a beautiful white stallion bursts out of the trees. It rears up on its hind legs, whinnying loudly. It gallops with majesty around my sad imitation, tossing a perfect, glossy mane as it goes.

"Thanks for rubbing it in." I glower at him and his horse.

"Don't fret; I know you'll get better with time. You simply need more practice."

I poke him lightly in the side. "And what about you? How are you doing with *your* newfound abilities?"

The expression on his face tells me I've caught him off guard. He stares pointedly at my abomination of a horse.

"Perhaps we should get rid of that thing. It might frighten someone."

"You'll never get the hang of it if you don't try, you know." I persist. He isn't likely to budge. For whatever reason, he hasn't embraced his dual magic in the way that I have. For me, it has been exciting to have the potential to expand my skills and learn something new. But he resists the change.

"I seem to have managed just fine until now."

"But you could get even better and have more control over it. Blake is a natural. I'm sure he'd help you learn if we asked."

"I'm not like him," Elm states.

Now I think I'm starting to understand. Elm doesn't want to be thought of as a Shaper because he doesn't want to be compared to Blake. It seems so childish, and yet in a twisted way it makes sense. The two of them haven't exactly bonded.

I reach for a lone flower in the grass, but the petals all puff away when I pick it. It's getting too cold for flowers. "Well then," I say, brushing a few stray white petals from my fingers, "if you won't be taught, maybe you'd be more comfortable teaching *me*?"

"I'm at your disposal. Except for the one subject you no doubt are about to inquire after."

I hesitate, then toss the flower stem away. I've been caught. "Dream hopping could be useful. You did it all the time." This isn't the first time we've had this discussion. And it never ends well for me.

"But I was already strong in my Mentalist abilities. Therein lies the difference. It's not a beginner's sport."

We both still at the crack of a branch. A horse, real this time, grazes a few paces off. We breathe again.

"Come along," Elm says, glancing around. "We really shouldn't stay here any longer."

It's immediately evident something in the cave changed while we were away. The normal hustle and bustle of everyday life has been replaced with anxious chatter. Elm and I share a worried glance and pick up our pace.

"You don't think it could be Brie, do you?" I can only imagine how Jazz would feel if Brie's quarantine didn't go well.

"I suspect not, but we're about to find out."

We move toward the voices, and I notice the tension in Elm's movements. He walks just ahead of me, his stance protective.

As we reach the main chamber of the cave, which is packed with tense bodies, I hear a girlish voice call out, "Would you all relax? I just need to see Elm. I'm not gonna hurt anyone." The shrill voice echoes through the chambers and sends a chill through me.

Someone here to see Elm? Friend or enemy? I can't risk it being the latter. I'll never let him suffer the way he did at the hands of the Benefactors again. I break away from Elm and hurry forward.

"Miss Ava!" His voice is sharp, and he tries to catch me, but it's easier for me to move through the crowd than it is for him.

I soon identify the source of the stranger's voice, a lanky young woman with porcelain skin and canary-yellow hair that falls in waves just past her chin. Her hair is slightly frizzy from being dyed a few too many times. She wears a yellow outfit with a tutu-style skirt and stands elevated above everyone else on a small rock shelf of the cave. All that yellow . . . where did she come from?

Elm pushes through to the front, looking frazzled. But the second his eyes land on the girl, a light goes on in them.

"Sammy!" he cries in delight.

Sammy?

"Elm!" The visitor's face glows with a wide smile, and she jumps down from her perch and flings herself into Elm's arms.

A raging heat explodes through me without warning. I grab the girl's arm and pull her sharply away. She looks at me with defiance and commandeers Elm's hand, locking her fingers tightly with his.

"Who are you?" I demand. I want to break her hand.

"It's alright, Miss Ava," Elm says, still smiling. He then looks around the room and raises his voice to address the worried faces of our group. "This is Sammy—Samantha, rather. She is a dear friend from my childhood. She's perfectly safe."

The doubt in the air is thick, and Elm's declaration doesn't make me feel any better. In this world—where anyone could be in with the Benefactors—a childhood friend is no guarantee of safety. Not even another Mentalist holds the promise of being on our side—just look at Jace. Aside from that, the possessive way Samantha holds Elm's hand has me reeling. She seems to just be really noticing me for the first time. She looks me over and narrows her eyes.

"Who is she?" she whispers loudly to Elm, as though I'm not there.

"Sammy, this is Miss Ava. She is exquisitely important to me."

I can tell by the twitch of her face that Samantha doesn't like his answer one bit, and my jealousy mellows. She may be an old friend, but I'm "exquisitely important" to him now. I have no reason to feel threatened . . . right?

I hold out my hand to her in an effort to start off on good terms. "Nice to meet you, Sammy," I say, in the most cordial way I can manage while she is still holding a possessive grip on Elm.

She looks down her nose at me and drops Elm's hand. "It's *Samantha* to you," she informs me and stomps away. Confused onlookers part for her, having no desire to be in her warpath. So much for extending the hand of camaraderie.

Elm gives me a flabbergasted look, then hurries after her. "Sammy, wait!"

I move to follow, but someone grabs my arm gently. Nikki. "Better to let them sort this out."

"But . . . but how do we know she's not dangerous?" I protest. Dangerous to all of us. Especially to Elm.

"Elm's a big boy," she says. "Let him handle himself."

"But—"

She places a calming hand on my shoulder. "I know this jealousy thing is new territory to you, but trust me. You're not doing yourself or Elm any favors if you butt in right now."

I close my mouth, stewing. Leave it to Nikki to see right through me.

Curious murmurs in speculation about the newcomer spring up everywhere. I don't know where she and Elm have gone, and I don't like it. Any of it.

It's nearly evening when I finally see Elm again. Thankfully, Samantha is not with him.

"Where have you been all day?" I'm unsuccessful at keeping the slight bite out of my voice.

"Catching up with Sammy. Figuring things out."

Sammy. The obvious endearment needles at me, and I chide myself for it. "Where is she now?"

"I finally convinced her that if she wanted to stay here and be trusted, she needed to go through the quarantine, just like everyone else."

"You're keeping her there with Brie?" Until now, we only brought in one person at a time so that everything could be managed carefully and safely. This newcomer is all kinds of trouble.

"Do you have another suggestion? I'm certain we have nothing to worry about," he assures me.

I don't know how he can be so sure, but telling him that would be saying I don't trust his judgment. "So . . . where did she come from? How did she get here?" I want to add *what's your relationship with her*? But I don't.

"We were great friends when we were children. Best friends, I would say. She says she has been trying to get through the barrier to find me for years. She's not sure how, but she was able to break through recently, perhaps because we weakened the Benefactors' forces."

"But I thought the world outside of the barrier was toxic."

"You really think it beneath the Benefactors to lie about that? Sammy has no reason to tell tales."

Well, he has a point there. My mind whirls at the possibility of a whole world outside that could be openly explored. I'm not about to trust her this easily, even if the Benefactors were lying about the world outside. Too much about Samantha remains unexplained. "How did she find you? We've stayed hidden for months, and she just pops in like it's nothing?"

"Oh, Sammy's very gifted," Elm says airily. "She can see through just about any illusion. She noticed the sinkhole as she was traveling through the forest and suspected I might be at the heart of it. There aren't many Mentalists within the barrier, after all."

"How do you know she's not involved with the Benefactors?" I press stubbornly.

Elm bursts out laughing. I'm not sure why the question is so funny.

"Believe me, Miss Ava," he grins, "few people hate the Benefactors more than Sammy. And in terms of the influence of the mind, you have a lot less to worry about if it's a Mentalist. You saw what they had to do to me to keep me controlled."

"And you don't think things could have changed in all these years?"

He studies me. "Why are you being so difficult about this?" The note of exasperation in his voice is clear.

"I'm just trying to keep us all safe. You're being careless."

"You're being jealous."

I feel the instant heat in my face. "I'm not . . . that's not what this is." That's totally what this is—at least, partially.

"You have nothing to be jealous of," Elm says gently. "Sammy is a dear friend. She does have feelings for me . . . she has for years. But I don't reciprocate. She knows this."

Somehow his honesty doesn't make me feel any better. "We have a lot at stake here. I think it's fair that we treat her with the same suspicions as any newcomer."

"Which is precisely why she'll be doing the quarantine." He takes my hand. "Please, Miss Ava, trust me."

"Okay," I sigh, "but I'll feel better after the quarantine is over." Part of me worries I won't feel better about Samantha being here until she's gone.

"And this is really the only option? Using this?" Samantha is disdainful as she points to our makeshift bathroom. We set up a curtain for privacy over a rushing cavern stream. Not exactly luxurious, but better than other alternatives.

Nikki shoots her a glare. "Got another suggestion, Goldy? We're all ears. This is no resort."

Samantha looks for a moment like she might say something more, but she doesn't. I'm glad I decided to have Nikki help me show Samantha and Brie around—Samantha isn't as eager to give her lip as she is with me, and Nikki is a lot less likely to take it.

We move through the bathroom chamber into a large, cavernous room with a particularly high ceiling.

"Welcome to the kitchen. We only cook in here, otherwise we'll be smoked out." I indicate the fire pit in the center of the room, surrounded by cookware. "We all take turns with the cooking. We'll add you two to the schedule, which is posted in this room every week."

At Samantha's expression, Nikki gives her a look that says, "I dare you to complain." Samantha holds her tongue.

"I like to cook!" Brie declares. "That will be fun."

"A few rules we have to cover," I say as we enter the great chamber once more. "Firstly, travel in pairs through the cave as much as you can. I think we've made it pretty safe, but it's still a cave. Plus it's better not to be alone just in case the Benefactors catch on. Second, don't ever leave unless you have a good reason and have spoken to Elm and me about it." Elm and I are the unspoken leaders of our remnant, likely because we were the ones who set this whole rebellion in motion.

Samantha lifts a haughty brow. "Why do I need your permission?"

I take a deep breath, trying to be the bigger person instead of losing my temper. "Samantha, look. It seems like you're used to doing things your own way, but you can't live like that here. The only way we stay safe and undiscovered is if each person follows the rules and is careful. We can't have everyone coming and going as they please and risk a Benefactor tracking us down."

"If I have to leave, I'll tell Elm. Not you."

"Fine. Don't talk to me if you don't want to, but if you act careless and put us at risk, you'll answer to everyone."

She shrugs. "Whatever." She takes an impatient step. "Are we done here?"

"I guess we are." I resist the urge to make certain she understands. She is going to be a constant challenge.

"Can I go find Jazz, now?" Brie bounces on her heels.

Nikki waves. "Yes, go. He's waiting for you."

Brie will settle in easily. She and Jazz were popular at Prism, many in the group knew her already. Samantha is another story. I'm not the only one who is suspicious of her, and she doesn't do much to help with her attitude. It's not going to improve if she keeps herself secluded from everyone. Well, everyone except Elm.

"So, do you think she's okay?" Nikki asks as we make our way to the gardens to look for fresh food to duplicate.

I shake my head. "I don't know. Elm seems to think so. I don't really trust her, but I do trust Elm."

"He seems to put up with a lot from her."

"Well . . ."—I try to be kind—"they were friends when they were kids, so . . ."

Nikki seems a bit uncomfortable, like she has more to say. I eye her curiously. "Me and some of the others wondered if you could talk to her," she finally says. "You know, about being here. She's rude to everyone. And it's not like anybody invited her. She has to treat people better if she wants to stay."

"I agree." But I wonder how Elm might react if I suggest such an ultimatum. More than that, would she expose us all if we force her to leave? I hate the idea of having to hold her as a prisoner. That's not who I want us to be. Then again, I hope taking captives is not the cost of our safety.

As we approach the garden area, Nikki gasps and comes

to a halt. I crane around her to see why, braced for any needed defense.

The gardens are destroyed. Plants uprooted. Soil overturned. Leaves scorched. Vegetables smashed. Even the gardening tools are bent and broken. Not an inch of it appears salvageable.

Neither of us can speak as we process the scene before us.

Nikki finds her voice first, and it's rigid with anger. "Why would someone do this?"

"I-I don't know." I go into leadership mode. "Round everyone into the main chamber. I'll find Elm."

Nikki gives a sharp nod. "Got it."

My heart pangs as I think of Elm and all the time he spent carefully tending to and nurturing those plants. Destroyed. Just like that. It's going to devastate him. It doesn't make any sense. Why would anybody here want to go without fresh food?

I find Elm tinkering with one of his light spheres. Samantha is there, watching his every move in awe. Just as she always does.

Elm looks up and, upon seeing my face, rises to his feet. "Miss Ava? What's the matter?"

"Your garden . . ." I try to find the words, but instead I just hold up a decimated carrot.

His eyes flicker and his jaw tenses. "How bad is it?"

No sense in trying to downplay it. "It's gone. All of it. I'm so sorry."

His face pales, and I reach out to touch him, but Samantha comes between us.

"Oh, Elm!" she simpers. "That's awful!"

I quash my irritation. "Nikki is gathering everyone to the main chamber. We need to go over there."

"Yes, Miss Ava," Elm says grimly. "Let's go."

The buzz of confusion and speculation infiltrates our ears when we enter the room, but the voices quiet down when they see us. Several people eye Samantha with dislike and give Elm and me pointed looks as if to say, *What are you going to do about her?* I wish I knew.

With every face turned to me, I again raise up the mangled carrot for display. "Today, when Nikki and I went to pick food, we found the entire garden destroyed. There's nothing salvageable."

The room erupts. Surprised eyes and outraged gasps. Exclamations and swearing.

"Who did it?" someone demands.

"We don't know," I reply. "But we plan to find out. It has to be someone in this room, and, whoever you are, this act hurts all of us. Including you."

An Augmentor speaks up. "Do you think it's a coincidence that something like this happens right after we let in two newcomers?"

Jazz steps in front of Brie protectively, his normally kind eyes challenging.

Blanca touches his arm. "Relax, Jazz. Nobody thinks *Brie* did it." She gives Samantha a direct glare, and several voices murmur in assent.

"You think *I* did this?" Samantha's voice is nearly a screech. "That's ridiculous! Why would I ever do that to Elm?"

"Sammy has been with me most of the time since her arrival, apart from the quarantine," Elm speaks for the first time. "She didn't do this."

"Exactly what you would expect a Yellow to say."

Gasps ring out at the statement, but there are mumbles of agreement.

"Who said that?" I demand.

Elm places a hand on my shoulder. "It's alright, Miss Ava. It's nothing I haven't heard before."

I turn toward him. "That doesn't make it any better." My voice is shaking. "After everything you did to help—"

"We need to figure out food," Blake cuts in, most likely to defuse the tension. "The longer we wait, the worse the problem."

I don't want to let the prejudicial accusation go, but he's right about the urgency of the circumstance. I have to keep a level head if I want everyone to continue trusting me. I take a calming breath and address everyone again. "We have the copier, so on the plus side, we don't need much. But we do need something."

"Violet City will probably be easier to get food from than Prism," Kaito observes.

He's probably right. It's a longer trip to the former, but it's much easier to sneak around in a bustling city than in an enclosed school, and after last time, I'm not eager to go back to Prism. The main issue is we would have to travel on foot since the hover carts are all being monitored. But our options for getting there are limited.

"I need a small team of Augmentors, then," I think aloud. "Since we'll be traveling on foot, it's better if we have people with speed and stamina."

"I'm in," Blanca says immediately.

"Thank you. And of course I'll be going. Maybe four more?"

In the heavy moments of silence that follow, I fear we won't be able to get any more help. But eventually four Augmentors raise their hands.

"Great," I announce, relieved. "We'll leave first thing tomorrow—after we do some planning. For now, everyone, please be on alert, and if you notice anything that seems odd, please tell me or Elm." I shoot a glance at his impassive face.

Everyone disperses, and I can't pretend I don't notice the dubious looks people give Elm and Samantha as they pass. The group dwindles down to a small gathering of my friends. I release the tension in my shoulders, thankful to get out of leadership mode.

Elm comes to my side. "I'll be joining you tomorrow as well."

More than anything I want him to come with me, but we also need someone trustworthy here to keep an eye on things. And we don't know who to trust. I look at him gratefully, but say, "Someone needs to hold down the fort."

"But you do need someone to go and charge the invisibility devices," Blake interrupts. "No offense, Ava, but I wouldn't trust your abilities for that yet. I mean . . . you remember last time."

I cringe at the memory of the broken device that my power surge rendered useless. Elm watches me. He and I both know it's true. We can't leave something so important in my unpracticed hands. With so many devices needing to be charged several times, it could be disastrous.

"Send Samantha," Nikki says suddenly.

"What?" Samantha and I blurt simultaneously.

But it dawns on me. Even as I balk at the idea of traveling with her, it makes the most sense. It allows me to keep an eye on her and leave Elm without distractions to observe things at the cave. I can't let my personal feelings get in the way of the most logical conclusion.

"Good idea," I begrudgingly admit. "Samantha, you'll come with us to charge the devices."

She glowers at me, then clings to Elm's arm and looks at him pleadingly.

"Please do as Miss Ava asks, Sammy," Elm tells her. "This is the best way for everyone."

5

ELM'S ARTIFICIAL LIGHT SPHERES
awaken me the next morning. He has their brightness timed
to mimic daylight. Thank goodness for that, as the time spent
in this cave would be all the more maddening without that
variation. I get ready quickly and prepare to meet the team
we assembled to go to Violet City. My stomach rumbles, but
I can't do anything about that yet. We could have been more
judicious with the food we pilfered from Prism, but none of us
expected the garden to be ripped out from under us.

"Want me to see you off?" Nikki mumbles, rubbing her
eyes and sitting up in her bed.

I shake my head, grabbing a water pouch from my nightstand
and stuffing it into my satchel. "Go back to sleep. But you'll
help Elm keep an eye on things while we're gone, right?"

"Of course. Whoever destroyed that garden is going
to answer to me." She pulls the covers back up and nestles
in. She's never been a morning person. But I know I can
depend on her.

I stuff a few more items into my bag and say goodbye to
Nikki, though I think she's already fallen back asleep. Now I
just need to stop by to see Elm and get the invisibility devices.
Besides ours, which the two of us always wear, he made six
more to use for outings like this. I'm grateful he was able to

repair the one I busted when I tried to charge it before—we'll need all of them today for five Augmentors plus Samantha.

Before I reach Elm's room, he is already standing in front of it, holding twinkling pieces of something in his hands.

"Miss Ava," he says gravely, "something is terribly amiss."

I recognized the crushed object he holds as an invisibility device. Or, what's left of it.

I glance up at him. "How many?" I fear I already know the answer.

"As far as I can tell from these fragments, it appears to be all of them."

First the garden. Now this. Someone is definitely trying to sabotage us. And it has to be someone on the inside.

"When could it have happened?" Panic pushes its way into my chest. Losing our invisibility will set us back on any sort of venture outside of the cave.

"I'm not sure. I haven't checked them since they were last used at Prism, so it could have been any time between then and now."

I take a deep breath. "It just means I have to go by myself, then," I say.

"Out of the question."

"We need food," I tell him. "We don't have a choice."

He looks at me steadily "Then I have to come with you, Miss Ava."

I glare at him. "We've been over this. One of us needs to be here. Now, especially." There's no way both of us are leaving with a traitor on the inside.

Blanca suddenly appears beside me in a too-tight shirt and olive-green tactical pants.

"Are we ready to get this show on the road?" She notices our expressions, and her enthusiasm fades. "What's wrong?"

"Someone broke the invisibility devices." I hold one out to show her.

Her bright eyes darken. "What is going on?"

I wish I had an answer.

"I was just informing Miss Ava that she isn't going into Violet City by herself," Elm comments. "All of us agreed that nobody should be traveling alone."

Still looking at the pieces, Blanca's face reddens slightly. She reaches into her pocket and slowly produces an invisibility device.

"How did you get that?" Elm asks in surprise, taking it and immediately beginning to charge it.

"I accidentally kept it from you last time," Blanca confesses. "After everything else that happened, I was too lazy and never got it back to you, and by morning I'd forgotten about it. In fact, I came here to have you get it ready for me."

I breathe a sigh of relief. "Well, in this case, thank goodness for laziness. But that still leaves us one short, since we have to hide Samantha too."

"I forgot she was coming," Blanca groans. "Can't we just take Elm?"

Elm looks at her briefly. "That would be my preference. But regrettably that doesn't seem to be in the cards." He pulls a playing card out of thin air, and it bursts into flames. His expression is ill-tempered as he flicks away remnants of ash with his cane. But there's no way we can leave Samantha here without Elm or me to keep an eye on things. Elm knows that.

"With everything that's been going on, we have to have someone here we know is completely trustworthy," I reiterate.

"I guess you're right," Blanca concedes as Elm checks the device in his hands.

"Perhaps we should only send you and Sammy. At least this time," Elm says to me.

My mind reels at the thought. I can't spend a whole day with her and no one else to help keep my sanity. Besides, if she really is untrustworthy, having another person around would be best. There has to be another way to do this.

I turn to him. "Elm. Nobody really knows who Sammy is, right?"

"I told you, Miss Ava, we can trust her," Elm says with a sigh. "*I* know who she is."

I give my head a shake. "No, no. I mean the Benefactors. She's not on their *wanted* list like you. Does she even need to be invisible?"

He considers this for a moment. "I guess she wouldn't be on their radar," he says thoughtfully. "We'd have to alter her clothes, of course. And her hair. The yellow would be a dead giveaway. But . . . I think it would be safe."

"It's settled, then," I proclaim. "Once we get Samantha entirely ready, we'll head out. Where is she?"

"Off pouting somewhere, I suspect," Elm replies casually. "I had to have a frank conversation with her about relationships and boundaries. She knows she is to be civil to you and that my friendship with her will be damaged if she is not."

This gives me a swell of satisfaction. Blanca just looks at us.

"And," Elm adds, "Miss Ava, if you would attempt to be kind to her as well, that would mean a lot to me. She is my friend, after all."

"Can *I* still be a jerk to her?" Blanca grumbles. Elm merely raises his eyebrows at her.

"For you, Elm, I'll do my best." I give him a quick hug, and we head off to find Samantha, while Elm continues to assess the damage to the devices.

We find her sitting by one of the cave pools, swirling the water with her staff and definitely brooding. I try not to feel too elated and speak cautiously. "Samantha?"

She turns her blue eyes up to me with an icy glare. "What do you want?" This person really hates me.

"We've had a slight bump in the road. Someone has destroyed all but one of the invisibility devices."

She jumps to her feet. "Why is someone doing these awful things to Elm?" Her petulant anger surprises me. "Can't you figure out what's wrong?" she demands.

"This isn't Ava's fault," Blanca snaps. "I'm hungry, and I'm ready for us to get moving. So shut up and listen."

Samantha looks like Blanca slapped her, but at least it quiets her.

"We need the invisibility device for Blanca. But we think you'll be fine without one. You haven't been to Magus for years, and you weren't a specific target. Nobody will pay attention to you if we change your clothes and hair."

She stares at me. "But I like my clothes and hair!"

"You'll survive for a day," Blanca retorts.

I play the one card I know will persuade her. "Elm thought this was the best idea. Remember this is for him too."

Her defiance disappears quickly at the mention of Elm's name. "Fine. Let's get it over with."

In order to fix up Samantha, we need to see Gemma—a slightly plump third-year Shaper with a flair for fashion. When we broke free from Prism, many students asked for her help in changing their uniforms into clothing more suited to their individual tastes. Since we've had the copier, we've been able to duplicate certain organic fabrics, and she often spends her time designing new creations.

One room of the cave is designated specifically for creative pursuits and practice, so long as they're done safely. Gemma can almost always be found there, and today is no exception.

"Hey, gals!" She flashes a brightly colored smile as we enter. I have never seen Gemma without a vibrant shade of lipstick. Today's is electric blue, which currently matches the tips of her spiked platinum hair.

"Hi, Gemma," I greet her. "We need your help."

Gemma's eyes scan over Samantha as we explain the situation.

"So you need something plain," she muses. "Too bad. I would have liked to dress you up. But, girl-next-door it is! Come sit in my magic chair." Gemma gestures toward a bold, rainbow-shaded armchair, where students sit while she's working on them. Samantha sinks down into the plush cushion, looking tense and skeptical.

"Is this going to hurt?" she asks. There is none of the biting sass in her tone. She sounds genuinely worried, and I almost feel sorry for her. Having come from outside the barrier, I wonder how often she has interacted with anyone besides Mentalists.

"You might feel a twinge of warmth," Gemma soothes her with another smile, "but it won't hurt."

She surveys Samantha once more, then pulls a jar of translucent powder out of her pocket. She sprinkles it on Samantha's hair and begins working it through.

"What's that?" Samantha's whole body is on edge.

"Colorbind powder," Gemma replies. "It's alright. Just relax." The powder melts as it is applied, leaving her tresses glossy. Samantha observes the effect in the mirror, and fascination eases her tension.

"Shapers can't make any changes to living creatures," Gemma explains to her, "only inanimate objects. The colorbind coats your hair, and then I can change the shade of the colorbind." Her face grows intent in concentration.

Samantha's eyes widen as her hair begins to dull from its

bright yellow to brown, and then lightens back up to a more subdued dirty-blond.

Gemma pauses and takes a breath. "Believe it or not, these neutral, in-between shades are actually harder than bold colors."

"Well, you've done amazingly," I say, admiring her skill. "What can you do for her clothes?"

By the time Gemma is finished, Samantha wears a white T-shirt and a simple gray skirt to go with her unremarkable hair. There is nothing about her that would stand out in the city.

Samantha frowns at herself in the mirror. "At least it's only temporary. Right?"

Gemma assures her, and I thank the Shaper. "It's perfect!"

The vibrant smile reappears. "Come see me for something more fun next time!"

6

"I'M TIRED!" SAMANTHA WHINES. "CAN'T we stop for a rest?"

Blanca and I halt. Having Augmentors along is always a good idea for traveling with speed and endurance, but a Mentalist, especially a particularly irritating Mentalist—not so much. It's not her fault she doesn't have the same abilities we do, but I'm also certain Elm, or probably any of the Shapers, would have handled this better.

"We only have about 30 minutes left," I say. "Are you sure you can't pull through?"

She scowls at me and drops down in the middle of the field we're standing in. She tosses her head. "You must give me a few minutes. Honestly! I'm not a workhorse."

"That's unfortunate," Blanca mutters. "Horses can't talk."

Thankfully, Samantha doesn't hear her.

"I still don't see why I couldn't have taken the hover cart and met up with you later . . ."

"Because Blanca's invisibility device wouldn't have lasted the whole journey," I point out. Again. "We already explained this." Also, the hover carts are monitored especially carefully, and a single person taking a multi-passenger cart would have raised questions. More than ever, I wish I were better trained so I could be relied on to charge Blanca's device.

RADIANT   43

Samantha groans again and flops her head down onto her knees.

I recall when I needed to heal myself after being tortured by Veronica. Elm gave me a mental boost when I thought I wouldn't be able to continue. Could I try something like that on Samantha?

I gaze at her as she hugs her knees to her chest. She needs to feel stronger. I imagine a little ball of energy flowing from my mind to hers.

At once she bolts up from the ground, glaring at me with fury.

Blanca looks at us in surprise.

"What do you think you're doing?" Samantha fumes, her voice nearly a shriek. "Do you want to kill me?"

"S-sorry." I stammer and step back. "I was just trying to help you feel stronger."

"Until you actually know what you're doing," she spits out, "keep your crazy, untrained abilities away from me."

Well, if nothing else, she's moving again. And in the right direction. Blanca shrugs at me and we follow.

At last we reach the city. Like Prism, there are Benefactors at every turn. However, there is so much bustle that as long as we're very careful, we run a lot less risk of being noticed here in our invisible states. Samantha wordlessly gives Blanca's device a quick charge, and we head off in search of food.

The big supermarket at the center of town is probably a better option than the smaller shops, because we can more easily avoid shoppers in the large aisles. Besides that, anything we take is less likely to be noticed among the ample rows of well-stocked commodities. I stuff down the guilt at the theft we're about to commit. *Life or death, Ava. You were forced into this position.*

Samantha takes her time strolling through the doors of the market before Blanca and I can get inside. We find the freezer aisle so the noisy refrigeration equipment will mask our quiet conversation.

"Remember," I say, "the copier can only duplicate plant-based materials, so stick to plant-based foods."

Blanca pretends to pout. "No cheese?"

"Sorry. Now remember, this is just a super-quick run. Be back here in five minutes. We can duplicate, so we don't need a lot." I hesitate. "I don't like being a thief, so please don't take anything we don't need."

"What am I supposed to do?" Samantha complains. "I can't buy anything." Magus only uses currency cards instead of physical cash, which makes purchases impossible. Anything would be tracked.

"Just browse around," I encourage. "Be normal." Assuming she even knows how to do that. Maybe that wasn't the best suggestion.

We split, and I hit the dry-goods aisle, grabbing small bags of beans and lentils so we have a good source of protein. A bag of rice as a filler. Some oatmeal and nuts. Blanca has a produce bag of fresh fruit and vegetables. Easy as pie. As an afterthought, I grab a couple of seed packets from the gardening section. Elm will likely want to plant again.

It feels strange to just leave the store with full backpacks and without paying, but since our only other option for food right now is to turn ourselves in, I'll deal with the guilt. Maybe someday, when all of this is over, I'll be able to return to this store and repay what we took.

Once outside, Blanca pulls a couple of candy bars out of her pockets and begins to peel back the wrapper on one.

"Blanca!"

She looks at me with feigned innocence and takes a bite. "We need strength to get home."

My stomach complains loudly as I'm about to argue with

her, so I just shake my head. It does not surprise me when Samantha demands the other bar.

As we make our way back through the city to follow our path home, the library across the street catches my attention. It's surrounded by red caution tape, and official-looking signs hang on the doors. A group of Benefactors enters, carrying hefty-looking boxes.

"Hold up for a second. I want to see what they're up to."

"We shouldn't push our luck." Blanca's eyes shoot darts at the Benefactors. "Forget them. Let's just go."

I'm already heading across the street. "I'll only be a moment." I have to know what they're planning.

The signs on the door read:

CLOSED FOR RENOVATIONS

The library is currently undergoing repairs as a result of the earlier attack by Elm. As always, please report any unusual sightings. We apologize for any inconvenience and hope to have the library running again soon.

I jump out of the way as another Benefactor enters and quickly slip inside behind him. I look over my shoulder and catch a glimpse of Samantha's and Blanca's equally horrified expressions as I enter the building.

Just as I feared, the Benefactors are implementing new tech. They place yellow devices on the innards of each digidome before the front panel is secured. Anger churns within me, although I don't know why any of this should be a surprise. The library was one of their main hubs for control. Of course they would want to get it up and running again as soon as possible.

I want to smash all the tech I see, right here and now. I'm

already gathering the energy in my fist. I could probably get at least a couple and be out before they could even process what happened . . .

But at what risk? At what cost? I relax my hands and clench my teeth instead. We will come back and take care of this. I can't do it without a plan or with so many others depending on me. Begrudgingly, I turn back toward the door and wait for my chance to leave.

Blanca and Samantha have crossed the street to my side. Blanca stands tapping her foot in impatience, while Samantha nervously fidgets.

"Let's get out of here," Blanca says as I reach them. "All these Benefactors are creeping me out."

I nod, then take one last glance into the library. "Although, they're pretty busy with their own plans. We're probably safe."

At that very moment, I notice him coming down the street. The one person who could possibly see through our illusions and blow our cover. Jace.

"Drat," I say under my breath. Blanca utters something much less appropriate.

"Samantha, keep walking. Act normal. It's very important— we'll explain as soon as we can." I grab Blanca's arm, and we duck into the narrow alleyway between the library and the shop next to it.

When I peer out, however, Samantha is acting anything but normal. She's frozen in place, staring at Jace with what is clearly fear. Then it dawns on me—if she and Elm were childhood friends, and Jace was Elm's teacher, they probably knew each other. I want to kick myself. She must know what Jace did to Elm. Why did he have to be here now?

At last, she lowers her head and stares down the sidewalk. Jace passes her by, but then stops. My heart stops with him. We're close enough to hear.

"Say," Jace says, "you look awfully familiar. Have we met?"

Samantha's face flushes. "I don't think so."

"Are you sure?" Jace leans in as he studies Samantha's face. "Even your voice . . ."

They both start as a red butterfly darts between them, hovering just in front of Samantha's face. She gives a nervous laugh and brushes it away, but Jace doesn't take his focus off her.

I bite my lip as Samantha responds. "I have a lot of siblings, so I've been to the color initiation ceremonies several times. Don't you help Selene there?"

So, she knows about Jace even now. Did Elm tell her or has she kept tabs on him somehow? Regardless, I'm glad she has some kind of excuse. *And she's handling things well*, I grudgingly admit to myself.

Jace nods. "Ah, yes. That's probably it, then. Have a lovely day." He continues on and disappears into the library. Blanca and I hurry out from the alley.

I grasp Samantha's arm as we rush by and pull her with us. "We have to get out of here."

She doesn't protest, and we begin to run.

7

THE FOOD IS WELL-RECEIVED WHEN WE
return. At Prism there was always a meal, so this is new
territory for most everyone. And I still have to face the reality
that someone here forced us into this position. For now, we
store the food in the quarantine area, since it's unoccupied,
and resume with guard shifts. Acknowledging we can't trust
one another feels like finding half a worm in your apple—
everything about it makes you sick, and you can't do a thing
to change what happened. But we can't take any more risks.
Nobody is getting near that food without someone else
knowing about it. No more worms sneaking by.

"There were no further incidents while you were gone,"
Elm states, glancing around the cave for probably the twentieth
time. "I trust you had a safe journey?"

I haven't told him about our experience. "More or less."
I shift. "Samantha was no problem." I omit her complaining
and my Mentalist attempt. I'll tell him about the library later.
"Samantha had a quick run-in with Jace, but I think she
handled it well."

He stiffens. His voice is taut when he speaks. "Because Jace
was my mentor and Sammy was always tagging along after
me, he got to know her quite well. Are you certain he didn't
recognize her?"

"He thought he knew her from somewhere," I admit. "But she said it was probably from initiation ceremonies, and he seemed to accept that."

"Perhaps . . ."

"It's okay, Elm," I soothe, tracing my finger down one of his arms, wishing I could pull the tension away. "Now that we have food, we can lie low for a while. It's going to be fine." Well, fine if ignoring the fact that there is an unknown wolf lurking among our sheep. I'm sure Elm is thinking of that too.

I study his face. He doesn't wear his mask of devil-may-care as easily now. Ever since our rebellion at Prism and letting the students into the cave, I only see flashes of the carefree Elm I spent so many months with. Now, even when he's trying his best to hide it, there is always a hint of apprehension beneath the surface. Somehow, I will find a way to get that old Elm back. It's hard not to look on the days before our rebellion at Prism with longing. The days when I could visit him here and have him all to myself. I know it can't be that way now—this is about more than us.

He gives me a gentle smile, the worry flickering away, and runs his thumb along my cheek. "How could I persuade you to divulge your thoughts right now? Those eyes have stories left to tell."

I should have known. I return his smile and shake my head. "Just wishing things could be simple. Wishing I could have an afternoon with you that didn't involve secrets and betrayal."

His lips widen into a mischievous grin. "Since when did afternoons with me not involve secrets and betrayal?"

"Fair point. But I'm not sure betraying the bad guys really counts as betrayal."

"Oh, yes it does. My favorite betrayal ever." He laughs and plants a welcome kiss on my lips. For that moment, the shadows go away.

Three days pass quietly with no new incidents in the cave. Perhaps whoever it was realized the error of their rash acts after the possibility of going without food. I can only hope their actions were simply misplaced anger or some petty slight and nothing more sinister.

After a morning spent checking the light devices and making sure everything else is maintained, Elm and I move into the main room of the cave to assess the current situation. Most of the students congregate here during the day. Today they are smiling. Laughing. The atmosphere feels more relaxed than it has in a while. But there's still one thing that's not right. I survey the tear-shaped pendants on the student's necks. A cluster of red here. A gaggle of blue there. We've come a long way in many aspects since Prism, but we've more to go.

"How do I get them to work together?"

Elm chuckles.

"What?" Does he think it's impossible?

"You don't see the irony? How do *we* work together, would be the better question, Miss Ava. You always attempt to take on everything by yourself."

"I feel like it's my responsibility."

He levels his eyes at me. "Responsibility can be shared."

I sigh. "You're right, of course." I have to get used to this whole teamwork thing. After spending so long working with Selene and looking out for my own desires, it's hard to adjust to the idea of working toward something with other people. I should take comfort in the fact that I don't have to do this alone, but because I dragged everyone into this, part of me still feels I should be the one who finds how to get us out of it. And, despite everything, they still don't trust Elm because he's a Mentalist.

"Those two, at least, manage to get along," Elm says, glancing at Blanca who is teasing Kaito near the stream. Honestly it's a miracle they became friends so quickly. An Augmentor and a Shaper, and not even in the same year—Blanca being older. He's quiet and analytical. She's boisterous and forward. Yet somehow they're always together. It gives me hope for the rest of us.

All at once my ears grate with the echoing squeal of the one person I'm not sure I can ever be at ease with.

"Where is Elm?" Samantha's shrill voice cuts over the noise of everyone else in the cave. "I need to see him *now*."

I don't even try to hide my irritation. "What does she want this time?"

"She sounds quite upset," Elm merely says, and I trudge after him over to Samantha.

She thrusts a paper in Elm's face. "Look at this! Look what they found!" I'm taken aback to see tears in her eyes.

I stand on my tiptoes to get a better glimpse of the paper Elm examines, and my stomach sinks. A wanted poster, this time with Samantha's face sketched on it.

"Who found it?" I ask.

Brie appears behind Samantha, slightly out of breath, followed shortly by Jazz, who says, "Brie found it on one of the trees down the path to Prism." He glances at us helplessly. "I know we shouldn't have been out, but she wouldn't stay put."

I give Brie a harsh look. "Why were you anywhere near Prism?"

She tilts her chin downward. "I was bored. I thought maybe I could do some spying, but Jazz made me turn around." Her voice is trembling.

I can't entirely fault her; I left the cave out of boredom

just a few days prior. She's younger than I am. So I save the safety lecture for now. Samantha fastens onto Elm's arm as her tears fall.

"So it appears Jace did recognize her." Elm places a consoling hand on Samantha's shoulder. "Chin up, Sammy. My face has been all over the city for some time now, and they haven't snagged me yet."

"You can't let them catch me," Samantha pleads with Elm. "You know more than anyone what they do to people like you and me." She really is afraid.

Elm's face pales. I'm sure he is not only thinking of what he suffered at the hands of the Benefactors, but of the countless other tortured and murdered Mentalists. I swallow. I use Yellow magic too. I carry the same risks. Likely the only reason I didn't meet the same fate as Elm was because Selene wanted my own power hidden from me until she thought I could be properly manipulated.

"It's safe here." Elm comforts her, though his voice is less sure now than it was a moment ago.

"I found something." Brie reaches into the bag at her side. "I was wondering if we could help it." She holds out a small glass jar where a red butterfly rests inside, twitching in an odd way.

"Another one of those?" I take the jar carefully. The creature looks to be in poor shape. "I've been seeing them everywhere lately."

"I told Brie I didn't know if I could heal it." Jazz sounds anxious. "I haven't ever tried on something that small before."

I examine the butterfly through the glass. Something is wrong with its eyes. They look almost . . . smashed? My heart plunges at the sight. "Brie, I don't know . . ." I twist the lid open, and as I do so, I hear a strange sound. A faint whirring that seems almost . . . mechanic.

Elm's eyes widen, and he grabs the jar from me, tipping the

creature into his hands. He holds it up by the wings and his face hardens. "This is electronic. Some kind of transmitter."

"Break it," I say without hesitation, my own fear reflected in the faces around me. Who is it transmitting to, and what have they seen?

But Elm continues studying the butterfly—robot—whatever it is. I see his Shaper mind kicking into action. That part of him that innately understands how things work. "Fortunately," he says, prodding the device, "this one can't transmit anymore. The lenses in the eyes are smashed, and the transmitter is damaged."

We all exhale at once.

Elm turns his head to me. "You say you've seen more of these?"

"Yes. In the city. Near Prism. In the forest. Pretty much every time I've gone out."

Samantha gives a little cry. "One of those things was in my face in Violet City. Do you think that's how they recognized me?"

Elm's answer is to snap the head off the device. "Just to be certain it's truly out of commission," he says grimly. "I'd like to examine it with Kaito's help, so we know precisely what we're dealing with."

"It was like that when you found it, right Brie?" Jazz asks.

"Looked like it was crushed by a rock."

Brie looks nervous now, so I touch her arm. "If it was already broken, it's not likely that it saw you or any part of the cave. That's good."

"Stupid buggerflies," she grumbles.

We stare at her. "Buggerflies?" Our voices in unison break the tension, and we laugh.

Brie quirks a smile and gives a small shrug. "Since they've been bugging us, it seemed to fit."

I look at Elm and he nods at me. I take a deep breath,

preparing myself for the news I have to deliver. "We need to warn everyone else about the . . . buggerflies. If they're sending information to the Benefactors, which is the most likely case, we all need to be diligent in avoiding them." Our list of things to be wary of just keeps growing.

I open my eyes, thinking I heard a noise, but the cave is quiet except for the usual faint echoes in the stillness. My brain feels muddled, as though I slept too long. The light spheres Elm rigged turn on at sunrise, and the cave is still dark, so it must be early.

"Ava."

"Nikki? What's wrong?"

"It looks like someone broke the light spheres."

"What?" I bolt upright. "Are you sure?"

"Yes. I've checked."

Another attack. I haven't even recovered from the news about the buggerflies. And here we are in pitch darkness with the attacker living among us. I fumble for the small book light I keep by my bed for late-night reading, relieved when it flickers to life.

"Is there any other damage? Is everyone is okay?" I can barely make out Nikki's face in the shadows.

"It's hard to tell when it's so dark out there." She answers my unspoken question, "Elm is aware."

This, at least, brings me some relief.

We stumble through the cave in the dim glow of my book light, taking care to avoid rough terrain and crevices. The sound of anxious voices grows louder as we approach the main room. I'm relieved to see light as we approach—it's amazing how comforting even a small light is when you're surrounded by shadow. The glow comes from Elm, who is in the center of the room by a pile of broken light spheres, already working on repairing them. Kaito assists, following Elm's directions with precision. Students huddle around them.

"I'm going to try and round up anyone else who's missing," Nikki says. "Can I borrow your book light?"

"Of course." I hand her the light. "You should take someone else with you, though, just to be safe."

She peers around. "Blake, want to come with me?"

Blake turns and spots us. He gives me a quick appraisal before heading off with Nikki as she explains. Blake is always looking out.

I kneel beside Elm, and he glances at me with a wry smile, though anger and concern line his countenance. "Forgive me for not coming for you myself, Miss Ava. The darkness created quite a panic. Nikki convinced me it was better if I set to work on this and let her see to your well-being."

"It's fine," I assure him. "I'm just sorry I wasn't here sooner."

I detect a change in the atmosphere and look up. Samantha just entered the room, and voices hush into hisses, eyes narrow to suspicious glares.

"It's gotta be that Yellow," I hear someone whisper. "None of this happened until she showed up."

I wish I could disagree. But it's true: nothing like this happened until Samantha's arrival. She holds her head up high and places herself in front of Elm.

"They think I did this. I didn't. I would never do anything that would hurt you. Never."

"I know, Sammy."

That's the fact I can't ignore. While all of the attacks have impacted everyone in the cave, they seem to target Elm most directly. Elm's garden. Elm's invisibility devices. Elm's light spheres. While it would be easiest to blame Samantha, her obsession with Elm seems genuine. It's hard to imagine her doing anything that would harm him.

One of the students nearby gives a pointed look at Elm. "Can't you just get into her mind or something and find out if she's telling the truth?"

Elm looks disgusted, and I cut in before he can reply.

"Nobody is getting into anybody's mind," I say rapidly. "We're going to figure this out, but we need to keep calm until then."

The accusing looks don't die, but most of the murmurs stop. I know some kind of action will have to be taken soon in order to keep everyone satisfied. And safe.

8

NOW THAT THE LIGHT SPHERES HAVE
been repaired, Elm and I brainstorm together as we attach
them back to their proper places. How can we track down our
attacker? If nothing else, we need ways to protect the innocent.

"We have to keep everyone focused and working together.
And not afraid." I wobble atop Elm's shoulders, securing a light
sphere on a higher alcove in the cave.

"There is still a great suspicion surrounding Mentalists."

"Not just that. But even among Augmentors and Shapers.
Everyone is getting suspicious of everyone else." I test the
security of the light sphere with a shake. "Okay, this one's good.
I'm coming down."

"Do mind your elbows this time," he teases as I slide back
down. "My nose can't take another hit."

I give a sly grin. "Sure it can. My Augmentor abilities will
have you fixed up in no time."

He laughs. "My, how fortunate I am."

We travel to the next section of the cave, my thoughts never
straying far from everything that has been happening. The one
solution that comes to mind is White magic, protective magic
that requires all three magic types. The problem with this,
however, is that Elm and I—and Samantha—are the only Yellow
magic users, and I barely count with my limited abilities.

"I've been thinking . . ." I pause as Elm prods a hook on the cave wall with his cane to test it for stability before securing a light sphere to it. Shadows dance in the space around us, like the weaving thoughts in my mind. "If we can combine all three magic types to create White magic, do you think it's possible to create other types of magic too? Like what you can do as a dual magic-user. If a Mentalist and a Shaper worked together, could they do what you do?"

Elm considers this. "Well, as we already know magic types can be combined, I don't see why not."

I haven't yet explored what I might be able to do by trying to combine my Augmentor and Mentalist capabilities. But if Elm can combine his two magic types, I should be able to do the same. Why shouldn't two individuals be able to combine their magic types too?

"Do you think we could get them to try?"

"It harms nothing to ask. I suspect most are growing tired of being at the mercy of our enemies without taking some kind of action." Elm secures the last sphere in place, his face illuminated with both light and pride in his work. "Let's give it a shot."

"Careful." Kaito extends a hand toward Blanca as she navigates from a rocky ledge to the cave floor. "There's a lot of loose sediment here."

She ignores his hand and jumps down, her boots crunching into the earth. "Jazz will fix any bones that break." She grins.

Jazz's face grows pallid. "Please tell me we're not doing anything that will break bones."

"No," I say with a laugh. "At least, I hope not."

The small group of Shapers and Augmentors meeting up with us are those we feel are trustworthy and whose skill level is strong: Kaito, Blake, and Nikki for Shapers and Jazz and Blanca for Augmentors. They each have strengths in different areas of their magic types: Blake is particularly skilled at changing the physical properties of objects while Nikki is particularly agile at maneuvering them. Jazz has a good handle on the healing components of Red magic while Blanca has perfected sheer brute force. Kaito is here because his analytical eye might help us identify any roadblocks to our success (and because Blanca insisted on it). The room we're tucked away in is further back in the cave, quiet and secluded—though I'm not quite sure why I feel the need to keep this a secret. Maybe just to avoid humiliation since I really have no idea what we're doing.

"Thanks for coming," I say. "We want to test something that can help us if we get it right."

Blanca raises her eyebrows. "Are we guinea pigs?"

I shake my head quickly and Elm speaks up. "You were asked because you can handle the responsibility." He gives me a slight nod.

"We recently learned about something called White magic," I begin. "It was practiced at Prism before Yellow magic was banned, and it's how the Benefactors formed the barrier around Magus."

Now I have their interest.

"We know little about it," Elm informs them. "However, Miss Ava and I used it accidentally on the day we escaped from the school. The one thing we can say for certain is it requires the use of all three magic types."

I watch their faces as they process this information. By now, our closest friends know Elm and I are dual magic-users. But we have never really talked about how we managed to survive that traumatic day.

"But that means there must be many more Mentalists working with the Benefactors." Kaito's brow furrows. "If it requires all three magic types, they couldn't keep the barrier up otherwise."

"You're right," I reply. "The Benefactors obviously know more about it than they've let on."

Nikki turns to Blake. "Your parents are Benefactors, right? Did you ever hear them talk about anything like that?"

"Never. But obviously there was a lot they didn't tell me." Blake floats a few pebbles into the air and idly twirls them around one another. He glances at Elm and me. "So, you want us to try and use this White magic?"

I have to explain in a way that doesn't sound crazy. "Not exactly. I mean, we should figure that out, too, for the extra protection. But we have something else in mind. Some of you have seen that Elm can create things out of thin air."

"A most extraordinary trait, I must say," Elm remarks to nobody in particular. Blake rolls his eyes.

I continue, ignoring them both. "Because of the way Elm combines his two color uses and the fact that magic types can combine to create White magic, we think it might be possible for two individuals to combine their magic types for even higher purposes."

"Isn't that something you and Elm could practice?" Jazz asks, looking slightly nervous. All of us had it drilled into our heads repeatedly at Prism that we shouldn't experiment. Many have been gravely injured by using magic irresponsibly. His anxiety isn't surprising.

"We could, but since we're both dual magic-users, it might be different. We want to know if it can work for single magic-users. If it does, it increases defense for everyone."

Blanca cracks her knuckles. "Just tell us what to do."

I pair them off: Blanca and Blake, Nikki and Jazz. Kaito hangs back, watching everything unfold. I feel somewhat foolish, because I'm really not sure what to do. When Elm and I formed the shield around ourselves, it seemed to happen spontaneously. How did we combine our magic? Everyone looks at me expectantly.

"Well . . . to start with . . . everyone hold hands?" Is physical contact necessary?

Elm grabs my hand at once and gives it a squeeze, his eyes lighting with a hint of the playful Elm I have come to know so well. I shoot him a small smile in return.

I turn back to the group, noting Blake's stiff expression as I do so. Each Shaper/Augmentor pair has linked hands. What do I suggest next? So much of Augmentor magic—and Mentalist magic for that matter—is about concentration and specific focal points. Perhaps that's the key here too.

"Focus on a spell and bring that energy to where your hands are joined." That seems reasonable enough.

A pause, a *bzzzzzzt* sound, and then a yelp of pain.

"Watch it, Shaper!" Blanca pulls sharply away from Blake and shakes her hand.

Nikki glares at her. "Watch it yourself, Red."

"He just sent some crazy magic jolt through my hand!"

"I'm sorry." Blake holds his hands out, looking defensive. "I wasn't trying to hurt you. I just did what Ava asked."

Jazz takes a step back, as though he might get pulled into the fray.

"Perhaps this isn't the best idea right now," Elm cautions, eyeing our now-heated companions.

He's right. What was I thinking?

Blake gives Blanca a challenging look. "Ava is just trying to figure out ways we can fight back stronger. We can't just hide forever."

Blanca crosses her arms. "Yeah, but I thought she had some vague idea of what she was doing before using us as lab rats."

"We have to start somewhere," Nikki defends.

"No, she's right." I drop my head. "I shouldn't have dragged you into this without having a better grasp on it. I'm sorry."

Blanca approaches Jazz and holds out her hand. "This still hurts. Can you heal it?"

Jazz nods and sets to work on her as we all watch.

"Thanks." Blanca breathes more calmly when Jazz has finished. She turns to me. "Next time, don't gamble on your friends." She promptly leaves the room.

"I should go too." Jazz is clearly uncomfortable with the tension in the air. "Sorry, Ava. Maybe another time."

I try to push away my embarrassment and shame.

Blake comes to me. "Don't worry about her. You're just trying to be proactive."

"I was an idiot," I say miserably. "I know it's dangerous to mess around with magic, and I have no idea if this will even work."

"It was kind of dumb," Nikki admits. "But we're not going to get anywhere without taking risks here and there."

Elm slides his arm around my waist. "We'll find another way. For the moment, we'll make do and stay extremely cautious."

As Blake's eyes go to Elm's arm securely around me, Nikki suddenly pipes up, "Hey, Blake! There's a weird-looking stalactite near my room of the cave. Someone could get impaled. Come help me round it off, will you?"

She grabs him before he can protest and steers him away.

With everyone gone but Elm and me, the room feels more cavernous.

"Go ahead and say it." I don't dare look Elm in the eye.

"Say what?"

"That I was stupid." My voice rises in volume and pitch. "That I could have gotten someone seriously hurt or killed."

"Miss Ava . . ."

"You don't have to pretend you think it was a good idea."

"Well, I said I felt it was worth exploring, did I not?" He tilts my chin up to look at him. "You have the right intent. We require strength now—not division. We'll find a way."

"I hope so." If we work together, does it mean putting everyone else at risk? Maybe I should just find a way myself.

9

FOR NOW, I PUT THE IDEA OF MY classmates joining two magic types out of my mind. But I haven't given up on finding other means to protect and unite ourselves. White magic is combined magic, and there has to be accessible knowledge on it somewhere. If I can unlock that, it will be easier to revisit the dual-magic idea.

One thing I know for certain is the Benefactors, or at least some of them, know how to use White magic. They use it to sustain the barrier around Magus. They used it to put that spell on Elm so that he couldn't approach students at the school. I may not be able to find that specific information about it in books, but there might be another approach. A way to tap into the knowledge from another person's mind without putting anyone else at risk.

Except maybe me.

It feels silly to be sneaking around in Elm's room like this. But he knows me too well. If he saw the book I was looking for, he would catch on.

My eyes run over titles as quickly as possible until I find the one I'm looking for: *Into Dreams: Mentalists and Dream Invasion.*

No sooner have I grabbed the volume off the shelf than

I hear a noise behind me. I whirl around and hide the book behind my back as Elm enters.

He raises his eyebrows. "Well, what a lovely surprise! I came to grab spare parts, but instead I find Miss Ava."

I smile at him in what I hope is a distracting way. "I just wanted to see you."

He approaches, and I back against the bookshelf, debating whether or not I can slip the book back without him noticing.

"I always want to see you." He stands just in front of me, his smile warm. "It seems we don't have enough time for each other lately."

My cheeks heat as he leans down, nose to nose with me.

"I have a question for you," he says.

I swallow. "What's that?"

His mouth quirks. "Do you want me to pretend I don't know you're hiding a book?"

Drat.

"Why the secrecy?" He tugs the book from behind me and dangles it roguishly in front of my face. "Miss Ava, this isn't Prism. If you want to borrow one of my books, you need only ask." He glances down at the cover, and his smile fades. "Ah . . . I see."

My face is hot with guilt.

"May I ask whose dreams you were planning to invade?" His voice is stiff.

"Nobody in particular," I lie. "I just feel like it's something I should know."

"You will eventually, I promise you. I would love nothing more than to show you everything I know. But, Miss Ava, believe me when I say it's not something you should attempt until you have mastered your other Mentalist abilities."

"Why do you get to decide what I do and don't know?" My voice is sharp and sounds petty, even to my own ears.

"If you're withholding knowledge from me, how are you any better than the Benefactors?"

I've gone too far and I regret it in an instant. The sting of my words reflects in his eyes.

He takes a deep breath. "I assure you I'm not trying to be difficult, and I'm not needlessly sheltering you. All Mentalist mentors save this aspect for last—for good reason. Many Mentalists don't even touch dream jumping because of the risks it poses."

But I still need to try. I stare him down and he stares back. Finally he sighs. "If I give you the book, do you promise not to test it out? Read and study it as much as you wish, but don't attempt anything until we can train together."

I already feel unsettled by my dishonesty. I have no intention of keeping my promise. But in this case, it's for the greater good. I'm certain he'll forgive me once we overthrow the Benefactors once and for all.

"Very well, then." He tentatively hands the book back to me. "I trust you, Miss Ava."

I'm such a rat.

10

"THERE YOU ARE, SAMANTHA! JAZZ HAS been looking for you."

Samantha glances up at me from where she's huddled with Elm. They looked like they were in deep discussion before I interrupted. I do my best to shove away the creature of jealousy that crawls through me and focus instead on the way Elm's face brightened when he saw me.

Samantha inches nearer to Elm, as though anticipating something might separate her from him. "What does Jazz want?"

"He said you're supposed to be helping him with dinner."

Elm raises his eyebrows at her. "You're not shirking your duties, are you, Sammy?"

Her lower lip juts out. "This is way more important, don't you think? Somebody else can cook."

"Everyone shares the load, Samantha," I say evenly. "But I'm willing to hear you out. What's so important?"

But it is Elm who replies. "We were just about to go find you. Sammy has some information that should help us tremendously."

"I think I know where the other Mentalists are being kept," she says, looking at Elm.

As much as I dislike Samantha, this definitely gets my attention. "Where?"

"I've spent a long time hunting around Magus—on the other side of the barrier, trying to find Elm. There's a place northwest of Violet City that the Benefactors seem to hang around a lot. It's some sort of large compound."

My mind swirls. "Then we should go as soon as possible," I say urgently. "We'll start planning now." I mentally pore over the logistics of cutting across Magus with a group of wanted individuals—particularly when we're short on invisibility devices.

As though reading my mind, Elm says, "Sammy thinks it would be safer to travel outside the barrier. It will take a little longer than cutting straight through, but nobody really monitors what's happening on the outside as far as we're aware. And she's familiar with traveling to the area that way."

Every part of me wakes up. "We can get out?" I shake my head at myself. What would it mean if we could go outside of the barrier? I should have realized this sooner. If Samantha got in, surely we could get out.

Samantha shifts, and I try to figure out the reason for her sudden discomfort. "I know a way," she says. "There are faults in the barrier that come at varied times. I've learned how to read them. It's complicated, but I can get us out."

"When can we leave? Do you know when the next fault is?"

"Uh . . . in two nights."

"Well then, we'll start preparing right away." Part of me feels this is happening too fast, but the mere thought that there are more Mentalists being kept in the same enslaved state as Elm was is unnerving.

"We shouldn't take a big group," Samantha states. "Even outside the barrier, we don't want to attract attention."

"The three of us will go, then," I say. "Once we assess things, we can return with a larger group if needed."

Elm has been quiet this whole time, and I see his mind is working out something. Finally he turns to Samantha. "Sammy, would you excuse Miss Ava and me for a few moments? You ought to be helping Jazz, anyway."

She doesn't make any effort to hide her distaste as she gives me an acidic look before huffing away.

"I anticipate you won't like what I'm about to say," Elm begins carefully, "so please just listen with a logical mind. That's all I ask."

"What is it?" I ask warily.

"We need a leader here. Someone to maintain as much security as possible."

I have a feeling I know where this is going.

"And the other students already seem to rely on you."

"Are you telling me I can't come with you?"

His eyes soften. "You know I would much rather we be together. But you're the only person in this place I truly trust. One of us has to keep an eye on the situation here so that we're informed. You said so yourself before."

I think of him traveling alone with Samantha, and my heart sinks. "Can't . . . couldn't I go instead?"

"I believe you and I both know that's not going to work. Two strong Mentalists to seek out the others is best. And you and Sammy aren't much of a team." Seeing the expression on my face he adds, "She's as much to blame for that as anyone."

I want to fight it. To clench my fists and yell and make him change his mind. But the logical side of me knows he's right. Aside from the fact that Samantha and I don't get along, I know many of the students still don't trust Elm. It could cause trouble. Besides that, he's probably in more danger than I am if he gets caught. His way makes the most sense. My emotional side protests, however, and I can't help arguing anyway.

"With everything that's going on, how can I be sure you'll

be safe going with her? How can you be sure Samantha wasn't the one who did all these things?"

"Miss Ava . . ." he sighs. "It wasn't Sammy. I know you dislike her, but I'm certain she wouldn't do this."

"How can you know?" I persist. "None of this started happening until she showed up."

"Because she loves me."

The words somehow manage to catch me off guard. I guess it's not surprising to hear it—she makes it pretty clear how she feels about Elm—but to hear it from him . . .

"Or at least . . . she loves me in whatever her perception of love is. But the point is that I know her well enough to realize she wouldn't intentionally do things that could harm me."

"All right," I reluctantly concede. I do trust Elm. Really, the only thing keeping me from agreeing at this point is my own jealousy, and I hate that side of me. Decision-making used to be so much easier.

I stand stiffly before him. "Well, I guess you'd better start making preparations, then."

The forest is dark and we're all jumpy. Blake came with Elm, Samantha, and me to the edge of the barrier so that I wouldn't have to travel back to the cave alone after seeing them off.

"Be careful, okay?" I watch Elm with uncertainty. I haven't exactly been warm toward him the past couple of days, holding a slight grudge over being left behind. Now I regret it.

Always forgiving, he pulls me into an embrace, warming me in the chill night air. I forget Blake and Samantha and hold him tightly.

Blake finally hisses at us. "Do you want the Benefactors to show up while we stand here?"

I break away, my face aflame. Blake and Samantha both glare at us.

Elm seems oblivious to it all, his fingertips lingering on my arms as he gazes at me. "I'll return as soon as I can."

"It's time to go." Samantha bumps me to the side as she approaches the barrier. "Come on, Elm."

She inhales deeply and cracks her staff against the side of the barrier, then straightaway grabs Elm and pulls him with her. They're through. Just like that. I brush my fingers across the barrier where they departed, but it's already solid again, sending a slight buzz through me at my touch. It feels so strange staring at them through the dome. This barrier that I have known my whole life, and suddenly they are on the other side. What does that even feel like? Envy stabs into my heart, and I could swear the breeze just got a little colder.

Elm mouths something, but I can't hear him. I shake my head and point at my ears to let him know. With a slightly sad smile, he blows me a kiss instead, and he and Samantha disappear into the trees.

11

ELM'S LIGHT SPHERES ARE ALMOST
cruel at this moment. They appear so much like sunlight, but
they offer no warmth. I wish I could bask in them. I'm so tired
of cold, damp cave air.

Although I wonder, if Mentalists can use illusions to
change how other people are feeling, can they do the same to
themselves?

You're warm, I tell myself. *Soaking in the rays of the sun.*

I feel it, just a little. The gentle pulse of heat against my
skin. It grows warmer. Hotter.

Too hot.

I cry out at the searing pain and force my magic to stop. I
hold up my arms, expecting to find them red and raw. Instead,
they look just fine. I laugh with relief, marveling again at the
power of illusions. I'll get it right eventually.

"Can I get in on the joke?" Blake is watching me as we
recline on the floor of the cave underneath the light sphere.

"There's no joke. Just practice."

"Mentalist stuff?" His voice is flat, but he looks worried.

I sigh. "Go ahead and say it—whatever it is."

"That other Yellow . . . she's just . . ."

"Annoying?" I offer. If he just wants to complain about
Samantha, he won't get any argument from me.

"Let's just say I felt sorry for Brie when she was quarantined with her. I almost feel bad for Elm being stuck with her right now."

I sense there's more to his rant than just a complaint about Samantha's behavior. I wait in silence for him to continue.

He runs his hand through his hair. "Are you sure you know what you're doing with Elm?"

A little spark fires off within me. "I thought we were past this." I glare. "We can trust him."

"It's just, well, the track record for Mentalists hasn't been great. Just look at Jace. Not that I'm saying the Benefactors are right or anything," he adds.

Has he been waiting for a moment where Elm was gone just to say this? He's wasting his breath. And getting on my nerves. "Just because Samantha is irritating doesn't mean Elm—"

Blake stops me. "Be careful, is all I'm saying."

"Don't be so worried about it."

"You're like my sister, Ava," Blake says. "And every time I see you close to him, I can't help but worry. I don't want to see you get hurt or make bad decisions."

I set my jaw. "I've made plenty of bad decisions in my life, but Elm isn't one of them." But Blake's attitude over the past few weeks makes more sense. "I know you care about me, and I appreciate it, but I'm not a little child you have to look after."

Nikki bursts in, eyes lively. "One of the Shapers just made this amazing dessert. You gotta come have some. It's not 'cute cafe in Violet City' good, but it's one of the best things we've had in this cave yet."

I force a smile as I get to my feet. "You two go ahead. I have things to do. Enjoy an extra serving for me."

The world sparkling around me isn't enough to distract me from Elm's book. Elm and I decided early on that we would set up an illusion to deter students from entering the fluorite room of the cave. So much power might be too much of a temptation. But, with Elm gone and nobody else aware of it, there's no better spot for me to hide out and study the art of entering dreams. If anything, Blake's words just made me more determined to master my Mentalist abilities. This is part of me now, whether he approves or not.

I read through the chapter once more, taking notes to be certain I haven't missed anything crucial. Elm wasn't kidding—this dream invasion stuff is complicated. First you have to be dreaming and have a solid recognition that you're dreaming. That seems easy enough. But from there, you have to focus on sending your mental self to the dream plane, which I'm guessing is the place where I first met Elm. The only reason I found my way there before was because of Elm entering my dreams. I'm not sure how to get there without Elm forming the bridge.

Once in the dream plane, I have to find the portal to Selene's dreams, which the book describes as something you discern with feeling rather than sight. Previous physical contact with a person is required in order to enter their dreams. That, fortunately, won't be a problem. The thought of the maternal embraces and pats on the shoulder Selene gave on so many occasions now sends a shiver of repulsion through me. All of it was a lie. But, I'll use that against her.

Once you enter the person's dreams, it's a matter of safely

navigating them. Since dreams are unstable, you have to be prepared for change at any instant. Any damage done to your mental self translates to your physical body.

I take a deep breath. I've read about it practically to the point of memorization. All I can do at this point is try it. First step: dream.

I have to slow down my mind to fall asleep. But all I can think about is Elm traveling alone with Samantha. How close were they as children? He obviously still has a fondness for her, and she's been very clear in her feelings for him. What would it be like with the two of them traveling together, Samantha throwing herself at him constantly? She has the benefit of sharing a nostalgic past with him. That's bound to conjure up something.

Hands shaking, I slam the book shut. This isn't happening today. If there's one thing I've learned from my mistakes in the past, it's not to practice dangerous or unfamiliar magic while distracted.

Next time for sure, I tell myself, slipping out of the glittering room and back into the bustle of the cave.

I leave the crystal room again, but something doesn't feel right this time. I'm light-headed and my steps don't seem to connect with the ground. Definitely time for a break. I pass one of the clear pools and kneel down to splash my face with cool water.

I stare at my reflection rippling in the pool. My eyes look too tired. Too . . . wavy.

Wavy?

The pool undulates, and suddenly Elm emerges from it. I jump back in surprise.

"Miss Ava," he says with stern disapproval. "What have you been up to, my dear?"

When did he get back? What was he doing in the pool? How could I not have noticed him?

Oh! My mind at once snaps into focus. *I'm dreaming!*

Once this realization hits, Elm disappears, and a peculiar sensation overtakes me. At first, I feel like I'm floating out of my body, but then everything begins to feel more solid. More real. I no longer have that slightly separated feeling that comes when dreaming. I can feel the cool cave air. Smell the dampness when I inhale. I pinch myself, and it stings. For a moment, I wonder if I'm actually awake, but that can't be the case. I search around for the portal I know must be there, fighting to keep command over my emotions so that I don't lose my chance to access the dreamscape.

I catch the faintest gleam of the portal; it's so small. I run to the swirling speck, and as I approach, it opens up bigger and bigger until it swallows me up. Now I stand in that pearlescent, undulating place where I first met Elm. This is where I'll find entry to Selene's dreams.

Several portals speckle the landscape before me. People I've had physical contact with. They all look a little bit different. I take a breath and reach a timid hand out toward the one nearest me. A jolt, and countless images bombard me at once. Blue eyes. Zap Blaster. Competitions. Too many and too fast for me to pick out each one individually, but I know without a doubt that this one is Blake.

A worrying thought strikes me: if I find Elm's portal, would he know? His pond appearance was just a dream—right? Would he be able to tell I was testing things, even if I don't enter his dreams? I stare at the remaining portals. They all look slightly different, but there's no way for me to know whose is whose without examining them. I have to take the chance.

I move to the next one. Soft. Shy. Admiration. This one is Sarah.

Caring. Healing. Concern. A bit of trepidation. Dr. Iris.

The next one hits me stronger than the others. Yellow. Warmth. Desire. Laughter. Protection—

I snap myself away. Elm's portal. It would be wise to memorize what this one looks like so I can avoid it in the future. It's striking, with a golden center that spirals outward into shades of deep blue and flecks of light around the edges. I take a moment for my heartbeat to slow before proceeding to the next portal.

Three more in, and then I find it, full of conflict. Anger and hatred mixed in with maternal warmth and high expectations. Everything awash in red. Selene. I'm not sure if I'm ready for this. My heart pummels the inside of my chest. But I have to do this. I have to do *something*.

I step through.

I expected a wasteland, or a barrage of weaponry. I expected chaos. I didn't expect this.

It's Prism, but not Prism. The halls are familiar, but everything is just slightly off. A doorway where there shouldn't be one, an extra turn here and there. And a faintly misty quality about the walls.

I turn around and startle as I see . . . me. I expect the dream-me to feel the way I feel, but she doesn't seem to notice me at all. Instead, she walks forward down a long, wide hallway.

Dream-Ava calls out, "Selene?"

I hide behind a corner as I hear the footsteps and peer around as much as I dare. Selene looks younger. The way I remember her from when I was a child. The dream-Ava has shifted now to five-year-old Ava. Selene's face goes blank.

"Why do you always come here?" Selene's voice is cold with fury. "Why did you have to ruin everything?"

The child Ava stares up at her as the anger intensifies on Selene's face.

"You deserved it for what you did," the child says in a small voice.

Selene screams like a wounded animal, and suddenly red slashes appear all across dream-Ava's body, who has somehow become a teenager again. Dream-Ava bursts into bloody nothingness.

I can't suppress a scream of horror and shock. Selene's eyes narrow, and suddenly, too suddenly even for an Augmentor, she is around the corner, face-to-face with me. How did she move like that?

Well, this is a dream.

Her dream.

I try to run, but my legs seem to be on a treadmill. I can't go forward no matter how desperately I try. Selene just murdered dream-me—what's to stop her now? She might restrain herself in real life, but she'd have no reason to hold back in her dreams. Panic rises. I'm going to die here.

Wake up. Wake up!

I'm still here, and a slash of red cuts across my arm. I shriek at the sharp pain. The very real pain. Selene slaps me, and I propel backward with far more force than should be possible. I try to run again, but I can't. I attempt to cast an agility spell, but my body feels cold and useless.

WAKE UP NOW!

My eyes fly open, and I shiver from head to toe, breathless. My heart won't stop its frenzied pounding. Blood trickles down my arm in several ribbons, and my cheek stings sharply where Selene struck me. I inhale and exhale slowly to calm myself enough to perform a healing spell.

Drat. Drat, drat, drat!

I didn't expect my first time in a dream to go so very badly, but maybe I should have. Elm wasn't exaggerating. If I continue this, I could very easily die in an instant. I struggle to remind myself Elm managed to survive. Other Mentalists have done it. So can I. There must be little tricks, creative mind maneuvers for survival. I just need to figure out a safer way to experiment before setting off after Selene again.

My arm is still in bad shape, but I think I've healed it enough that I can pass it off as an injury from the cave. Jazz is a much more skilled Healer than I am and can help complete the healing.

I move from the deserted corridors into more populated areas and follow the sounds of echoing laughter. Blanca and Kaito are engaged in a game of tug-of-war with a broken stalactite, Kaito tugging with his mind while Blanca pulls physically. She seems to be winning. I find Jazz among the watching cluster, next to Brie. He is rarely far from her side. He glances up as I approach, eyes growing wide at the sight of my arm.

"Ava! What happened to you?"

"I scraped it in a silly fall," I say, wincing for effect. "Would you mind healing it for me?"

"Are you sure you trust him to do that?" Brie teases. "He'll probably tear your arm off."

"Go pester somebody else," Jazz grumbles, but with a twitch of a smile.

Suddenly a scream echoes through the chambers. Everyone freezes, then I spring to my feet mid-healing, which causes one of the gashes to burst open again. Jazz calls after me, but I'm already bolting in the direction of the cry, using Red magic to propel me there faster.

I catch sight of the dark spirals of Nikki's hair and Sarah's hysterical face before my eyes focus on Blake lying stone-cold on the ground. Blood runs down the back of his head.

No.

I scramble to place my ear to his chest and hear the faint murmur of his heart. I sag in relief.

"What happened?" I ask. It's becoming our theme question. I immediately begin a healing spell, though my hands are trembling.

"I found him this way," Sarah chokes.

Nikki looks shaken. "I came as fast as I could when I heard Sarah scream. Ava, I've searched the area, but there is nobody else around."

Jazz shows up then, and once he sees Blake, I don't even have to ask before he is by Blake's side to assist me. My mind is already running over the students who were with us a moment ago, trying to think of who was missing. But it was just a portion of our group, so it really isn't helpful. One thing I know for certain, though, is that it couldn't have been Samantha. Part of me already knew, but my own feelings made it hard to admit. I can't pretend anymore that any of this is her fault.

"We have to figure out what's going on, Ava," Nikki says, her complexion ashen. "This is more than an attack on our resources. Now they're actually hurting people."

She's right. And whoever is doing this isn't only targeting Elm. I determine to practice going into dreams again. Not just for White magic, but to see if I can detect any snippets of information about what's been happening here. If dream invasion allows me to get insight without leaving the cave and drawing extra risk, then I simply have to do it.

12

"AVA, REALLY, I'M FINE." BLAKE NUDGES
my hand away from his head. "You're like an old mother hen."

"You're sure it doesn't hurt anymore?"

"Jazz knows his stuff." He throws off the covers and pushes
himself out of bed.

"Wait! You should rest more. Jazz says if there was any sort
of internal injury, he isn't sure if—"

Blake's pillow hits me in the face, propelled by Shaper magic.

"I said I'm fine," he repeats and grins as I try with little
success to push the pillow away.

"Okay, okay! Get it away!"

He floats the pillow to his bed, and I straighten it back into
place. "So you still don't remember anything?"

Blake shakes his head. "I wish I could. All I know is I was
making my way to the main room of the cave and suddenly I
was waking up in my bed with you and Jazz patching me up. I
don't remember being attacked."

"Well, we're thankful you're okay. That's what matters. But
we do need to find out who's responsible." Things have been
different since Blake was attacked. Destroying objects and
food is one thing—actually harming a person is another. Every
action that seems carefree on the surface carries a weight of

fear and uncertainty deeper down. We're not going to become more unified with a traitor among us, that's for sure.

"We could try and practice that magic merging thing again," Blake offers.

I shake my head vigorously. "No."

"It was a good idea. Just maybe not great execution."

"No," I insist firmly. "I'm not putting anyone at risk without knowing what I'm doing." I really do want to test the waters with combined magic more, but can I really ask that of anyone? At least going into dreams is only putting me at risk.

He shifts. "What if just you and I practice?"

"Like I said, I'm not putting you in danger, Blake. Especially while you're still recovering."

He points to his head. "Already recovered. And you're not putting me in danger. I'm volunteering to help. You can't do this by yourself."

He sounds just like Elm. And I know he's right. For this particular task, I really do need someone to practice with, and I do trust Blake. So much can be accomplished if we can make this work. "All right. We'll try it. But not until I know for sure you're totally healed."

He smirks. "If my head's as hard as yours, you have nothing to worry about."

"Are you ready to let me carry it now, hotshot?" I cock my head at Blake while he stares at the splash of water across the stone floor of the cave, the fallen cauldron beside it.

"No," Blake replies stubbornly, bending down to turn the now empty cauldron back over. "What we need is a respectable bucket for carrying water instead of this huge thing. I can't use my magic to keep this steady with all that water sloshing around." He raps the side of it. "Where the heck did Elm get this anyway? And why?"

I can't help but smile. "He said it felt more mysterious cooking with a big black cauldron than a simple pot."

"Sounds like him."

I cast a quick strengthening spell to lift the hefty cauldron with one hand, and grin. "We still have pasta to make, so why don't you let me take care of the water this time?"

At once, the cauldron floats just out of my reach. I raise my eyebrows at Blake.

"Or," he remarks, "why don't we try to make a bucket?"

I'm not sure now is the best time to practice when it's our turn to make dinner and we have a cave full of hungry people waiting for us. But it is also vital that we learn how to bring our magic together so I agree. "All right, just put that thing down before you hurt someone."

The cauldron floats back to the ground with surprising control. I guess it really is easier for him without the water inside. Blake reaches his hand out to me, and I take it. We still aren't sure if the touch is really necessary, but it did something before.

"What kind of bucket are we making?" I ask.

"A normal one."

"What is a 'normal' bucket?"

"I don't know. A regular-sized metal one with a little handle?"

"Regular-sized?"

He sighs. "About half the size of Elm's stupid cauldron. How about that?"

That gives me something more specific to work with. I place it in my mind: The silver curves. The tinny metal. The swinging handle. I imagine the heft of it and the way it might feel to carry it. Hopefully, Blake is doing the same. My head feels warm, and the current of magic moves down through my arm to where Blake and I have joined hands. My eyes open as I feel a little spark, and I see a glow of Green magic between us. I gasp in surprise at the bucket that appears in the air ahead of us.

Blake whistles. "Now the question is, does it hold water?"

I reach for it, and my hopes fall as my hand slips right through. Simply another illusion.

"Your illusions are getting better, though, Ava. So that's something, right?"

"Maybe my Mentalist abilities are still too weak in general . . . maybe that's why we can't combine our magic."

"I don't think it's you. I think this is just complicated. We don't even know what's possible."

"White magic is combined magic, though." The thought of it being impossible depresses me. "Come on." I sigh. "Let's get this water taken care of."

Nikki is waiting for us in the cooking area. "Need any help?"

"You're not on duty tonight. You should take a break."

"It's more fun with you two. Besides," she winks at me, "we have to make sure you're not too lonely with Elm gone."

I roll my eyes.

Nikki and Blake share a loaded glance as we set to work getting a fire started. I wait, preparing myself for whatever they're about to say.

"Hey, Ava," Nikki begins, "Blake said you're trying the color mixing stuff again."

I shoot him a look. "I told you I didn't want anyone else involved!"

He shoots me a look back. "It's Nikki. And I figured the more help the better."

Nikki tosses a few more sticks into the fire. "I want to stop the Benefactors, too, you know. Let me help."

I open my mouth to refuse, but the words halt on my tongue. Should I really be a gatekeeper here? They're in this too. "All right. But let's try to keep it under wraps from here on out. Until we know what we're doing, I don't want to take any chances."

13

SO MUCH YELLOW. AND SPARKLE. A room full of sunshine and glitter. Samantha's dream. I decided to practice on someone else who isn't harboring as much animosity as Selene, but who doesn't have pleasant feelings for me. At the very least, I'm confident Samantha wouldn't try to hurt me when she knows Elm wouldn't want that . . . right?

My eyes widen as I look ahead, and angry flames seer my insides. Perched atop a giant sunflower I see Samantha and Elm, and she's positioned cozily in his arms, toying with one of his curls.

Just a dream. Just a dream.

Elm leans in and gives her a passionate kiss. Everything inside of me goes blank. I don't know why I came here or what I was trying to do. I don't know how to tear my eyes away.

A wet droplet on my head makes the world around me ripple. Then another. Slowly the edges fade, blurring and darkening, and finally, I'm freed from the sight of Elm and Samantha tangled up together.

I open my eyes and feel the *drip, drip, drip* of water from a stalactite overhead. A sob tightens my chest, and my eyes mist. *Just a dream.*

But I can't help wondering if the dream was Samantha's fantasy or if it was based on reality. They've been gone almost a week now. Just the two of them, with whatever their history is. And what if Elm was really in her dream? Can two Mentalists go inside the same dream? Did that happen for real?

I resist the impulse to ransack all of Elm's books to find out the probability of that dream being more than a dream. I should go see Nikki. It would be nice to spend real time with a friend and not worry about dream worlds.

Laughter floats in toward my ears as I approach the room Nikki and I share. I watch from the doorway as Nikki and Blake, oblivious to me, take turns using their magic to throw pebbles against a makeshift target. Nikki places a hand on Blake's arm, and he leans in and says something, which sets them both off laughing again.

A mélange of emotions overtakes me, seeing them smile at each other like that. Happiness for them. A loneliness that there's something there I can't share. Wavering back and forth between images of Elm and Samantha. I take a step backward.

I'm just so confused about everything. Angry. Sad. Isolated. The emotions set my feet in motion before my head can process them.

I'm not sure what brings me here, but I plunge into Elm's room. I dive into his bed and breathe in his soft, lingering scent. Missing him is hard. Seeing my friends work together without me is hard. It's all hard.

This was so much easier when I was alone. I didn't have to worry about anyone but myself. It's good that Nikki and Blake are getting along so well. And it doesn't mean there's no room for me. I'm acting like a child. Everyone else seems to be able to understand the whole people thing. Why can't I? Did Selene isolate me for so long that there are parts about myself I can't change?

Selene's puppet.

No, not anymore. There's more to me than that.

Isn't there?

I just want to sleep.

14

THE BOY WEARS A YELLOW PRISM
uniform. Golden-tan skin and a cascade of dark curly hair.
Strong facial features that have a vague familiarity about
them. And the eyes—I would recognize them anywhere. Elm's
eyes. Who is he?

Selene has a shyness about her when he is near. I can feel
her heart flutter. This isn't the Selene I'm used to seeing.

She likes him.

"Hello, Selene," he says, smiling.

She smiles shyly back. "Hello, Andres."

Something flickers in my mind, and my thoughts change.

*I'm utterly fascinated by Mentalists. Such a unique power.
They could easily dominate everyone if that's what they wanted.
But it seems like most of them don't enjoy using their abilities
that way . . . Mother being the exception. So interesting.*

Andres looks like he has somewhere to be.

*"Thanks for your help on my paper the other day," Andres
says. "You've really got a brilliant mind."*

*He glances over his shoulder. "I must run for now, but I'll see
you around, I hope."*

*My heart glows, but then I notice where he's going. To her.
That Mentalist with the perfect golden curls and honey eyes.*

I open my eyes. A dream? No, that felt more like . . . a

memory. Selene's memory? Did she really once pine after a Mentalist? Confusion jumbles me with lingering feelings of Selene's jealousy. How did I end up in Selene's memories?

I'm still in Elm's room, and the security of it mingles with guilt. I've been sulking when I should have been taking care of things. I probably made Nikki worry when I didn't come back to our room. Or maybe she was too busy with Blake to even notice.

They don't need you. You don't need them.

Of course we need each other if we're going to make progress and figure out this magic-blending thing. Blake shouldn't be playing around with Nikki when I need him. I should find him and get back to the grindstone.

I cross paths with him coming out of the main room.

"There you are, Ava! Ready to get back to work?" he asks.

Didn't they even think to come looking for me? With a traitor hiding among us, didn't it matter to them that I never came back?

"I was ready to get to work last night, but I guess you were busy with Nikki." The coolness in my voice is evident.

He just stares at me. "You're upset that I was with Nikki?"

"I mean . . . you're allowed to play games if you want, I guess. But there are bigger things at stake, don't you think? I know you don't take anything seriously, but maybe you should for once." The hurt in his eyes is real, and it hurts me too. Why am I acting this way? I know it's wrong, but I can't seem to stop. The angry words continue to bubble out of me like boiling water. "You're always nosing into my business, but you can't be here when I actually need you?" *Stop, Ava.*

His expression darkens. "You know, you've always been a jerk to me, but this is probably the worst thing you've ever done."

He may as well have slapped me. "Excuse me?"

"When you stayed with my family. I get that you didn't really want to be there, and you only had one thing that was important to you. But we lived in the same home together. You practically ignored me for years. But I was always watching you, waiting for you to spend time with me. And here I thought we were finally becoming closer."

My true feelings try to break free of this haze of malice. "I know I treated you badly. I'm sorry. Believe me when I say I'm a different person now, or at least, I'm trying to be. Back then, my vision was a straight line toward being a Benefactor, and I couldn't see anything that didn't fall on that line . . . it wasn't just you." I hope I'm making sense. "Blake, I'm sorry."

"And now"—he continues as though he didn't hear me—"you don't want me to be friends with anyone else either? What's going on with you, Ava?"

The twisting cloud of anger that has been billowing inside of me rolls to the surface, suffocating any of the remorse I just felt. "Nothing is going on with me," I say. "Just that apparently I'm the only person in this cave who cares about getting out. I'm the only one who's doing any work to try and fight back against Selene."

"It's Elm, isn't it?" Blake's voice is bitter. "He changed you. Or maybe now that you know you have Mentalist abilities, too, it was just a matter of time."

"What?" I spit.

"Listen, Ava. I'm trying hard to get on board with you that Mentalists are good. But everything I'm seeing says something else. Just look at you now."

I'm taken aback by his words. But I think of the things I've seen. What Elm's power can do. It's no wonder everyone is afraid. "I'm not really a Mentalist," I mutter.

I turn away from Blake, and he grabs my arm. "Seriously, something isn't right. Let's talk about it."

"Let go." I try to shake him off, but he tightens his grip. I struggle.

Wait, why am I struggling? I'm an Augmentor.

Strengthening myself, I shove him away from me, and he falls hard, looking stunned.

"I wasn't kidding." My voice is deep and clear. The power

feels . . . delicious. Mentalists aren't the only ones who can take control. Why shouldn't Augmentors be able to rise to the top too? We're just as capable as anyone. More so. I draw my fist back, pulling power as I prepare to strike. I shriek as a shower of rocks from the cave floor flies at me, leaving tiny fissures on my skin. How dare he?

"Ava?"

I detect something in the way Blake says my name—fear. Concern. It shakes something loose in me, and I feel like I'm coming back from an unknown place. My strengthening spell cuts off.

Blake gets to his feet.

"Don't touch me," I say.

He doesn't walk any closer.

"I'm sorry I did that, Ava. Really. But after . . . you . . . you didn't look like yourself for a moment."

"What do you mean?"

"Your face . . . You looked like you were lost."

I am lost. What is happening to me?

"I think we need a break from each other," I say slowly. "But I meant it when I said I'm sorry about before."

The world blurs as I retreat from Blake. But I can't escape from myself.

The halls are deserted. Nobody here except for me, Selene, and Andres.

Selene is speaking. "The spring formal is in two weeks. There's nobody I would enjoy going with more than you."

"I'm really flattered, Selene, and I do enjoy your company. But I'm already attending with someone."

"It's Delia, isn't it?" Selene's friendly tone is forced. "I've seen you in the halls with her. I think you'll have a wonderful time."

He smiles. "I must be going, but I hope you have a fine evening."

Selene nods and busies herself with her locker. The door exiting the school clicks shut.

"Just because he doesn't want to go with you doesn't mean you can't have a good time," says a strange voice.

Somebody named Dillon and two of his cronies. All Yellows.

Selene slams her locker shut. "I have to go."

"Don't be like that," one tsks.

Dillon grabs her arm. "Always so unfriendly!"

"Let go."

"Or what?"

Selene is trying to build a strengthening spell. Before he knows what hit him, she jerks her arm away and sends him and his friends slamming into the lockers. She races down the hall, focused on the exit.

"Hey. We're not finished with you."

Selene stops suddenly midrun. Her feet start to move, but in the wrong direction. She is walking back to them? No . . . no.

Her mind is foggier with each step. There are smirks on the boy's faces, and Dillon taunts, "Let's dance."

Her legs bend. Too fast. Too far. There is a crack, and Selene tries to scream, but Dillon won't let her. Her arms are next. The pain is horrific. Somebody, please stop them!

I scream myself awake in a cold sweat, terrified and in tears. In spite of all the hatred I have felt for Selene over the past several months, I can't stop this current of sadness for her now. And the rage I feel for those . . . those *Yellow* monsters.

The Mentalist blood running through me is repulsive. A disease. But I've survived this long as an Augmentor. I don't need to hone my Mentalist abilities to be competent. Not many people know about my dual magic. I could continue living as an Augmentor, and nobody would be the wiser. The poison power within me would just be my dirty little secret. My eyes feel heavy again as I catch another whiff of orange blossom and cedarwood.

"Andres, do you have a moment?"

He clicks his locker shut and turns. "Selene, something on your mind?"

"I need you to teach me how to defend myself against Yellow magic."

The tone of his voice turns stiff. "Why?"

Her mother's cruel laugh and Dillon's smirk shudder through her mind. "Someone hurt me. I don't want it to happen again. Ever."

"Look, Selene, if someone hurt you, I am sorry about that. Truly. But you're trying to be a Benefactor, aren't you?"

"Yes." Her reply is curt. "What does that have to do with—"

"Did you know that it's been six years since a Mentalist was hired as a Benefactor?"

"I didn't, but—"

"Did you know that every day more Mentalists are arrested by Benefactors without cause?"

"I'm sure there's a good explanation."

"Oh, there's an explanation, all right. Pure, undiluted hatred. I apologize, but if you're going to be a Benefactor, I will not help in giving them another weapon."

"I'm not asking for a weapon. I'm asking for help combating the problem that Mentalists created for themselves."

"I can't help you."

Her helplessness quickly becomes resolve. If they won't help me, all that remains is to help myself, and to make sure nobody else gets hurt. By any means necessary. Andres will regret turning his back on me someday.

Me? Where is that coming from? My brain swims in a confused mist. I'm awake, right? Did I even fall asleep again? Am I experiencing Selene's memories even while awake now?

The pain of Andres turning his back wrenches my gut.

I have to get out of Elm's room. I've taken to practicing dream intrusion here instead of the fluorite room, but all the reminders of Yellow magic are sickening to me right now.

What time is it? Late afternoon? How long was I dreaming this time? I bump into Brie as I barrel from Elm's room.

She looks startled, then smiles. "Looks like you can use some air. I know I could." She peers behind her. "Jazz hasn't noticed I'm gone yet," she whispers loudly. "Can we please go outside for a bit?"

I know I'm supposed to scold her for repeatedly leaving the cave, but who can really blame her? I'm going stir crazy myself, and she's much younger. Besides, I'm suffocating here.

"Just a quick outing, okay?"

Brie beams and gives me a hug. Letting her express fondness for me feels like deceit.

Once outside the cave, Brie stretches in the golden, dimming sunlight and then immediately goes poking around for rocks and sticks. She reminds me of a puppy who has been cooped up for too long. She really is just a child. None of us should have to worry about running and hiding. None of us should have to worry that the adults around us could decide at any moment to forfeit our lives.

The low caw of a raven sounds in the distance, and I quickly scan our surroundings as Brie gathers pine needles and twists them together. Normal forest sounds shouldn't make me so jittery. I remember a time before all this, when I would have enjoyed just sitting in the woods with a book, taking it all in.

Why are we fighting this fight? We were okay with things before, weren't we? Is it really so bad to have someone in charge? Yellow magic *is* dangerous, so isn't it really better to protect people from it? Life was so much easier . . . so much less complicated.

Brie hums happily and balances along a fallen tree. In the

distance, I hear the crack of twigs. Maybe just an animal, but we can't take that risk.

Or can we?

What would happen if I just let us be caught? Would Selene give me another chance? If we fell under Jace's mind control once more, could we all just resume our lives and be students again? Blissful ignorance. Everyone safe in a perfect snow-globe world.

My heart beats as I hear the distinct murmur of voices. Brie is oblivious to it, trusting me to assess and warn of danger. After all we have gone through, and how far we've come, I can't believe I'm seriously considering this. But if I'm going to maintain our cover, we need to act now. We should go. We should—

And then the voices emerge in the dusky glow, eliminating my need to choose.

"Well, hello, Miss Ava."

Elm and Samantha both look travel worn, but Elm looks genuinely happy to see me. A part of my heart sings at seeing him back and unharmed, but my mind feels muddled and repulsed as he approaches. He touches my face, concern and questioning in his eyes. The fog lifts, and I throw my arms around him.

"Welcome home." I didn't realize how badly I needed him here until now.

He leans back and studies me. "Something's wrong." He is not deceived for an instant. "Tell me what happened. Were there more attacks?"

"One. But that isn't really the problem right now."

Where should I even start? Blake being attacked? The crazy thoughts going through my head? The fact that I went against his warnings?

"You didn't let them ruin anymore of Elm's stuff, did you?" Samantha narrows her eyes at me, her voice high and accusing.

"Sammy, why don't you head in?" Elm steers Samantha away from me. "I'm sure you're ready for some rest, and I would like to speak with Miss Ava alone. Take Brie back with you, perhaps?"

A storm flashes in her eyes, but at last she nods and stalks away into the cave. "Let's go, Brie," she shouts.

"It's good to see you, Elm. Thanks for the break, Ava!" Brie skips off after Samantha, and I feel like she took all the sunshine with her. Elm guides me to the log Brie balanced on moments before and sits, pulling me down beside him.

"Now, what trouble did you all get into while I was away?"

The tale spills out as I tell him about the attack on Blake. About my failed attempts to merge our magic. But not everything. I know I need to tell him about the dreams, but the words freeze in my throat every time I try to shove them forward.

Elm furrows his brow, listening. He slowly runs his thumb along one of the scratches from Blake's shower of rocks. Then another. And another. I never did bother to heal the marks. It seemed important to keep them there as a reminder in case I felt out of control again.

"What happened?"

"Blake flung some pebbles at me. We were fighting," I admit. I'm getting closer to the subject now, but I still can't make myself tell him.

"He *what*?"

"He was defending himself," I say quickly. "I started it."

Elm has an odd frown on his face and doesn't seem focused on what I just said. "Elm?"

He doesn't respond.

I'm a little worried. "You're not plotting against Blake, are you?"

"Well, obviously I'm considering numerous satisfying ways to torment him. Did he apologize sufficiently for harming you? I could make him very sorry."

That cloud overtakes me, and I feel the mistrust and anger seeping in again. Sneering faces. Twisted, cracking limbs.

"Well, if you really wanted to, you *could* make him sorry, couldn't you?" I retort. "Isn't that what being a Yellow is all about?"

"I beg your pardon?"

"You could make Blake—or me, for that matter—do exactly what you command. Is that what you want?"

His eyes widen in shock, an undercurrent of pain twisting his features. "Of course that isn't what I want." He is looking at me peculiarly. "Just because someone has the ability to do something doesn't mean they should or would. And I thought you"—his voice drops—"you, Miss Ava, of all people, would understand that."

He stands, and the moonlight reflects off the silver now lining his eyes. Something shatters within me, and I clutch his hand, my knees suddenly feel weak.

"Please," I plead. "Oh, Elm, I'm sorry. Please. Please, don't go."

He stares down at me, his expression unreadable.

"I didn't—I *don't* mean any of that." I cling to his hand. "I think something is really wrong with me." My voice rises in panic.

Despite the emotional wounds I just inflicted on him, he gently pulls me up and places his hands firmly on either side of my face. I fight against the intrusive repulsion that tries to mask the warmth his touch brings.

"Tell me."

Tears come to my eyes. "I ignored what you told me about going into dreams."

His body goes rigid.

"I went into Selene's dreams . . . and . . . and now I think something is wrong."

Elm closes his eyes and takes a breath. When he opens them, they are grave. "Miss Ava. What did you do?"

I tell him everything. About Selene attacking me the first time I entered her dreamscape. About the memories. The violent thoughts. He listens in a deadly stillness. The silence is heavy and amplifies the cool touch of the air on my skin. The glitter of stars in the sky above the flickering dome. He's far too calm. When I can stand it no more, I finally blurt, "Are you mad at me?"

He doesn't say a word. He sternly takes hold of my arm and pulls me up. His reaction is too distressing for me to dare ask what he's thinking. We return to the sinkhole, and he takes me to his room and pulls a book off of the shelf.

He thumbs through the pages and shoves the book into my hands, stern and commanding. "Chapter 27," he says. "Page 536, paragraph 4. Read it."

My eyes begin to skim, and he snaps, "Out loud."

I comply. "An imbalance of magic use can cause a number of undesirable effects. Inexperienced Mentalists entering another person's dream may have access to their memories. While this may seem harmless or even useful on the surface, this means the Mentalist has also opened up to vulnerabilities of their own mind. In other words, by opening a bigger door into the mind of another, the initiator's mind is opened as well. The Mentalist will start to confuse his own ideals with those of the person whose mind he entered, and his own thoughts and memories are vulnerable to examination."

"Oh," I breathe.

"'Oh' indeed."

He stares at me in silence again, his face eerily calm.

"Please say something," I finally beg.

"I'm extremely angry with you."

"You should be." *Oh, Elm. Please, please forgive me.*

"But," he sighs, "I'm also relieved. Relieved there's an explanation for the things you said." He gazes at me. "And that you haven't had a change of heart about me."

My heart swells and my lip quivers. "I'm sorry." It's not enough and will never be enough, but I can't stop myself from saying it again. "I'm truly sorry."

"You disregarded everything I told you."

"I know."

"You didn't trust me enough to listen to what I asked."

"I know."

"And yet," he throws himself onto the chair beside his bed, "I can't help but be a little impressed."

I stare at him with wide eyes, bewildered.

"The fact that you even managed to get into the dreamscape and target Selene specifically, with no training beyond what you read, is quite impressive. I am, of course, furious about the harm you've put yourself in, but really, I'm not sure why I'm surprised. We *are* talking about the girl who spent her whole life trying to be a Benefactor and then went rogue with a Mentalist because she had questions." He flourishes his hand at that last word. "This is par for the course, really. I can't control you. Nobody can." He grins.

"This isn't funny."

"It's a little funny."

Now the anger is all mine. I want him to yell at me. I want him to cut through the guilt I feel. To show some sign of imperfection or just . . . something.

I put my hands on my hips. "You know, I've been worried sick this whole time. About the intruder. About what's happening to me. Worrying that you might be kissing Samantha." I can't believe I just said that.

Elm's laughter stops, and he looks at me. "Miss Ava. Do you really think I would do that to you?"

"I guess I was more worried she wouldn't give you much choice."

"Ah, fair enough, I suppose. But count on the fact that you would hear of nothing else from Sammy if that had occurred."

"Why is she like that, anyway?" I huff.

"Like what, precisely?"

"So clingy. She acts like she owns you. And she behaves like a child."

A shade of sadness crosses Elm's face. "I think poor Sammy has been caught in a bit of a time capsule of herself. She put everything into finding me, and I suspect she hasn't changed, because she hoped everything would be the same. I was her safe harbor."

"What do you mean?"

"Things weren't good for Sammy at home. Her parents were abusive."

It's amazing how quickly those words extinguish the fire in me.

"She stayed with my family often, and we became fast friends. I felt more like her brother. Her protector. But she saw us differently." His eyes are soft and distant. "She asked me to marry her when we grew up so that we'd always be together. I loved her—not in the way she wanted—but I wanted to make her happy."

"And she still thinks you're held to that bargain?" I bristle at the thought.

"Oh, I don't believe she really thought she could pin me to promises we made when we were children. But in case there was any doubt, I did clear that up with her while we were away." He gives me a glance, those hazel eyes both disconsolate and caring. "And, understand, Miss Ava, I wouldn't hold you to any promises either."

My heart stutters. This is it. I've messed up too badly this time. He's going to find some nice way to say he's ending our relationship. "What do you mean?"

He stares ahead, choosing his words carefully. "I always felt that you may eventually want to experience something or someone other than me. Selene hoarded you for so long that you never really got a chance to explore other relationships. I don't suppose I can blame you."

"So are you saying . . . you don't want me to be with you?"

He looks startled and jumps from the chair to stand directly in front of me, placing his hands on my shoulders. "No, Miss Ava. I'm only saying it's new to you. If it were up to me, I would turn all the world to dust in order to keep you by my side. To hold you close always and banish anyone who even so much as thought about taking you away from me." His eyes soften. "But that's not entirely my choice. You have your own mind. Your own heart. And if you decide you want another, that's not up to me."

I have goosebumps.

I can't believe I was so worried. So this is what it feels like to have unconditional love. To have someone who is loyal no matter what and accepts all the mess and cracks that are part of me. I want to become the kind of person who really deserves that.

The layers of stress and fear come undone and dissolve into a stream of tears. Elm holds me close and lets me empty the well of my emotions as I snuggle into him. "I promise I'm going to be better."

"I know you will," he replies, then adds pointedly, "Swear you will not go into any more dreams until we can do so properly."

"I promise. But will that be enough to fix me?"

"I certainly hope so," he says fervently. "But I'm afraid I don't know for certain."

I nod. "We'll take it a day at a time." I wipe away my tears and look up at him. "For now, though, there's someone else I need to talk to, and I want you to be with me."

Blake looks up from the droplets of water he toys with at the edge of the stream, and his eyes darken when he sees Elm, fingers entwined tightly with mine. Shame washes through me, and I have to fight to maintain eye contact.

"So," Blake sits back, "I guess now that he's here you can start ignoring me again?"

Elm's voice sounds casual. "I'd advise you to speak to her carefully."

"Or you'll do what?" Blake says derisively. "All you have are parlor tricks. You can't even hurt me."

No sooner does he say it than his eyes widen, and he clutches at his stomach, groaning.

"I believe I just did," remarks Elm. "Or perhaps more accurately, *you* believe I just did."

"Elm," I snap. "Don't. This isn't why we came here."

Elm ignores me. "I believe you were the one who intentionally marred Ava's skin with rocks."

"Only because her mind got poisoned by Mentalist ideals."

Before I know what's happening, the room is suddenly full of Elms. Just like the time we sparred in the crystal room. All of it is done simply as a distraction, and Blake's eyes dart in every direction. At once the Elms vanish, and the real Elm holds Blake tightly by the collar, looking him dead in the eye. "Do not lay a finger on her again. Is that clear?"

One of Elm's cufflinks pops suddenly off his sleeve and hits him in the brow. Elm blinks, surprised, and then ducks as a chunk of cave rock comes flying toward him. He waves his cane to swat away stray bits of rubble.

"Blake! Knock it off!" I shout.

The rock starts to move toward Elm again, but then it stops. Blake looks confused as he runs and snatches the rock out of the air and throws it. Toward his own head.

"Elm!"

Neither of them is going to pay attention to me. Their fighting continues until I stand suddenly in between them. I hold out my arms and send a Red-powered punch into each of them. "STOP. IT."

My voice reverberates as both Blake and Elm get to their feet from the cave floor.

"Honestly, what's the matter with you two?" I shake my head. "Ridiculous. Both of you."

"Elm, Blake was right to try to stop me; he just didn't handle it well. Blake," I say, looking directly at him, "I've treated you really badly, and we came here because I wanted to set things straight."

He eyes me skeptically.

"Please, just listen." I tell him about the dreams and about Selene, continuing in such a torrent that neither he nor Elm can say something stupid. "It doesn't excuse my bad behavior toward you," I finish, "but there's been a lot going on, and my head isn't on straight. I wanted you to know."

His expression has calmed. "I get it. I do. I just . . . wanted to help."

"I know," I say. Elm listens to the side, though I know it's taking a lot for him not to engage. I take a deep breath. Being raised with Benefactor parents, this has to be a particular challenge for him. "Blake, I haven't always treated you well, and I want to be better friends, but if that's hard for you with my Mentalist abilities and Elm and I as a couple, I understand. There's a lot to overcome."

He looks defeated, and it stings to see him that way. But he finally gives a short nod. "I got it." He shifts. "I've got things to do." He heads to the door, then turns. "Thanks for the apology, Ava." He doesn't look at Elm as he leaves.

I watch him as he goes, glad to have all cards on the table, but still feeling guilty over the whole situation. I turn to Elm, who watches me sheepishly.

"Please, don't ever do that again," I say sternly. "I don't need you fighting like a dog on my behalf."

"Woof," he grins, but then becomes solemn. "My apologies, Miss Ava. I should have been better behaved."

"I guess I'm in no position to scold you for bad behavior." I sigh. "Oh, Elm, can we just . . . pretend the last few weeks never happened?"

"No," Elm says, bonking me lightly on the forehead. "But we can learn from it and move on."

I smile at him. That's good enough for me.

15

THE MOTHER HAS THAT CRAZY LOOK IN

her eyes.

"Did you do this?" She holds up a pair of blue pants with a hole in the knee.

"I-I'm sorry." The brother stammers. "I didn't mean to. I tripped on the steps on the way to class."

"Do you know how expensive these uniforms are? Do you know how hard I have to work to provide them for you?"

The brother doesn't speak. Fear in his own eyes grows.

"Answer me, you careless brat!"

"It was an accident." The girl Selene intervenes. "He's a Shaper. He can fix it. I'll help pay for new ones if he can't."

"You and that Red power of yours, Selene." The mother's face transforms into a cruel smile. "Teach your brother a lesson."

"What?"

"I said make your Augmentor-self useful, and teach your brother a lesson."

"No."

Selene's arms lift without her permission, and she can feel them strengthening.

"No, please! Don't make me do this!"

"It's not your fault, Selene," the brother says in a small voice.

"Last chance to do it on your own. It will be easier for both of you if you simply do what I say."

Selene relents, and the brother looks at her with pain in his eyes. But the instant she is released from control, Selene unleashes her full force on the mother instead. The hateful glee in the mother's eyes vanishes as she is sent crashing back into the china hutch. The brother has fled from the room.

The mother lies on the floor, her body broken. Broken by Selene.

Footsteps approach. A man and a woman in Benefactor uniforms appear.

At once everything shifts and spins, the view taking place from my own eyes.

"I didn't mean to," I say immediately. *"She was going to hurt my brother—"*

The man puts a hand on my shoulder, but not in a reprimand. "You did the right thing. Your mother was dangerous. All Mentalists are. But all is going to be well now."

"You're Selene, correct?" says the woman. "We've heard about your talents. You've now proven how much you care about keeping Magus safe. We are her to recruit you."

"As a Benefactor?"

The man indicates the sofa. "Sit down."

I comply and the woman sits beside me. "All is going to be well."

They keep saying that. It must be true.

I gasp awake and shove the hand away from my shoulder, prepared to fight.

"Miss Ava."

The soothing voice brings me back. I blink a few times, shaking away the remnants of the memory of starting off as an observer, then ending up one with Selene. Elm sits at my bedside as he promised to be while I work through my scrambled mind.

"What if it never stops?" I whisper, ghosts of voices and faces still trying to claw their way to the forefront of my mind.

"If it never stops, I'll still be here."

I pull myself from bed, fighting down the panic that always rears its monstrous head every time Selene's memories overtake my own. "I need air. I need to get out of here. I—"

"The sunflowers need attending to," Elm remarks. "Perhaps you'd like to go tend to them with me?"

"I would love to, but one of us has to stay here." Something within me says that our time of safety grows thinner by the moment. There's no way we can both leave. Not now.

"I'll stay here. I'm certain Blake and Nikki would be willing to go with you." I can tell by the slight tension in his voice that this isn't easy for him. But he's willing to put his own reservations aside to help me.

"Thank you." I rest a timid hand on his cheek and go off to find my friends before any memories can swallow me up again.

I'm a little embarrassed by how quickly Blake and Nikki agree to join me. Everyone acts like I need to be handled with extra care, and I guess I can't blame them. I haven't used my best judgment lately, to say the least.

"Did he really need to plant these where they could only be accessed by boat?" Blake says, regarding the worn vessel bobbing on the river before us.

I think back to my frantic rush through the wild woods to reach Elm after Selene took my powers, remembering the harsh sting of the branches. "Well, you can get to it on foot. But this way is better. Trust me."

We teeter onto the boat, which doesn't seem suitable for three people, but we make it work.

"You sure those flowers aren't dead already?" Nikki shivers as we bob down the river, surrounded by red and orange foliage. "It's getting pretty chilly now."

"Elm says they're still doing well, but it *is* a bit strange." The thought of the flowers dying sends sadness through me, but I know I've been fortunate to have them as long as I have. "As long as they're growing, we'll take care of them."

"These were a birthday present?" Blake asks. "In April?"

"Yes?" I'm not sure why he looks so confused.

"When I was getting my parents' garden back in shape, I was reading a book on plant care. It said sunflowers bloom in late summer."

I shrug. "Maybe the book was wrong. Sunflower husbandry isn't exactly common knowledge these days."

"I guess it was about some kind of red sunflower. Maybe the yellow ones are different."

"Maybe."

We maneuver the boat to shore as the river slows and make our way onto the grassy bank. I inhale deeply through my nose, though I know we're not quite close enough for the perfume of flowers to reach us.

"Why does he still bother with these?" Blake wonders out loud as we walk. "It seems like with everything going on it would be easier to just leave them be."

Nikki elbows him. "Because he's romantic. I wish someone would do that for me."

Blake bumps into me as I stop short, and he huffs. "Give me some kind of warning before you—"

Nikki and I throw our hands over Blake's mouth at the same time as we take in the scene before us. Elm's sunflowers—my sunflowers—are a sea of fluttering red. Buggerflies resting on nearly every petal, gently flapping their wings. The sight might be enchanting to anyone not in the know, but to me it's like a vision of the blood that's yet to come. Ice fills my veins.

"Should we run?" Nikki whispers.

I shake my head and hurry to the spot where one of Elm's devices for hiding the sunflowers should be. My fingers fly roughly through the dirt, in search of what I already know I'm going to find: nothing.

The devices are gone.

"Ava, they're going to know we're here!" Blake warns.

"They already know." I stand and brush the soil from my hands, narrowing my eyes at the buggerflies. The only reason for there to be so many of them here, along with the missing devices, is for the Benefactors to send a message: there is no safety in this place anymore. Well, I can send a message of my own.

I walk slowly into the center of the field and remove my necklace so I'm visible again, causing Nikki to gasp and Blake to utter something incoherent behind me. The buggerflies whirr into action, already transmitting videos and data to the Benefactors. They begin to lift off of the sunflowers, and I stare straight into them.

"Ava!" Blake's whisper is urgent. I ignore him.

"Hi, Selene." I gaze fiercely up into the swarm of buggerflies. "You may have found this spot, but know this—you won't win. You can't. This world will only tolerate evil for so long. Even if this battle ends with me, you will lose the war." The whirring of the buggerflies grows louder, and now I spark into action. I reach for the nearest buggerfly and use a strengthening spell to crush the tiny mechanical insect. Then I use agility and set to work on as many as I can, swiping them from the air and destroying them one by one. Blake and Nikki join in, using their Shaper abilities to scramble the devices and send them falling from the sky.

After we have laid the whole crimson swarm of them to waste, I glance at Blake and Nikki. "*Now* we should run."

As we disappear into the trees, I turn and soak in one last look at my beautiful gift from Elm. This may be the last time I see it. But sunflowers will grow on Magus again. I will make sure of that.

16

THE INCIDENT WITH THE BUGGERFLIES
adds a new weight to our circumstances. Every day it's as
though I can hear a clock ticking the seconds away. Feeling the
movement of time pushing forward to that inevitable moment
of catastrophe. Something deep within me gives a low hum of
warning.

Soon. It's all going to happen soon.

Elm and I tried to brace everyone, but I feel like they don't
fully understand. In their minds we can just keep hiding here
forever in complete safety.

I pause in filling the basket of vegetables that we planned
to duplicate for dinner. Sarah and I are in charge of cooking
tonight, and she seems a little sluggish. "Are you alright?"

She looks up from the bag of rice she holds, seeming to
come out of a daze. "Oh, yes. I guess I must not be sleeping
well. I'm so tired lately."

The dark circles under her eyes add truth to her statement.
A pang of guilt hits me. I've been so consumed with myself
that I haven't paid much attention to many of the others. Sarah
really doesn't look well.

"Are you worried about what's been happening lately?"
Sarah is the type who doesn't share her feelings very openly,
but I know she worries.

"I . . . I don't know."

I set the vegetables down. "Maybe someone else should help tonight. I'm sure Elm would if I asked. I think you need to rest, or maybe even go see Jazz." I reach toward her, but she steps backward.

Sarah stares at me, her eyes suddenly growing cold. She lets the bag of rice fall from her hands with a thud, seeming not to even notice. She blinks a few times and says, "They're here."

A chill runs down my spine. "Who?"

At once I hear the shouting. I listen, straining to make out words through the chaos. I catch the only word I need to know: an air-shattering cry of "Benefactors!"

I bolt, but find myself pulled back. Sarah grips me with a strength I didn't know she had.

"Hold her," Sarah says robotically.

"Let go!" I power myself up and rip free from her, her nails leaving streaks of red across my skin. She lunges at my legs in an effort to keep me in place. I kick free and call on a short burst of power to push her away as I take off again.

I don't look back as I run. I'm certain she's not acting of her own accord. The Sarah I know would never voluntarily hurt anyone. My mind races faster than my body. Benefactors. Here. It was only a matter of time, wasn't it? I knew it was coming. But I didn't expect it now.

"Elm!"

I recognize Samantha's shriek, and panic overtakes me. I imagine what they'll do to Elm if they capture him again—if they would even take him alive this time. I draw from the red blouse I'm wearing and increase my speed.

At last I reach the cave's main chamber. Chaos. Students fighting against black-uniformed Benefactors across every inch. Shouting. Falling rock.

Blood.

My eyes scan the room quickly, but I don't see Elm. Or Samantha. Could they have been taken already?

A high-pitched cry makes me turn to see a Benefactor grabbing Brie from behind, pulling her toward the exit of the cave.

Jazz appears from nowhere, rage filling his normally placid eyes, "Not my sister!" He barrels into the Benefactor and punches him squarely in the jaw. The Benefactor is hardly fazed, and seconds later, a gash blossoms across Jazz's stomach, sending Brie into hysterics.

I have to fight.

No sooner have I had this thought than something connects with my head, sending stars before my eyes. A Shaper Benefactor manipulates bits of debris, sending them my direction. I duck out of the way, disoriented, but manage to avoid her attack. I urge myself back to Brie and her assailant, barely processing the sight of Jazz motionless on the cave floor.

Brie is holding the attacker off—just barely—and I note the Benefactor's now-colorless uniform stripes. I slam into him and put him in a choke hold until he falls to the floor. Brie rushes to her brother, sobbing.

"Start a healing spell as soon as you can, Brie!"

She nods through her tears, steadying herself to build her strength. I see her mouth move, but can't hear her through the pandemonium in the room.

Something collides with my ankle, and I stumble as a chain whips around it. *No, no, no.* I rip it off, but it keeps coming at me. My strengthening spells are coming slower, and it's progressively harder to keep the weapon at bay.

"Remember, the girl and the Mentalist are top priority!" a Benefactor barks, and at once, they all focus on me. Then Garren, sweet, gentle giant Garren, comes barreling through, throwing punches left and right, tears streaming down his face. A Benefactor leaping for me gets taken out of commission by a broken stalactite, and I see Nikki coming through like a warrior with Blanca close behind, firing off a stream of curses with every hit she delivers. Everyone looks like they've taken a few blows. I spot a few students making for the cave exit, and I just hope they can get away somewhere safe. Anywhere is better than here right now.

The addition of my friends allows me enough breathing room to use an agility spell to get closer to my attacker. My fist connects with her middle, and I dodge as her chain whips back toward me.

"Miss Ava!"

Even within the chaos around me, the sound of his voice soothes me. He's alive. For the moment he's still free.

I maneuver past the Benefactor and work my way to him. Once we finally reach each other, he says breathlessly, "We have to lead them to the crystal room. If I can get more power—"

I see what he's getting at. If Elm can access more power, even for just a second, he can take control over them. We won't have much time, because once they take in the details of the room they'll know they have access to more power too. But if we can time it just right . . .

Another Benefactor lunges for me, and Elm and I take off at a run, shouting at any students who can, to follow. Nikki, Blanca, and Garren pull from the fray to join us. Elm grabs one of his light spheres from the cave ceiling and then starts smashing each remaining one with his cane. "The less they can see, the more time I'll have," he pants.

"Good thinking." I surge forward, putting out the lights ahead of us, hoping the students can keep up in the dark.

At last, I see the twinkling of the room ahead. I put out the remaining lights and hold my breath. Elm's light bobs erratically toward me, the stampede of footsteps and shouted orders are close behind. Then, in an instant, the footfalls stop, and all I hear is ragged breathing next to me.

"You did it," I manage.

"But I can't hold them forever," Elm warns. "Even with the power of the stones, exercising my abilities will tire me eventually."

"Just kill them all," Blanca growls, appearing beside us.

"We can't do that, Blanca. We're not murderers." Even knowing who they are and what they've done. Some of these Benefactors are so young, many of them probably have no idea that they're fighting for the wrong side. Slaughtering them while they're under Elm's power would be wrong.

Samantha tumbles in, battered and breathing heavily. She immediately goes to Elm.

"How long can you manage to hold them?" I ask Elm.

"A while. Certainly long enough for you to assess the rest of the situation."

"I'll help." Samantha offers staunchly, and Elm accepts. I'm actually grateful for her.

I turn to Blanca. "I need you to find Sarah."

"Is she hurt?"

I search for the right words to describe the way Sarah behaved. "I think she's . . . compromised. I'll explain later. But for now, just find her, and Blanca, don't trust her. At all. Bring her to me as soon as you can. And please try not to hurt her."

"Got it."

"I'll be back as soon as I can," I say to Elm and Samantha.

The scene when I return to the main chamber stops me short. So much blood. My classmates, fallen. I see wounds that are far beyond my own healing capabilities. Probably even beyond Jazz's.

Is he even alive?

He has to be. They all have to be. The possibility of the alternative threatens the little strength I have left. I try to numb the hurricane of tumult inside of me to, as Elm said, assess the situation.

Across the room, a few Benefactors are still brawling with students. A handful of our group, who aren't severely injured or engaged in the struggle, approach me with haunted eyes.

"What do we do, Ava?"

They look to me, beseeching me, as their leader, to make this better.

"I . . ." I can't tell them that I don't know; I feel utterly defeated.

I *don't* know how to fix this.

My heart stops as two more adults rush into the room. Dr. Iris and a woman I don't recognize. I grab my arm in reflex, remembering the hot flash of pain where she wounded me before. Will she use that same power here and now?

"Stand down," Dr. Iris shouts. "Selene's orders!" The remaining Benefactors pause, looking at her in confusion, but comply.

"Assemble!" she orders. The Benefactors shove away any students in their path and stride to her. It stings to see Dr. Iris in this role, commanding in Selene's place. She was always so kind to me and healed countless numbers of students. Was all of that an act? Was she just following Selene's orders the whole time without any real care for the students she assisted?

Once all the Benefactors are gathered to her, Dr. Iris quickly pulls a tiny red pistol from her jacket. She fires beams of red light at the Benefactors.

I gasp. They are all incapacitated in a matter of seconds.

"They won't be down long," Dr. Iris says briskly. I nearly faint with relief. She's who I always thought she was.

The woman with her pulls a syringe out of her pocket and

jabs it into the arm of the Benefactor nearest her. "A heavy sedative. Primitive, but effective," she declares and looks around at us. "It will keep them out longer than your Red magic can."

I'm so confused. But through the bewilderment, a thought rises to the surface: we have a Healer here.

"Dr. Iris," I plead. She turns to me. "We need to heal people. Quickly." I spot Brie kneeling over her motionless brother, her face contorted with sorrow, and tentatively call out to her.

"He's alive," she chokes out her response, "but he doesn't look good."

"Please heal him first," I beg Dr. Iris.

Dr. Iris glances at the woman. "Hazel, can you patch up the minor injuries so I can focus on the bigger ones?"

Hazel nods and sets right to work. But rather than using Augmentor magic, she floats a satchel full of medical supplies toward her that I hadn't noticed before. A Shaper working as a Healer?

Dr. Iris has already started a healing spell on Jazz, and I begin checking students to see who needs the most help. Blake comes toward me, limping, but alive. I embrace him and immediately start healing his ankle. He nods his thanks, then rushes off to find other wounded. We need no words

A moment later, I hear Jazz groan, and I take a deep breath. I can tell Brie is filling him in on the situation. Once fully revived, he'll be eager to help.

"Trisha!" Hazel calls out. "This one here could use your attention."

It takes me a moment to realize "Trisha" is Dr. Iris.

"Can you manage?" Dr. Iris asks Jazz.

"Yes. Thank you." He rises to his feet. "I can help."

"Over here, Jazz!" Blake waves at another injured student. No time to waste.

Blanca enters, carrying a limp form in her arms. Sarah. Blanca drops her unceremoniously at my feet and sets to work healing the series of scratches all over her skin that weren't there before. "You were right," she huffs. "Sarah's gone looney. I had to knock her out just to get her here." She glances at me. "Oh, don't look at me like that. I only did what I had to."

Dr. Iris notices Sarah. She stops what she's doing to come to us. "Hazel!"

Hazel is there instantly, summoning a scalpel from her satchel. She carefully turns Sarah over onto her stomach and glances at Dr. Iris. "You'll want to heal her quickly."

Dr. Iris nods, and I cringe as Hazel slices into Sarah's neck at the base of her skull. She removes a small oval-shaped device, glittering and yellow. Dr. Iris is already healing the cut.

"What is it?" I ask.

Dr. Iris holds the device out to Blanca, who doesn't even flinch at the blood covering its surface. "Will you destroy this, please?"

"My pleasure." Blanca takes the device and crumbles it easily.

Dr. Iris explains, "It's a mind-control device. It was placed in your friend the day you invaded the school for supplies."

I recall Sarah's disappearance. Never once did I suspect anything could have happened to her. My eyes go to my arm where Dr. Iris spontaneously cut and healed me. She notes my glance and nods. "A tracking device. I wanted to be able to find you so that I could help you when the time came." She indicates Hazel. "My sister made it. She's always been the smarty"

Hazel smiles ruefully. "Unfortunately I made things for the Benefactors as well. Including the prototype for the device in Sarah."

"You didn't know what you were doing." Dr. Iris waves a dismissive hand.

"I didn't want to work for them to begin with," Hazel explains. "But I was desperate at the time, and they seemed to treat my sister well enough." She turns to me. "I had a traditional medical practice in Violet City, but it closed down last year."

I connect the dots in my head, recalling the battered office I saw near Chrysanthemum Street. "Dr. Thompson?"

She nods. "Thompson is my married name. My husband was killed in an accident several years ago. That's actually what motivated me to learn traditional medicine in the first place. When he got hurt, I wasn't able to get him to a Healer in time. I just kept thinking if I had only been able to help him myself . . ." she trails off. "Anyway, none of that matters now."

As Hazel speaks, I notice the gaunt look to her face. It doesn't look like her time working for the Benefactors has been good to her. "Did the Benefactors tell you what sort of work you would be doing?"

"At first, it was just assisting my sister. But they separated us more as time went on. Eventually, they forced me to start creating the devices, using Trisha as leverage. They threatened to torture her. But Trish eventually figured something was up."

Dr. Iris shakes her head. "I didn't realize it soon enough. But once I did, I helped her form a plan to retaliate."

Sarah stirs and her eyes open. She stands up, her face confused and disoriented. She sees me and falls in her effort to put distance between us. "Get away from me! I'm dangerous!"

"Easy, Sarah." I kneel beside her. "It's okay now. You're alright." I gently explain Dr. Iris and Hazel's healing.

Sarah is instantly in tears. "I did it. All of those terrible things. The garden. Elm's devices. Even hurting Blake. I couldn't stop." She is jittery, still seeming to grapple with the urge to fight or to flee. I help her up

Blanca gives Sarah an incredulous look. "If you knew you

were doing all that stuff and you didn't want to, why didn't you say something?"

"But I didn't know!" Sarah's teary eyes beseech us. "I feel like I've been in a constant fog, and there are moments of complete blackouts that I couldn't remember. It must be when the device was gone everything came back."

Blanca's anger is mollified, and her expression softens. "I'm sorry."

"It's not your fault, Sarah," I add. "Everyone knows you would never have done those things if you could help it."

I want to keep myself together for Sarah and everyone else, but Dr. Hazel's revelation tremors through me like an earthquake. The Benefactors are devising new and creative ways to turn the populace into puppets and pawns. I can't help but consider the irony of the Benefactors using a device to control Sarah when that's the very thing they insist they're protecting us from. More pressing, though, is that we have a whole room full of Benefactors to deal with, and we need to get out of this cave before those numbers grow.

Dr. Iris zaps a Benefactor who begins to stir. "I'm sure you've thought of this already," she remarks, "but there are probably other Benefactors on their way here. We must move."

I nod and spy Blake. "Blake, start rounding everyone up. We need to get out fast."

"Where are we going to go?" he asks.

"I don't know yet. But since we have no choice, we need to leave as soon as possible."

I wave over several Augmentors to lift the remaining Benefactors and transport them to the larger group. Dr. Iris accompanies us, stun gun ready in case any of them begin to cause trouble. We near Elm and Samantha, who are still engaged in their prolonged holding of the Benefactor's minds. But Elm balks at seeing Dr. Iris. Understandingly, she and Hazel move away.

"She's with us," I say quickly. "She's been wonderful. I'll tell you later, but right now we need to get out of here. Any ideas?"

Elm thinks for a moment. "Perhaps we could find a secure location in the forest. If we can disguise ourselves." There is a slight sheen on his forehead as he speaks. His expended effort was harder for him than I thought.

"The forest probably isn't safe anywhere with all those buggerflies."

"Ah, true," Elm acknowledges. "And anywhere near Prism is likely out of the question. Violet City as well."

Samantha has been silent through the exchange, her face growing steadily redder. When she speaks up, her voice is quiet. "I can get us out. Out of the barrier."

"Where?" Elm is startled. "And how?"

"I lied when I said it was faults and timing. I've been able to do it all along. I can send a surge of Yellow magic through my staff." She gestures toward the yellow star tip on the end of it. "Focusing it on a fixed point like that creates a small blip in the dome for a few seconds. It will allow us to pass through."

I stare at her, but before I can say anything, Elm speaks.

"Sammy." The sharp reprimand and disappointment in her name is enough to drive Samantha to tears.

"I'm s-sorry," she sobs. "I thought it was the only way I could get things back to the way they were supposed to be. J-just you and me!"

I take a deep breath, swallowing the words I want to lash her with. "We just need to get out. That's what matters right now."

Samantha is still weeping as we look at the Benefactors, frozen under Elm's spell. We have to do something with them. Once we depart, they will no longer be under the influence of Elm's magic. And once in command of themselves again, who knows what will happen.

"Suggestions on what to do with our Benefactor friends, Miss Ava?" Elm looks to me, allowing me the choice, though I wish someone would take this away from me. It would be a relief to let someone else make the hard decisions. Things could still go horribly wrong, but at least the burden wouldn't be on my own shoulders.

Samantha speaks in a small voice. "I feel like . . ." she swallows. "Blanca's suggestion from before might be the best way."

I eye her warily. "You really think we should kill them?"

"After what they did to Elm? After what they did today?" She shudders. "Don't you think so, Elm?"

Elm purses his lips. "There's no denying it would weaken their forces. It would give an advantage. And I'm truly not certain how we get out of here otherwise."

My head feels at once too empty and too full, every thought spinning into a void. Are we really talking about killing a group of people? "How?" I hear myself ask.

"The room is fragile," Elm gestures to the space around us. "You may recall me saying I nearly collapsed a portion of it once by mistake. I'm sure it wouldn't take much. It would be quick," his eyes level at me, "if that's what you wish to do."

Is that what I want? Well, no, of course it isn't. But it's war. Choices have to be made. Sacrifices have to be made. Is this what needs to be done to keep everyone else safe? It's worse if I choose the Benefactors over my friends, isn't it? I work to keep my voice strong as I say the words I don't want to say. "Let's bring it down."

"Are you certain, Miss Ava?"

"Yes." Do it fast. Get it over with.

I build the power in my fist, red hot. Ready to bury our problems. I pull back, but just before I connect, I stop, millimeters away from my target.

I can't do this.

My lungs beg me to relax the tension in them, and I exhale, then fall to my knees and release the energy of my balled fist into the floor.

"I thought as much," Elm says. There is a pleased smile on his face.

"They've hurt and killed so many people." I'm angry at myself. I made the decision and can't carry it out. I am unable to stop the falling tears. "Why can't I do this? It's for the greater good. Why am I not strong enough?"

"Because you *are* strong, Miss Ava. Because people matter to you. The entire reason you entangled yourself in all this is because you care about others. You wanted to be a Benefactor so you could protect people. Now you're simply viewing the same goal from the other side of the fence."

"Some people are worth protecting more than others," Samantha tries to argue, still hesitant in her speech. "You can't save everyone."

"Maybe not," I get to my feet, "but I don't want the weight of any lost life if I can help it."

"Agreed." Elm reaches for my hand and gives it a gentle squeeze. "I am proud of you, Miss Ava."

I cling to his hand a moment, then say, "So, that just leaves the option of running for it and hoping for the best." This might be a decision I live to regret, but for now, it's the best I can do. "Elm, do you think you can hold them off long enough for us to get out of the cave?"

"If you can get nearly everyone out, I should be able to hold the spell long enough for Sammy and I to escape also. We'll have a small head start."

Is this really the right choice? Am I putting us all at risk with my hesitation to act more forcefully? *You are not Selene. You never have to be Selene.*

"Okay," I breathe. "Let's do it, then."

Elm and Samantha stay behind to keep the Benefactors

at bay, while the rest of us gather in the main room of the cave. Some of the Benefactors are showing signs they're about to come to.

"Can you put them out again, Dr. Iris?" I ask.

She shakes her head. "The weapons would have to be recharged. This was our chance."

"Move fast, everyone!" I shout, adrenaline hitting me at Dr. Iris's words. "If anyone near you is hurt, as long as it's not life-threatening, get them out, and we'll heal them later. More Benefactors could arrive at any moment."

Students scramble, faces petrified and world worn. I hear the sound of frantic footbeats heading toward the mouth of the cave.

"Ava, go back to Elm and Samantha, and let them know it's time. We'll get everyone out," Dr. Iris assures me.

"Thank you." I race back to the crystal room, pleading in my heart for even just a few more seconds of time before Benefactors arrive.

Elm sees me coming. "Time already, Miss Ava?"

"Just about. How far away do you think we'll get before they break out of the spell?"

"It's hard to say. They all have different abilities and resistance. It could happen very quickly for some of them."

"On three, then." Elm nods and Samantha straightens. "One. Two. Three."

We run toward the cave exit. I keep my pace even with Elm and Samantha's even though my instincts urge me to go faster. There's no way I'm going to leave them behind. The cave is eerily still, which must mean everyone has made it out. This, at least, brings a measure of relief.

The sunlight I longed for not long ago sears as it blazes across my skin. It feels too open. Too exposed. I blink a few times at the hazy group in front of me, taking a moment in my disorientation before realizing it's my classmates. Why are they still here? Then I realize: We have no idea where we're going. It's Samantha who knows the best route to get through the barrier.

Elm has already processed this. "Sammy! Take the lead!"

She runs obediently to the front of the group. She, of all people, doesn't want to be anywhere near here when those Benefactors show up.

We all barrel after her. I wonder if I should take the Augmentors up in front so we can be on the lookout for anyone in our path. But I decide against it—I do rely on Samantha to get us there, and it would take excess energy. I'll save that strength to fight again if that's what it comes down to.

There is a distant rumble, a flash, and smoke. I look in the direction it's coming from, trying not to slow my run as I glance behind. The sunflowers. My stride falters. I don't have to see them to know that they're all gone. The Benefactors are coming this way, and they're letting us know.

Elm appears at my side and takes a firm hold of my hand.

"Those won't be the last, Miss Ava. There are many more flowers in your future."

I toss him a quick smile. I have to keep believing that. I have to believe that we have a future at all.

Our group is slowing. Everyone is tired. Everyone is in shock. We've already been through so much in a few short hours. How are we going to get through this? The shadows stretch long as we make our way to the edge of the barrier, I imagine sinister shapes within them, clawing toward us. We haven't run into any Benefactors yet, though. Are we really going to make it out without a conflict? I'm suspicious of any good fortune at this point.

We watch for buggerflies as we go, Shapers crumpling them from the sky the moment they're spotted. I'm not sure how quickly they transmit information to the Benefactors. For all we know, they're giving our enemies a clear sense of our path. *Hurry. Hurry.*

At last we reach the barrier, and Samantha rushes to its flickering surface. Almost there.

Brie hesitates. "We're really going to go out there? It's really not toxic?"

"It's not," assures Elm. "I've been beyond the barrier myself, and there is a whole colony of people where Sammy is from who will welcome us."

Or at least, we hope they'll welcome us.

Samantha taps her staff to the barrier, closing her eyes for a moment in concentration. A jolt seems to go through her, and she says, "Three seconds! Go!" As many as can make it in three seconds pile through the opening, and she repeats the process. My anticipation builds until everyone is on the other side except me.

This is it. My turn. I push through, and just like that, it's done.

I'm outside the barrier.

17

I INHALE DEEPLY AND PAUSE BEFORE exhaling. Even knowing what Elm said, it's hard to let go of the idea that this place is poison after being trained to think that way. My senses tense, screaming at me to run. But the air feels beautiful. Magical. Energized. My body relaxes as I take a moment to stare at the sky, which looks somehow more vibrant without the barrier blocking it. A glowing shade of blue that I had long forgotten. The sun feels brighter. Warmer. I never noticed how much the barrier impacted life until I got out from under it.

Dr. Iris gasps. I see tears sparkling in her eyes, and she's not alone. The feeling outside of the barrier is overwhelming. It's as though we've all been underwater, struggling to breathe, and have finally broken the surface.

"So, is there a plan here, Ava?" Jazz asks, breaking the spell of wonder dazzling our group.

"Samantha is going to take us to the magic users that live here." I raise my voice for the others to hear. "From there . . . Elm and I want to figure out how to free the other Mentalists who are still trapped by the Benefactors. But we understand not everyone feels that's their mission. We won't ask anyone to go with us."

Jazz ponders for a moment. "Most of the folks outside the barrier are probably Mentalists, right?"

"Many of them, yes," says Elm. "But not all. I suspect most of them will be greatly delighted to have more Augmentors and Shapers on their side."

Jazz nods thoughtfully and then falls back beside Brie. I'm not sure how everyone will feel about suddenly living with so many Mentalists. It's been hard enough for them to get used to Elm, but maybe it will be easier with faces they haven't seen on Wanted posters for months.

We continue walking in a staggered line, silent. Wide-eyed. I can only guess that everyone is feeling similar. They gaze at the scenery, probably with the same emotions that are fluttering through me right now. Wonder at this new world. Nervousness at what is to come. Will we be greeted peacefully? Will we make it to any destination at all? Everyone is on edge in spite of exhaustion. After living so long in hiding, this feels far too vulnerable, as though Benefactors could come raging down on us at any moment.

Blanca's voice comes sharply behind me. She has tripped on a large tree root.

"Guess we better watch our step?" Kaito extends a hand to help Blanca. She ignores the gesture, but I catch a ghost of a smile as she begins walking alongside him once more.

Really, we all should be traveling more carefully. The terrain here is so different. Lush and green and tangled in vines. The air has a heaviness to it, full of moisture and warmth. Even in the dim light of dusk, I can tell it's a far cry from the forests near Prism. Is it the barrier that makes the land and climate so different?

Stars begin to twinkle into view overhead, and I catch glimpses of them through the canopy of trees. Even they seem to shine brighter here, and I notice a new depth to the sky. Deep purples and blues with more silvery specks than I could have envisioned. All at once I feel very small.

"Sammy, how much longer of a walk?" Elm casts a

concerned look over our companions, whose pace slackens by the minute.

"Well, I guess we could stop," Samantha replies after a pause. "I don't really want to camp out here, but we have at least a two-hour walk ahead of us. This spot is as good as any."

I hear the groans and internally release one of my own. Two hours. But we have to keep morale up. I muster strength to address everyone. "Once we all get a good night's rest, it will look better in the morning. Just think—when we start out again, it's only two hours before we see a whole new city outside of the barrier. That's pretty exciting, right?"

No verbal answers, but a few tired nods.

"There's a stream about a quarter mile from here, if I'm remembering right." Samantha points to a thicker canopy of trees.

Elm nods in agreement. "We should all rehydrate."

As our travel-worn group refreshes with water from the stream, I stare at the moon's light reflected on the rushing water. We have nothing. No blankets. No food. No possessions. But we do have each other, so I guess that's not really nothing. Overwhelming emotion suddenly floods over me. We didn't lose a single person today.

Soft pink light bathes the world around me as I open my eyes, filling me with an odd sort of peace. Elm lies a distance away to my right, still asleep, and Nikki to my left. All the other students are bunched around us, with Dr. Iris and her sister leaning against a tree a ways off. They insisted they should keep watch as the oldest of the group. A few of the Shapers used their magic last night to turn Elm's cloak into a giant blanket for us all to sleep on. Not exactly the best accommodations, but we were all too tired to notice the difference.

I stretch and sit up, taking in our surroundings in the daylight. The air has just a hint of a chill to it this morning with a light, humid breeze. Yellow sand spills around the edges of the enlarged cloak, and I can hear the lazy call of some kind of bird. Behind that, my ears strain to catch another sound. A faint roar.

No, not quite a roar. This is a gentler sound. Water?

"Do you hear it as well, Miss Ava?" Elm is sitting up, hair tousled from sleep.

I nod. "It doesn't sound far. Do you want to check it out?"

Elm stands and extends a hand to help me to my feet. We follow the sound of the water, and my heartbeat increases with giddy excitement as we grow closer to the source. I have a feeling I know what this is. We break the tree line, and my breath catches. Waves lap at the shoreline, morning sunlight cascading over the glittering surface of the water. For the first time, I see what I have only read about in storybooks.

"The ocean?" My voice is a pitched whisper.

Elm reaches down and removes his shoes and socks, setting them carefully on a nearby rock, and then grins back at me. "Let's get a closer look, shall we?"

I hastily remove my own shoes and relish the feeling of the damp sand beneath my feet. It soothes the ache from yesterday's events, and I can't help but give a satisfied sigh. Elm and I walk hand in hand to the surf. We reach the water's edge, and I squeal as the chilly water encases my toes. It's biting at first, but it feels better as I adjust to the sensation. I jump as something tickles my feet, but it's just a bit of a sea plant instead of some creature as I had feared. Elm laughs, then rolls up his sleeves, and reaches into the light waves. With a flourish, he produces a pastel pink seashell. "A souvenir for you."

"It's beautiful." As my fingers circle its smooth surface, I can't stop smiling. Elm's face is alight with joy. After pocketing the seashell, I bend down and skim the surface of the water with my fingertips as sea spray tickles my face. All at once, I'm drenched. I gasp, sputtering and turn to Elm, the surprise on his face reflecting my own at the unexpected wave attack. He blinks droplets from his eyes and shakes out his hair.

"It's so salty!" I sputter again, giggling.

"Yes. And you seem to have acquired a new hair accessory." Elm plucks a slimy strand of a sea plant from my hair. "Green is so lovely on you."

We laugh, all dignity and decorum forgotten, and plunge into the waves. The water doesn't feel so cold now, and we wade as deep as we dare, feeling the gentle pull of the undertow.

I hear a loud "whoop!" behind us, and we both turn to the sight of Blanca charging forward into the surf. Kaito watches with wary interest until Blanca goes back and pulls him straight in with her. He gasps as the water hits him, but recovers quickly, repaying Blanca with a tremendous splash. Jazz and Brie follow, and soon our whole group stampedes into the sea, wild and joyful.

So this is what freedom feels like.

After an hour or so of beach frolicking, the temporary high wears off, and our situation catches up to us again. We need food and accommodations. We let the sun and wind dry us out, stop at the stream for a long drink, and set out once more on our way. All the energy I had before is gone, and I'm tempted to draw on the red plants I see to strengthen myself. But, since not everyone here is an Augmentor, I don't. It feels wrong to strengthen myself if I can't do the same for my companions. After all, they're only here because they're following Elm and me.

"We look like we washed in off a shipwreck." I hear Blake laugh.

I survey everyone and cringe a little. Sandy, unkempt hair. Slight sunburns. Rumpled clothing. Maybe the beach wasn't such a good idea. I want to make a good impression for the people on the other side of the barrier. There's bound to be some mistrust when we first arrive—it's only natural, especially when we come from a world controlled by the Benefactors. Likely, it's not going to help the situation if we show up looking like riffraff. I rake my fingers through my hair as we walk, wincing as they catch in the tangles.

Elm lays a hand on my shoulder. He always seems to know. "It's going to be fine, Miss Ava. This is just one more step on the road to a free Magus."

"Do you think they'll like us?" I can't help wondering.

Nikki comes up alongside me, grumbling, her curls in a wild, frizzy state. "I don't really care what they think as long as they have a shower."

"Hazel and I should go into the city first," Dr. Iris says, looking resolute. "We can make sure they'll be receptive before bringing everyone in."

"No, we have to go together." I don't want even Dr. Iris and Hazel in a strange city fending for themselves.

Samantha has been listening from her position just ahead, and she stops and turns, hands on her hips. "You are talking about my home. They aren't the Benefactors. They're not savages. You're not walking into a lion's den, and they'll be happy for anyone who's against Selene. Now can you stop your yammering and just walk? I'm ready to go home."

Elm shakes his head and looks apologetically at Dr. Iris.

But Samantha's words do seem to lift everyone's spirits a bit. Our pace regains its speed.

I start as I catch a flutter of red. It can't be a buggerfly here. But this insect has black-tipped wings with flashy white spots. A real butterfly. I sigh and enjoy its beauty as it glides out of sight. It may be awhile before anything feels normal again.

Elm suddenly grasps my hand and points in the distance. "Look, Miss Ava."

I gaze up and catch something glittering high above the treetops.

Skyscrapers.

18

WHY IS THE SIGHT OF A TOWERING CITY
so surprising? Somehow I expected a ragtag group camped in
tents or other makeshift shelters. But life has existed outside of
the barrier for years— for all I know, much of this could have
been here before the barrier was ever implemented. Of course
they would have a city.

"Welcome home!" Samantha beams. She looks more
relaxed than I have ever seen her. This is her sphere. I'm sure
she has friends and maybe even family here. Does anyone else
in this place know Elm? My heartbeat quickens. Does anyone
here remember me? I search the crevices of my mind, suddenly
wishing I could remember any of my parents' friends, whether
they made it out or not.

We halt outside of a large brick wall at the outer edge of the
city. It looms, imposing and unwelcoming.

"They don't seem warm to outsiders, do they?" Blake
stares at the wall.

"Just a precaution," Samantha tells him. She's so much
more comfortable here. She's almost a different person.
"We've never seen a Benefactor outside of the barrier, but
we do want to keep our city safe. You have nothing to worry
about. C'mon."

Our group cautiously approaches the guard station. The

woman on duty raises her eyebrows, but her expression changes when she notices Samantha.

"Welcome back!" She smiles broadly. She looks at all of us gathered behind her. "Will you introduce me to your friends?"

It seems like everyone, including Samantha, blanches at the word *friends*. Samantha replies a bit stiffly, "Former students of Prism, driven out by the Benefactors. Rebels against Selene. They're with us now." She turns and takes Elm by the arm, ushering him forward. "And this is . . . Elm."

"My word!" the woman exclaims, and I wonder if it's possible for her eyes to be any wider. "This is *the* Elm? My, my. Well, you'd all better get inside."

The gate opens and she waves us in.

"So you already have a reputation." I nudge Elm lightly as we follow Samantha through the gate.

"Oh, I do hope it's something scandalous." He grins, though I catch a touch of unease in his eyes. Infamy did not serve him well inside the barrier.

Now that we're within the walls, my focus shifts toward the city itself. Glass seems to be the favored material for the outside of the buildings, and it shines in all colors. The entire city is a sparkling rainbow, reminding me of the suncatchers I used to paint when I was very young. Most of the towering buildings finish in ornate peaks, giving the whole city an almost castle-like appearance. Somehow we found a fairy tale in the middle of the tropics. Violet City has nothing on this place.

"What's it called?" My words come out breathless as we come to a halt beside Samantha.

She laughs. "This is Neo Prism. The name is a bit cheesy, but the founding rebels thought it would be a sort of victory to claim back the name of Selene's precious school."

Even the pavement, a bright silvery color, sparkles. For a moment I wonder if it's all illusions. A city full of Mentalists would make it easy to present something flashy.

Elm looks around and smiles fondly. "Typical Mentalists. Always ready for a show."

"So this really is the city?" I can't help but bend down and brush my fingers across the glittering sidewalk.

"Of course it is, dummy." Samantha shoots me a glare. "Just because we could make an illusion doesn't mean we want to do it all the time."

"Be fair, Sammy. Most of them don't have much experience with Yellow magic."

"And," I wink, "I know a certain Mentalist who made his cave pretty flashy the first time he had a visitor."

Elm turns a shade pink. "Well, perhaps I was simply trying to impress that specific visitor. Though I won't deny we Mentalists tend to favor spectacle."

As though proving Elm's point, my eyes are drawn to a street performer across the road, dressed from head to toe in a suit of white-and-yellow checkers. She entertains a group of children with a cyclone of candy-colored fish, and we watch them swimming through the air with elegance and shimmering grace.

A thought strikes me. "Elm, they must know those fish aren't real, right? I certainly know. How can we all still see that illusion?"

"Simple, Miss Ava. You see it because you want to. When you know the illusion is there for your entertainment, it's easier to accept it. Much different from a hidden illusion meant to deceive."

I can see why the best Mentalists are the ones who get to know people before using an illusion on them. All they have to do is play up their own desires to make the illusion more palatable. An unwanted prickle of disgust for Yellow magic threatens to surface, and I'm once more left to question how much of that is me and how much is Selene.

If the thought makes you uncomfortable, change it. It doesn't matter whose thought it is. The last thing I want to do in a city full of Mentalists is start out with negative impressions of them.

We draw attention as we continue down the streets—no illusions needed. I'm once again conscious of our tattered appearance. The people here are every bit as extravagant as those back home—maybe even more so. But sandy beach hair and salt-dried clothing aren't in style. We garner curious looks, and every now and then those passing by give us much more space than needed. Perhaps it's just as well until we're more grounded to our situation.

We pass a strip of restaurants, and my stomach rumbles uncontrollably as tantalizing spiced scents waft toward us. I catch Brie looking with a longing expression into the large, curved window of a restaurant.

Dr. Iris produces a currency card. "Let's get something to eat. I'm buying."

"I'll go half," Hazel offers.

Samantha scoffs. "You won't be able to use that here."

Dr. Iris lowers her card with a quizzical expression. "You don't use currency cards?"

"We do have a card system, but not on the same network as the Benefactors. We don't need them tracking everything. I mean, seriously. Are you crazy?" She looks at the hungry group before her and gives an exasperated sigh, digging through the ruffles of her tutu until she produces a small pouch. She pulls out a handful of pastel-colored bills and hands them to Dr. Iris. "Get something to eat. We'll have to figure out the money situation."

If none of us can access our currency accounts, that means we're all starting with nothing. Aside from Dr. Iris and her sister, we've all been living off the grid for a while anyway, but there was always the hope that someday we'd be able to access our funds again. As students, most of us didn't have much, but it was nice to think of something to fall back on.

The best we can hope for now is that Neo Prism will have the necessary resources to give everyone a fresh start and chance to be successful.

Our group piles into the shop, eager to eat, but Samantha grabs Elm. "Not you, Elm. I'm taking you and . . . Ava,"—she acts pained to say my name—"to see Ivan."

"Ivan?"

"He's sort of the one in charge. He'll figure out what to do with you all."

Elm and I exchange a glance.

"And what might that entail, Sammy?"

Samantha heaves a sigh. "Ivan is a good guy. A fair guy. Will you please stop being so suspicious?"

She walks us to a hover-cart station, which I'm a little surprised to see. Only this one doesn't require any sort of ID card. Nobody tracking who's coming and going or what their destination might be.

"This will take us downtown to Ivan's office." Samantha climbs in the four-passenger cart and immediately stares out the window, looking sulky again. I have a feeling if she had her way, she wouldn't be within one hundred feet of me. Elm and I situate ourselves in the seat behind her, and none of us speaks as we zip down the path, each lost in our own thoughts.

I'm only eighteen, but I've been marked, along with Elm, as the leader of our group. And now, I'm meeting with the leader of an entire people outside of the barrier. Talk about intimidating! My heart won't stop beating. Can we really trust this Ivan? Will the people here trust us? Samantha says so, but I don't consider her the most reliable source.

"I'm with you, Miss Ava," Elm assures, seeming to read my thoughts again.

"Thank goodness for that." As long as Elm is near, I know I have at least one person I can trust.

The cart stops outside a set of several industrial buildings.

None of the glitz and glam here. Just boxy buildings surrounded by heavy fencing and large gates. I feel claustrophobic, and I'm not even inside yet.

"They don't present the warmest welcome, do they?" Elm glances around as Samantha continues to lead the way.

"Oh, Ivan's just pragmatic. It's fine."

A glance upward reveals a security camera pointed directly at us. Elm pauses, strikes a gallant pose, and flashes a look into the lens that would stop anyone in their tracks. Or at least, it stopped me in mine.

"W-what are you doing?" I manage to ask.

Samantha just gawks at him.

Elm tips his hat and strides away from the camera with a cocky grin. "It's just something I do. If they're going to take my picture, it may as well be a striking one. How do you suppose the Benefactors got such a dazzling picture of me for their posters?"

"You're unreal." I shake my head, but smile.

Samantha walks on ahead. "Let's not keep Ivan waiting. C'mon."

I can't help but notice Samantha seems to know her way around this space extremely well. Has she seen Ivan often? Maybe I'm unfair for thinking it, but she doesn't seem like one who would hold a high-ranking position in society. What business has she had with the leader of Neo Prism?

We stop in the hallway outside a set of gray double doors. Samantha lowers her head slightly. "This is it. I need to talk to Ivan for a minute first. I'll be right back."

She hurries inside, and Elm and I exchange a look.

"She seemed a bit nervous, don't you think?" I ask.

"Somewhat, yes. But Sammy can be that way around other people."

As we wait, I comb a strand of hair away from my face and frown, brushing off another stray grain of sand. "We're meeting with this city's leader. Don't you think we should be more . . . presentable?"

"You're perfectly presentable, and anyone who says otherwise will answer to me."

I give him a wry smile just as the door opens once more. Samantha emerges, avoiding eye contact.

"I'm going home now, but Ivan will tell you what to do from here, I'm sure. See you, Elm. Soon, I hope."

As Samantha makes her quick exit, I turn to Elm. "So we just go in?"

"It would seem so."

We push the hefty door to the office open and step inside. Immediately a powerful force knocks me to the ground.

19

"IF YOU HURT MY DOG, WE'RE NOT
going to get along."

Elm helps me come out from under the giant mass of paws
and brindle fur.

I stand a little wobbly, then address the person who spoke—a
stocky man dressed in green-and-yellow camo. "W-what kind
of dog is it?"

"A big one."

I chuckle awkwardly, and the man releases a boisterous
laugh, throwing his head back. "English Mastiff mix of some
sort. Get over here, Dawz."

The massive dog bounds over to his master, heavy paws
thudding across the dark wooden floor. "Sorry about that,"
the man says, scratching Dawz behind the ears. "He gets
overexcited, but he's a cinnamon roll."

"You're Ivan, I presume?" Elm studies Ivan with keen eyes,
showing no trace of humor for the situation.

"That's me." Ivan goes to a massive desk and kicks his boots
up on top of it, leaning back in his chair and surveying us. "So,
you're the little scamps who have upturned all of Magus."

"We didn't do it alone."

Elm puts his arm around me. "Now, Miss Ava, you don't give

yourself nearly enough credit. You're practically responsible for the whole thing."

My cheeks heat, and Ivan's brown eyes assess me, full of amusement. "Well done. It's about time someone shook things up for Selene." He shifts his focus to Elm. "And you're *the* Elm Ridley. We've heard all sorts of things about you."

"He's not a criminal," I say quickly. It's impossible not to be on the defensive, knowing how Elm has been viewed in the past.

Ivan leans back further. "Obviously not. Anyone Selene hates that much can't be all bad. Tell me, Elm, what was it like finally breaking free?"

"Perhaps another time." Elm's voice is polite. "We have other matters pressing."

"You're in charge here?" I ask, ready to get to the point.

"Yes. More or less. We're more of a democracy, but I guess I run the place." He idly picks up a pen from his desk and rolls it between his fingers. "What was your purpose for coming here?"

"Safety, mostly," I reply. "But allies wouldn't hurt either."

"The first, I can promise you as long as your people don't cause any trouble here. We're happy to let you call Neo Prism home. As for the second . . . well, we'll just see."

"Are we not fighting the same battle?" Elm raises his eyebrows.

"More or less. We defy Selene's rules, but we do it within our own community. People like their security, and nobody's interested in stirring the pot. Let them rot in their own little bubble."

"I see." While Elm sounds civil enough, I detect the slight ice in his words. I feel it in me, too, but we can't risk conflict right now. Not when we could potentially have them as part of our own forces.

"Outside the barrier," I say, changing the subject, "do other nations still exist?"

"I have no idea." Ivan shrugs. "I assume so."

"Nobody goes to visit anymore?"

"Not for decades."

Elm beats me to the question. "By their own choosing, or because they are no longer allowed?"

Ivan regards Elm more carefully. "Look, we keep no prisoners, all right? People are here because they want to be. No, people don't leave anymore because *Magus* won't let them."

My eyes widen. "What do you mean?"

Ivan pauses a moment to scratch Dawz behind the ears. "People used to travel to and from Magus freely. Our communication with other nations was open. This was before my time, you understand. But after a while, people set out for Magus and never came home. Things got messy. Folks in other countries started accusing us of being hostile."

"What happened to everyone?"

Ivan waves a hand. "Different things. Swallowed by the sea. Icebergs. Torrential winds. Anything to keep them out and, eventually, to keep us in. People on both sides stopped trying. Too much risk. We have no communication with the outside world anymore."

"And you suppose this is the doing of Magus itself?" Elm asks.

"Maybe you've noticed," Ivan cocks his head at Elm, "that something odd is brewing. Magus is restless. The animals behave oddly—except tame ones like this loaf." Another pat on Dawz's head. "The plants grow quicker. The weather misbehaves."

I consider the things he mentions, and it's hard to ignore Ivan's observations. The overgrown woods, Elm's sunflowers, odd animal behaviors, seasonally uncharacteristic weather.

This is a different threat from the Benefactors entirely. Something we may not be able to fight.

"Anyhow," Ivan continues, "suffice it to say that nobody has been in or out for a while, and maybe that's for the better."

How can he show such minimal concern knowing nobody can travel to or from the continent? It was one thing to accept that the world was toxic and Magus was only preserved because of its magic, but thinking the rest of the world has been there this whole time and Magus itself won't allow travel is more than a little unsettling.

Dawz paws at Ivan, and he produces a bone-shaped biscuit from his front pocket. The dog downs it in a split second. Ivan watches with affection and amusement, but that all disappears when he turns his attention back to us. "So, now that your little crew is free of Selene, what are your plans? Are you continuing your education or just ready to work?"

School? Work? Neither of those things have been on my mind. I remember the card system. We will have to get funds somehow.

But Elm answers. "Well, considering we are in the middle of a revolution of sorts, those things might come secondary."

Ivan drops his feet to the floor. "You're not seriously thinking of going back to that blasted dome, are you? Not after you finally made it out."

"There are still many students under Selene's control," I say stiffly. "We can't just abandon them, can we?"

Ivan scoffs. "Kid, a lot of them are there because they want to be. If I were you, I'd cut your losses and just be glad you got out. Never look back."

I think of a polite but noncommittal answer. "Well, I guess that's something we'll have to consider. We all want a chance at a normal life." But at what cost? And can any of us be happy in that normalcy knowing what we left behind?

Elm crosses his arms. This meeting isn't going as either

of us hoped. "We don't want to take up much more of your time. What would you like our group to do for now? We're somewhat at a loss."

"Well," Ivan says, "we have apartments downtown with some empty units. Your people are welcome to stay there. I'll send someone to escort you. We'll even supply you each a small living stipend for a while, provided you'll give me what I want."

"And what is that?" Elm asks.

Ivan laces his fingers together. "Intel."

I think I know what he's getting at. "On Selene?"

"Bingo. If Selene and her cronies ever do decide to come through the barrier, we're going to be prepared. If I have my way, we'll never need to use this information, but I won't be a sitting duck."

"Agreed," I say almost immediately without waiting for Elm. I'm willing to share anything that could work against Selene someday, and while I don't really know anything about Ivan, I can't see any way giving him this information could hurt us. Besides, that means more opportunities to hopefully sway him to our efforts.

"Peachy. We'll give you time to find your feet and decide what you want to do long-term. If you want to become part of our society, we're happy to help you find jobs, school, whatever it is you need. You may feel like outsiders now, but this can become home if you want it to be. Can't imagine why you'd even give a second thought when the alternative is life on the run in a bubble."

"Thank you," I say, trying not to clip my words.

"And," Elm says carefully, "if we should choose to instead continue our fight?"

Ivan shrugs again. "If it doesn't disrupt our life here, I don't give a rip."

"I don't expect we'll be getting much help from him. Not as far as our rebellion is concerned." Elm gazes out the window of the hover cart, an edge in his voice.

"That was the feeling I got too."

"It's incomprehensible. With so many Mentalists living here, how can he be so blasé about the whole ordeal? What have they been doing all this time? While I was rotting away in restraints, what were they—"

I wrap him in a hug. "I know."

He lets out a long sigh, and I feel him relax in my arms.

"I'm sorry, Elm," I murmur. "I can only imagine how hard this is for you."

"Disappointing, I suppose, is the best word for it. We finally find other Mentalists, and I thought certainly we would have allies. But instead, they are entirely unconcerned with what's happened inside of the barrier."

"Well, we don't know for sure that they won't be our allies. Remember, that was just Ivan. There has to be others here who would be sympathetic to our cause."

"And you really think Ivan would let anyone assist?"

"Yes." I hesitate. "Well, I mean, he said he keeps no prisoners. I assume anyone who wanted to help us would be allowed to do so."

After living under Selene's rule and the Benefactor's thumbs, it's hard not to be suspicious. Even if Ivan appears to be all about free will, he also seems very intent on keeping his city safe. I have a feeling that eclipses anything else as far as he's concerned. And, as I watch Neo Prism racing past, a part of me understands. This place is beautiful. Even only being here a short time, I can feel its energy. Its life. Why wouldn't anyone want to preserve that?

The hover car arrives at the station where we initially boarded. Our group is clustered around a bench outside, looking utterly lost.

"Saved you both some food," Nikki says, thrusting a carryout container into my hands. I open it to some kind of pillowy flatbread topped with spiced meat and vegetables.

Brie bounces over. "You have to try it, Ava. It's the best food I've ever tasted. They have these things called banana peppers here. They don't taste like bananas . . . not that I've ever tried a banana, but I'm going to! Anyway, it's good!"

Jazz shakes his head at his sister, but he's smiling. "She's a little wired. She hasn't felt this safe in a while."

"I think we're all feeling that. I'm glad she's doing better." Even if it's only for this moment, right now, I want Brie to be a kid. Who knows what tomorrow holds? In spite of the uncertainty in the air, everyone seems to be in better spirits having eaten, and the immediate threat of the Benefactors off the table. There is one person, though, who hasn't said a word this entire journey.

I pass the food off to Elm and approach Sarah, who sits quietly on the bench, staring at her feet.

"Hey, Sarah." I sit down beside her and notice her eyes are full of tears. "Sarah?"

She turns her head slightly to me, then it drops. "This all happened because of me."

"No, Sarah, no. It wasn't your fault. You were under Selene's control. Everyone knows you never would have done any of those things on your own. Besides, it got us where we needed to go."

Tears streak down. "I wish I was stronger. I should have been able to fight them off."

Dr. Iris has been hovering nearby, listening. She comes over and places a hand on Sarah's back. "You're still a student, and you were up against fully trained Benefactors. You did the best you could. It is I who am sorry I wasn't able to protect you at the time. Perhaps I was too cautious.

"And, if we're playing the blame game," I interject, "I basically opened a network between Selene's brain and mine. For all we know, I'm the one who led them to us."

Out of the corner of my eye, I catch Blake watching us, his expression unreadable. I wonder if he does blame me for that. And really, why shouldn't he? I give an inward sigh. Maybe Neo Prism will be the place where we can repair our friendship. Elm and the others join us.

"Sorry to interrupt—" Kaito yawns. "But do we know what we're doing tonight? We're all pretty beat."

"The leader of Neo Prism, Ivan, said he has accommodations for us," Elm tells the group.

I look around. "Someone was supposed to escort us." No sooner have I said it than a young lady with bushy red hair in pigtails appears, wearing a tight dress with colorful geometric patterns. She tips the brim of a black paperboy cap. "Are y'all the domers?"

"Domers?" Blake asks in confusion.

"The ones who came from inside the dome."

"That's us." Elm smiles.

"I'm Marabell. Ivan sent me to make sure you all get settled for the night." She wrinkles her nose. "Ya'll look like you've had a time. Is everybody ready?"

Elm and I do a quick head count to make sure the whole group is still with us, and we follow Marabell, ready for a comfortable place to lay down our heads.

"Whoo-wee!" Marabell breathes as we reach the hover-cart platform. "Looks like we have some company. They must have heard about y'all and wanted to have a look."

The platform is a crowded mass of people, craning to see inside the carts. They really came here because of us? I feel as though we'll be set upon the moment we step out, like a pack of wolves on an injured animal. How did the word travel that quickly?

"Dang it," Gemma says. "If I had known we were going to have a big audience, I would have given everyone the red-carpet treatment."

"Well, I'm going to give this crowd the 'get-the-blast-outta-the-way' treatment," Blanca grumbles.

Nikki chuckles. "Well, walking out looking like survivors of a natural disaster makes a better story anyway, don't you think?"

The crowd sends a tight feeling through my stomach. I don't want to face all these people. What could they possibly want? To ask questions? To confront us? Just to stare? Although to be honest, we probably all would do the same in their situation.

"Nobody's gonna bother y'all," Marabell assures. I'm not sure how she can promise that. She's a fairly petite woman, and there's only one of her. I would guess Ivan never anticipated the extra attention we would receive, or he would have sent more security.

"Everyone wait until I give the all clear, all right?" Marabell pushes her way through the crowd in order to carve out a space for herself and steps onto the platform. She takes a deep breath, and in a booming voice that's a far cry from the belle-like hospitality we heard a moment ago, she bellows out, "Everyone off the platform! Ivan's orders!"

Is she an Augmentor, then? I can't imagine her pulling that kind of power into her voice otherwise. The crowd certainly responds, and a path clears for us, though a low murmur fills the air. In spite of curiosity that's almost tangible, the crowd allows us room to pass.

We arrive at a simple but tidy apartment complex. The smell of fresh paint tickles my nose. The walls are a clean and calming shade of pastel blue.

"These buildings are new," Marabell explains. "Ivan had them built as a place of refuge. Now that we discovered how to go back and forth through the barrier at will, Ivan suspected some folks might end up coming here. He wanted to make sure there was a place for them when they came. Looks like the timing was right." She waves at a woman sitting at a desk in the reception area. "Evening, Shayla!" She glances back at us. "First floor is currently being used as rentals. So y'all are on the second floor."

"We are grateful for any accommodations," says Elm.

I nod. At this point, I would take almost anything. My eyelids are weighted, and the thought that we're just moments from a bed seems to make the exhaustion grow. We climb the stairs, and I'm grateful it's only one level up.

"Y'all look like you're about to fall asleep standing up," Marabell says, eyes full of compassion. "Let's get you assigned and settled into your rooms." She seems to have a natural understanding of our group. She puts Jazz and Brie together, and the rest of us get our own rooms.

"I trust y'all can get settled on your own. Each room is stocked with the basic necessities, and I'll be coming later with clean clothes once I've gotten your sizes, but if there's anything else you need, Shayla downstairs can take care of you. Ivan's orders are to make sure y'all are comfortable. Have a good evening."

Everyone unanimously agrees to turn in for the night. I enter my room and flick the lights on. It's a small studio space but plenty big enough for one. The faint smell of a vanilla and cinnamon candle lulls me into a small sense of repose. The bed looks comfortable and welcoming, everything from the powder-blue comforter to the lacy pillow shams is clean and tidy. A cute kitchenette is already stocked with herbal teas and a bowl of fresh fruit. The last time I was in a private room was my room at Prism, with its deep-burgundy decor. By contrast, this room is light and airy, everything decorated in whites and soft-hued accents. It feels strange to be alone after spending so many months in the cave with everyone. But the sounds of life through the walls remind me that I'm not truly alone. Friends are a wall away.

The first thing I do is hit the shower. I close my eyes and sigh deeply as the warm water runs over me. It soothes my tension and relaxes my muscles. This is a luxury I had almost forgotten. A little basket on the shower wall is fully stocked with soaps and shampoo. The invigorating citrus fragrance of the shampoo envelops me as I scrub the last of the salt and sand from the beach out of my hair. Was that really just this morning?

After my shower I feel better, except for the blanket of fatigue that I can't shake away. I fall onto the bed, letting the gentle softness of the sheets caress my skin. Heaven. My eyes fall closed, and I'm almost out when I hear a noise.

I sit up at once, heart palpitating. But it's just friends chatting in the hall.

We're safe, I remind myself. The Benefactors aren't coming after us tonight. No traitors are lying in wait. It's going to take some time getting used to that.

I lie down again and pick up Elm's locket from where I set it on the nightstand earlier. The familiar feel of it helps soothe me to sleep.

20

ELM IS FRESH-FACED THE NEXT
morning when I find him in the hall, wearing a cozy-looking
black sweatshirt and jeans. I'm not used to seeing him so
casual, but it works in his favor. He's gone longer than any of
us without creature comforts, so I can only imagine what the
night was like for him.

"Sleep well, Miss Ava?"

"Mostly, yes."

"A little jumpy, perhaps?"

"Yes," I admit.

He puts an arm around my shoulders. "I experienced this
also. I suspect it will take us all some time to adjust." He
smiles down at me. "Shall we join the others for breakfast?"

Everyone else has already gone to a quaint cafe across the
street. It's decorated in shades of lilac, and every table has a
vase of fresh white orchids.

"Ava! Elm!" Nikki waves us over to a booth where she's
already seated with Blake. The rest of our group fills most of
the booths. "Marabell said we can order whatever we want.
Ivan's paying."

Elm and I slide into the booth next to one another. "That's
nice of him." I'm grateful for the gesture, but I'm also really
uncomfortable accepting this kind of generosity, especially

when I suspect he has his own agenda. Nobody else has the same reservations. Plates are filled to bursting with eggs, bacon, sausage, pancakes, and fresh fruit. The sight of the yellow scrambled eggs immediately sets my mouth watering, and I join in.

We all devour our food in euphoric bliss. Having yellow items on the menu is such a change. When I feel I can't eat another bite, I gaze sleepily out of the window. There seems to be quite a crowd outside. Are the streets of the city always this busy? This must be the start of the work day.

I turn my head as a bell signals the opening of the cafe door, which brings in the clamor of noise from outside. Marabell walks in, looking flustered.

"Hey, there. Hope y'all enjoyed your breakfast." She gets our attention. "Listen, I know this isn't ideal, but there are spectators and reporters outside. Ivan likes transparency. It would be really great if you could do a quick interview."

We all exchange uneasy looks. I don't think any of us are ready yet to relive our experience for an audience.

"They'll just keep pushin'. If you give them a little taste of information now, they're more likely to go about their business." Marabell holds out her hands to us. "Please?"

What can we say? They are providing food and lodging for us, and I can understand why the citizens would want to know what's happening. They have to be just as curious about the inside of the barrier as we were about the outside of it. "I can talk to them," I say.

"And Elm also?" Marabell looks to Elm with hopeful eyes. "To be honest, they're all a little obsessed with you."

"Well, who could blame them?" Elm gives a lopsided grin. "Of course I'll join Miss Ava. I can't very well just feed her to the wolves, can I?"

Marabell looks relieved.

"Anyone else?" I glance around.

"No." Blanca swipes a piece of bacon from Kaito's plate. "They're all yours."

When we walk out the door, the crowd is on us in an instant, and Elm's earlier wolf analogy doesn't seem too far off. I feel like a sheep about to be taken down by a pack. Everyone is shouting at us at the same time.

"Is it true you defeated Selene?"

"Are all the Mentalists inside the dome dead?"

"Is Jace still working with the Benefactors?"

"Elm, are you attached to anyone?"

"Oh, shoo!" Marabell says, brushing a group of teenage girls aside. "Honestly, I can't keep them away."

I steal a glance at Elm, who looks both perplexed and entertained.

"Just a few questions for the press?" A reporter with a loud voice waves Marabell down. "Don't keep everyone in the dark!"

"A few quick questions," Marabell says firmly. "These folks have been through an ordeal as it is."

The reporter takes out a recording device, ready to go. "Who's in charge of the group here? First and last names, please."

Marabell pushes Elm and me forward and answers in a clear voice on our behalf. "Ava Locke and Elm Ridley." I don't recall telling her our last names. Exactly how much information does Ivan have on us?

"Elm, is it true that you single-handedly overthrew the Benefactors to make your escape?"

"Oh, not single-handedly," Elm corrects. "Miss Ava here did much of the work."

"Were you under Elm's control, Miss Locke?"

Elm jolts beside me, and I shy back from the reporters. "No, I wasn't," I quickly reply, recomposing myself.

"Really? Not even once? We wouldn't blame you, Mr.

Ridley. You were in a desperate situation. Would you care to tell us about that?"

Elm raises an eyebrow at the reporter. "Not particularly, no."

The reporter isn't fazed. "How about you, Miss Locke?"

"Locke? Did somebody say Locke?"

A voice rings through the crowd, and something about it makes me pause in my response. A man's voice. It's hauntingly familiar. I stand on my tiptoes and strain to see who it is.

A man and a woman come to the front of the crowd, and my breath catches in my throat. I gape at the couple, and my heart accelerates to a speed I didn't think possible.

It can't be.

More lines around their eyes than I remember, and an occasional wisp of gray hair that wasn't there before, but there is no mistaking who they are. Or at least, who they appear to be.

I force the quivering words out of my mouth. "Mom, Dad?"

21

A SOB CHOKES OUT OF THE WOMAN
with the face of my mother, and she rushes forward, crushing
me in an embrace. I hardly notice Elm stepping aside. "Ava!"
She weeps. "Oh, Ava! My dearest girl!"

My body won't move. Am I dreaming? Is my head so
badly wrecked from my encounters in Selene's mind that I'm
hallucinating? Is this a cruel illusion? I'm vaguely aware of
Marabell shooing the reporters away.

"Elm, is this real?" I know it doesn't make sense to ask.
How would he know anything about my parents? But nothing
makes sense right now. I ease back from the woman's arms,
studying her features for some sign of the trick. She stares
back at me like I'm a unicorn.

The man . . . my father? He also tries to hug me, tears
shimmering in his eyes. Those eyes I know so well, yet don't
know at all. I evade him.

"Who are you?" I finally ask, my voice on the verge of
a whisper. "I . . . Selene—the Benefactors—they killed my
parents." My thoughts struggle to form.

"We are your parents, Ava. You recognized us right away.
It's really us." Their expressions have saddened a bit.

"How? I saw them kill you. I watched you die!" My voice

rises in pitch, and Elm steps near to place a steadying arm around my waist.

"This isn't the best place for this conversation," my father says, eyes weary as he watches the growing crowd and the reporters still arguing for a chance to interview us. "Will you come home with us?"

Home.

Do I trust this man who says he's my father? Do I trust anything anymore? But how can I not at least hear what they have to say? If there is a chance that this really is my mom and dad, how can I let that go?

I turn to Elm, who feels like my only lifeline to reality at the moment. "Come with me?"

"Of course. Allow me to tell the others that we'll meet up with them later. I'm sure they'll be in good hands with Marabell."

My parents—I don't know what else to call them—live in a small apartment not far from the cafe. It's simple, but well-kept. We all shuffle inside, and my mom motions to a plush, cream-colored sofa.

"I'll stand, thank you." I can't keep my body still right now. But Elm quietly sits, observing with his usual acuteness, but politely distancing himself from the conversation.

My father looks out the window of the little apartment. He always did have a way of avoiding eye contact during situations that made him uncomfortable. The familiar mannerism is somehow unsettling.

He speaks after a weighted pause. "The whole thing was an illusion."

My hands start to shake. "What? An illusion of your deaths? You made me watch that?"

"It wasn't meant for you. It was for the Benefactors." My mother looks on the verge of tears again. "We didn't want you to see it. We had no idea you were watching."

"But why? I can understand about the Benefactors. But why did you let me believe it? Why didn't you ever come back for me?"

"It was the only way we could think of to keep you safe." My mother's face pleads for understanding. "The outlook for Mentalists was bleak as it was, and we knew Selene wouldn't rest until she had you under her watch."

"If she didn't have you with her," my father says, "she would have viewed you as a threat. And if Selene views someone as a threat, they end up dead. The safest place you could have been was in her care."

My mother adds, "That was how we felt at the time. We've regretted it over the years, wondering so often if there was a better way . . ."

"Of course there was!" I snap, surprised at the growing fire within me. "You could have taken me with you! You could have *not* left me alone to mourn your deaths and to be brainwashed and raised by the enemy!"

"Try to understand . . ."

"You were too young," my father says. "You don't remember what it was like. There was fear everywhere. Our friends were being killed or captured every day. Their children were dying. Everything we did was to keep you alive, because at the time we didn't even know if we would make it out. War has always led people to desperation. We just wanted you to *live*."

"We never intended to leave you so long." My mother can't keep her eyes off me, and her hand twitches as though she wants to reach out. "We were going to come with reinforcements from Neo Prism to bring you back. But then the barrier went up, and it was too late."

I don't realize how much I'm trembling until Elm squeezes my hand. I never even saw him leave the sofa. There's a rushing in my ears, and the world around me goes in and out of focus. I know I should be feeling joy at having my parents here, but the anger and yearning for those lost years overtakes everything. Grief for the childhood I never had.

They could have taken me with them.

They're alive.

They could have taken me with them.

I take a sharp turn for the door, unable to contain the weight of these emotions for another second. "I just need some time," I manage to say before rushing from the room and into the complex hallway as my mother cries out my name. I assume Elm is behind me, even though I don't look back for fear that my parents will see the tears cascading down my cheeks. It feels too intimate to cry in front of them right now.

I don't know where I'm going. This city is still too foreign, and when I try to orient myself to think of where my own apartment is, I feel like I'm being sucked into a maze. My legs just start walking. Finally my eyes zero in on a park bench, and I sink into it, letting the torrent of feelings sweep me away. Elm gently settles his hand on my shoulder. He doesn't say a word until the last of my tears have squeezed out.

Then, with such tenderness that it almost makes me cry again, he says, "My dear Miss Ava. That was quite a shock."

I nod wordlessly and fixate on a purple-gray pebble on the sidewalk.

"But they must love you terribly." He sits down beside me. "I'm sure it can't have been easy to leave their only daughter behind. I imagine many parents would have done the same if they thought it was the difference between life or death for their child. And," he lifts my chin with his finger, "Prism did provide you with a first-rate education, I suppose. Quite a talent you are."

I sniff and smile slightly in spite of myself.

Elm smiles tenderly back. "Cry a little longer, if you must. But when you're ready, perhaps consider that you've been granted a rare chance that most of us could only dream about." He idly produces a few vibrantly colored bubbles from his fingertips, and I watch their pearly sheen in the sunlight, trying to determine if they're real or fake. It seems I have to question everything in this place. Elm blows an errant bubble over to pop on my nose. It certainly feels real.

He leans back while the remaining bubbles pop. "I wish my parents were still alive, fighting somewhere."

I berate myself. How insensitive I've been. How selfish. To be upset when Elm lost his own parents. His parents . . .

"Elm," I say slowly, remembering something that's been gnawing at me. "What were your parents' names?"

"Delia and Andres," he says promptly. "Why?"

I think of the boy's hazel eyes, exactly like Elm's. "I saw them in Selene's memories. She knew them."

He nods, his own eyes darkening. "I know. They sometimes talked about how they knew her . . . before."

Oh. He never told me. But I don't want him to fall into those shadows again. "Can you tell me your favorite memory about your parents?"

As I hoped, he lightens in an instant. "It's not my own memory, but a story they told me several times. Ridley, you see, is actually my mother's surname. My father's surname is Osorio. Shortly after they were engaged, my father told her, 'You know, there's not one thing about you I would change.' My mother responded, 'Except my last name.' She was joking, but he said, 'No, not even that. From henceforth I shall be a Ridley.' It was their joke all throughout their engagement, and in the end, they really did take her surname as our family name. They were both rather sweet." He smiles, eyes alive at the memory.

I can't help but smile with him. "I see where you got both your gallantry and your humor."

He is silent for a moment, then looks at me in a way that is both apologetic and yearning. "I know you prefer not to dwell on Selene's memories, but can you tell me what my school-age parents were like?"

"They were beautiful. Like you." Looking at him now, I can see the ways he complements the two of them so perfectly. A touch of his father's golden skin. The shine of his mother's hair. Lines and features of their faces and smiles. How unfair that I get to see the young man he has become when they can't. I swallow a lump in my throat. "You could see even back then that they loved each other very much. I know how much they must have loved you."

"Your parents love you just as much, Miss Ava."

I know he's right. This is a gift I never saw coming. Instead of mourning the years that were lost, I should be thinking about the ones I have yet to gain with them.

"I have forgiven them," I say at last. "It's just hard knowing they were here this whole time while I was with Selene. Life could have been so different."

"But perhaps we wouldn't have met."

I start. "Well . . . that's true. That is one thing I have no regrets about. But I still can't help but wonder."

"It does no good to dwell on the *what if*s," Elm tells me. "But you can choose to make the best of this fresh start."

And I really do want that. A flicker of joy stirs within me. My parents are *alive*. They're here, part of this outside world that the Benefactors can't touch. How they must have been aching for me over all these years. Did they wonder how I was doing? Did they even know I was still alive? And did they ever dream that they would meet me again someday? This has to be as challenging for them as it is for me. I suddenly feel small thinking of my reaction to them.

I take a deep breath. "Let's go back."

My mom—yes, *my* mom!—looks like she's going to fall apart when she sees me at the door. She flings opens her arms, then hesitates. I finish the motion for her, and she holds me in silence for a long time. I soak in the warmth of her embrace, and her smell. The same apricot perfume I remember from all those years ago.

"I'm sorry I treated you so badly just now. I'm all jumbled inside."

"Hush," she says. "You're so beautiful." She smooths my hair. "Oh, how I wish we could have watched you grow up. But I'm just so happy you're here now."

"I'm sorry." I fight the quiver in my lip.

"Don't be," says my father. "I can only imagine what you felt when you saw us. You're not the one with anything to apologize for."

"Come inside!" My mother motions to Elm, who is lingering awkwardly in the hallway. "You've been with Ava all these past months, watching over her. Thank you for helping to bring her back to us."

"So you're her . . . friend?" My father seems to size Elm up.

Elm grins pleasantly. "Oh, certainly. We'll call it that until Miss Ava is ready for that conversation."

My mom studies him a moment, then bursts into a broad smile. She likes him. I feel the heat in my cheeks. I didn't plan for one of my first interactions with my parents to be introducing my boyfriend to them.

We spend the next several hours catching up, although my parents have already heard most of what has been happening at Prism and with the recent rebellion.

My father leans back against the sofa. "For years, we had no idea what was going on. We couldn't find a way into the barrier. It's only more recently that we discovered a surge in power could disrupt it."

"Wait. How long ago was that?"

My mother raises her eyebrows, thinking. "Around last November, I think? Nearly a year ago."

"That timing . . . it matches up with Elm's escape." I quickly glance at him.

His face is thoughtful. "Is it possible that without me there to power it, the barrier was weakened enough to allow a disturbance?"

My father bolts upright. "You powered the barrier?" He suddenly looks very wary of Elm.

"Not by choice, I assure you."

My father nods.

"We understand," my mother says.

I wonder if my parents knew any other Mentalists forced to use their powers against their will. What things might they have witnessed all those years ago?

There is a squeal of a tea kettle, and my mother goes to the stove as she says, "But you are here, and the barrier is still there. Are there other Mentalists inside?"

"We know of at least one other," I say.

"Yes, Selene's crony. Jace." My father's tone ices over. "We know about him. That traitorous—" His jaw clenches, and my mother murmurs something to him as she returns with a tray of teacups and a sugar bowl. She pours an aromatic amber liquid into each cup.

I pick at a thread on my clothes. "We want to go back and

find the other Mentalists. There has to be more than just Jace keeping that barrier going."

"Yes," says my mother. "I hate to think what their lives are like." My mom turns to Elm. "If it's not too much to ask," she says hesitantly, "would you mind sharing the details of your escape? You're somewhat of a celebrity around here," she adds, blushing a little.

My dad leans in with interest.

"For Miss Ava's parents, of course. Particularly since she was largely responsible."

My parents' interest grows as Elm recounts his tale. It still feels a little too close in time for me, and hearing him praise me so lavishly makes me overly self-conscious.

One thing I learned from the cave standoff is that I don't want to fight the Benefactors if I can help it. Not in physical combat, at least. While some of them may truly believe in Selene's ideals, there's no way for us to really know for sure how many are under mind control or have had their loyalty shaped by what they've been told is the truth. After all, if I hadn't met Elm, I would likely be among them. I flinch, imagining myself in a Benefactor uniform, using my powers to bring Elm down. It would have been my utmost desire over a year ago. Well, I want no part of it now. I just wish there was a way to protect us until this is all over. A way to shield us . . .

"Oh!" I gasp. "White magic! White magic?"

My parents and Elm stop their conversation and look at me curiously.

"Ava?" my mother says, puzzled.

"Do you know about White magic? About how it works?"

"You didn't learn about it at Prism?"

"How could they," my father reminds her, "if no Mentalists are allowed to study there?"

A thrill runs through me. If people in this city know about

White magic, and if we can master it, then we might be able to figure out how to combine other magic types.

"Beyond the logistics of White magic without Mentalists," Elm remarks, "I believe Selene intentionally wanted awareness of it limited, since it's another form of defense that could be utilized to defy the Benefactors."

My father's face darkens. "I don't doubt it."

I look at my parents. "I want to know about it. Please, tell us," I plead. "Do you have books?"

My father laughs. "I see your enthusiasm for learning hasn't changed."

My mother smiles. "The concept is very simple. It's the execution that can be a challenge. The foundation of White magic is unity. The wielders have to be at one in their goal and united with one another."

I recall the time Elm and I used it by mistake. All we both wanted in that moment was to protect. We didn't care about anything but keeping each other safe.

"That shouldn't be that hard," I insist. "If we're working together against the Benefactors, we should want to protect each other. Our goals are already united." There has to be more to it.

"Yes," says my father slowly, "but conflict can arise between people for all sorts of reasons. You may all want the safety of a shield in a given moment but be experiencing animosity amongst yourselves in various other ways. If there is any conflict between those trying to summon White, it won't work."

This only confirms what I've known from the beginning. We have to be united. That's where our strength lies.

I take in this new information that is both encouraging and disheartening. It means White magic is well within our grasp, but we have to make some changes. I swallow. It has to start with me.

I'm suddenly very tired.

My mother is watching me. "You must be exhausted." She rises from the sofa. "This folds out, but we can make a space for you in the bedroom if you would be more comfortable." She turns to my father. "Can you travel back with Elm since they're not familiar with the routes yet?"

I shift, uncomfortable. "Thank you. But for now it would be better for me to stay in the quarters Ivan arranged for us. I need to be close to our group until we have all this sorted out."

Silence.

I wish I didn't see my mother's quivering lip as we stand. But despite that, she nods. "We understand." She wraps her arms tightly around me. "We've missed you terribly, dearest. To have you so near—" she breaks off. "We're proud of you. You must do what is best."

In some ways, it's like we were never separated; in others, they are still complete strangers. And the students from Prism need me more than ever.

My father puts his hands on our shoulders. "And I imagine this is all quite a shock to you. You need time—for many things—first."

Their understanding breaks something in me, and I begin to cry. "I missed you so much."

We weep together, my parents and I, but there is happiness in these tears.

22

ELM AND I STAND IN HESITATION
outside the door to Samantha's small apartment—Marabell
was happy to give us the address when we asked last night.
But the dawn of a new morning hasn't made me any more
optimistic about what I have to do.

"You're certain you don't want me with you?" Elm asks.

"I do want you here," I admit. "But this is between me and
her. So it's something I need to do alone."

Elm gives me a quick kiss on the forehead. "Then I will
meander around nearby, anxiously. Best of luck, Miss Ava."

I take a deep breath and give a sharp knock. A moment
later the door opens.

"Oh, it's you." Samantha scrunches her nose. "What do
you want?"

"Can we talk?"

For a moment it looks as though she'll slam the door in my
face, but she says, "I guess so."

Samantha's apartment looks just like her. Bright yellow
decorations and childish trinkets everywhere. Teddy bears.
Canary-yellow glass stars, similar to the stone on the tip of her
staff, hang from the ceiling. The light streaming through the
windows jumps off of them and bathes the room in dancing

gold. Samantha gestures to a nook with two poofy yellow beanbags. "Have a seat."

The beanbag is squishier than I expected and feels like it's going to swallow me whole. She smirks as I struggle to get myself into some sort of position that doesn't look completely ridiculous. Once I'm seated semi-upright, she slips daintily onto the other beanbag, cross-legged.

"I came here to apologize."

Samantha's eyes widen, but then narrow in suspicion. "Go on."

I stare at my hands and twist them in my lap. "When you first showed up, I was instantly suspicious of you, and that wasn't fair. Part of that is because in spite of everything, in spite of the fact that it's part of who I am, I still have deep-seated negative feelings about Mentalists. I hate that about myself, and I'm trying to change it, but years of indoctrination are hard to shake."

I wring my hands tighter. "It's confusing because I . . ." I pause. "I really care about Elm. But when I saw you, ingrained feelings came to the surface again."

Samantha says nothing, waiting for me to continue.

"I guess I felt threatened because of your relationship with Elm. It's not easy for me to say, but jealousy got the better of me."

Pain flashes across her face. "You don't need to be jealous of me. I'm not the one Elm wants."

At least both of our raw emotions are out in the open.

"The relationship you have with Elm is unique, one I can never have," I tell her. "You're special to him, and you always will be. You—"

"Don't patronize me!" she snaps. "We're friends, but it's not enough. We'll never have what I want, and it's your fault." That childish pout enters her voice. "Why couldn't I have found him before you? I've been searching for *years*! I never stopped. And then he meets you, and in just a few months, you're his world."

Anger threatens to boil up, but I steady myself, remembering why I came to begin with. "It's because you never stopped searching that we aren't trapped with the Benefactors," I say evenly, "because you came here and knew how to get us all out. No matter how you feel about me, I'm thankful for what you've done. No matter what else may happen, no matter what our relationship is going forward, I will always be grateful to you for getting us out and for never giving up on Elm."

She stares at me.

When it's clear I'm not getting anything else out of her, I fumble awkwardly off the beanbag. "That's really all I wanted to say, I guess. Just that I'm sorry for how everyone—especially me—has treated you, and that I'm grateful."

"You're not going to tell me to stay away from Elm?" she asks, voice lush with disdain.

"No. I trust Elm, and I won't ask him to give up a friend from his childhood." Then, in a true attempt to make amends, I say, "But, Samantha, you'll drive him away yourself if you keep acting this way."

I let myself out and leave her standing silently in the vibrant yellow room.

"My, that was quick. How did it go?" As Elm promised, he wasn't far.

"I don't know. I'm pretty sure she hates me." I can't decide whether I feel good about talking to Samantha or not. I tried to reconcile in the best way I could.

"She'll warm in time, surely. She's hurting right now. But I can't imagine her hating you once she gives you a chance."

"You're biased. But I promise I'm going to try really hard to make things better, not just so we can be united for the magic, but because I know she matters to you."

"Thank you, Miss Ava. I do appreciate the effort," Elm says somberly. "I hope it's returned to you."

"So, what should we do for our first full day in Neo Prism?"

Elm rests his arm on my head playfully. "We could go frolic with the rest of your classmates."

"Frolic? Where are they?" Frolicking a bit myself, I spin out from under his arm and surprise him by getting him in a headlock.

"Still at the top of your game," he says with a laugh. "Let's go join them in the square. Nikki said that's where they were headed."

And we do find them there, but they aren't alone. Several school-aged Mentalists have joined them. Gemma has a Hula-Hoop around her waist, bursting with uncontrolled laughter as she maneuvers it. "There's no way I could do this on my own!"

I freeze, realizing she's letting one of the youngsters control her. A bright-eyed boy with auburn curls. Nausea threatens my stomach, but I tell myself everyone is having fun, so there's nothing to worry about.

"Try it on me! Please?" Brie begs.

Jazz looks on nervously. "Brie, I don't think it's a good idea . . ."

"You're so boring." She sticks her tongue out at him and turns to the Mentalist boy. "Ignore him. Do it!"

The bright-eyed boy grins. "Okay. You won't know what hit you."

Brie suddenly starts to dance, elegant and graceful. Calm in a way that I have never seen her. I flash back to a memory of young Selene and the taunts of Mentalists at her school. I imagine her limbs bending. Breaking.

"Okay, I think that's enough," I say.

Brie continues her eerily beautiful dance.

"Stop," I say again, louder.

Elm glances at me. "He's not harming her."

My breathing comes faster as I watch, panic squeezing my chest. "Stop!" I finally shout.

Brie stops abruptly. Everyone stares at me.

"What happened?" Brie asks, coming out of her trance. "Did I do anything?"

I mumble an apology and turn to bolt, but strong hands hold my shoulders as Elm stops my retreat and spins me around to face him. He takes one look at my face, now wet with tears, and pulls me to him.

"What's going on, Miss Ava?"

"I think my head is still messed up. Selene's memories . . ."

His concern turns determined. "Surely someone here knows how to assist you." He brushes the tears from my cheeks. "With so many Mentalists about, there must be someone that can help."

"You said yourself you weren't sure if it could be fixed."

"It hurts nothing to ask."

We track down Marabell. "Do you have Healers here?" I immediately feel silly for asking. Why wouldn't they?

"Well, of course. I just sent your Healer friends to one of our centers, in fact. They wanted to see if they could be of service there. Strange to know someone who practices traditional medicine still, isn't it?" She stops, scrutinizing us. "Are y'all feeling sick?"

"No, not really. It's just something personal."

Marabell glances between Elm and me with curiosity. But she respects our privacy and waves us along. "C'mon. I'll escort you there."

The medical center is a full-fledged hospital with a bustling ER and various recovery units. Attendants hurry by with carts of red Colorsticks, so the various Healers have plenty of power at their disposal. I can only imagine how much of a toll healing others all day long would take.

Marabell puts in a word at the front desk, and we're able to track down Dr. Iris and Hazel—Dr. Thompson, rather—without too much trouble, and Marabell graciously departs.

After we explain, Dr. Iris leads us to the head of the hospital. "I'm curious what she'll say. If she knows how to heal you, I want to observe and learn."

Dr. Root, a woman with short sandy hair, gives me a sad smile as I relay the situation to her.

"Well, messing with the unknown wasn't the best choice, was it?"

As though I need to be told that again, I think ruefully.

"Unfortunately," she says, "I think you'll just have to give it some time. And some of it might never truly leave you. Those feelings of hate and suspicion that are so deeply ingrained in Selene are now part of you too."

"It's not something that a Healer could help with?" My voice is as desperate as I feel. Hopeless.

"No. This is more of a mental illness, and Healers address physical maladies. We've never been able to figure out how to heal a person's mind."

Her words sink deep. Will I really feel this way forever? Will I always look at Elm and have my feelings for him tainted by this darkness? Just the thought deflates me.

I turn to Dr. Thompson. "What about your traditional

medicine? How did you treat patients with mental illness before?"

"Medicines," she replies. "Therapies. But those were genetic and situational issues. Not something inflicted by magic, which is quite different. I'm not sure how we would undo something in a mind set there by a spell."

"So . . . there's really no way?"

The pitying silence of the Healers is all the answer I need.

Elm's hand closes around my own, and I almost sob with relief that this, at least, feels normal and secure. My connection to Elm is a part of me, and no part of Selene can erase that. He'll always be there to wrench me back from the shadows.

"We'll find a way to get through this together, Miss Ava," he murmurs. "We will overcome it."

23

"THIS BUILDING IS HUGE!" I CRANE MY neck to try and see the decorative peaks surrounding the top of the structure. The sight of the circular theater is astounding from the outside. The inside must be even more magnificent.

Today, November 30th, is a special occasion. Elm's birthday. When I asked him what he wanted to do, The Mirage Theater—a live theater troupe that performs with Mentalist abilities—topped his list. *"I want to show you some of the good things Yellow magic can do,"* he had said. Nikki and Blake are joining us as well, and as we wait in line for our tickets, I can feel the buzz of excitement for the show. Even the ticket line is fancy, lined with royal-purple velvet.

"What was I doing on your birthday last year?" I try to remember what seems like an eternity ago.

"Probably cursing my name," Elm grins. "That was only shortly after my escape, when I was still the forbidden, terrifying Mentalist."

My thoughts are pulled to him alone in the cave, not a friend in the world, and the image sends a pang of sadness and guilt through me.

Elm suddenly boops my nose. "You look much too serious. This is a birthday, not a funeral."

"You're right," I say with a laugh. "Which is why everything today is on me." I'm determined to make sure he has a good birthday. One he can enjoy without looking over his shoulder.

Once I've purchased tickets for Elm and me, and Nikki and Blake each buy theirs, we follow the crowd away from the box office and into the foyer. The air inside the theater smells like cinnamon almonds and caramel corn. And, thanks to Ivan's stipend, I can actually afford to buy some. Elm and I get a bag of almonds to share, and I savor the sweet, nutty crunch of them while we wait for the show to begin.

"Have you been to anything like this before, Elm?" Nikki asks, diving into her bag of caramel corn.

"My parents took me to Mentalist theater a few times as a child. If it's as I remember it, we're in for a treat."

Blake sits quietly, looking like he'd prefer to melt into the plush velvet of his seat. Of all of us, Mentalist abilities make him the most uncomfortable.

"Hey, Blake," I tease, "should we go to the opera instead?"

But Nikki is regarding him more seriously. "I was looking forward to seeing this, but if you're uncomfortable, Blake, I'll leave with you."

Blake straightens in his seat. "I'm fine, Nikki. Can't wait!"

I smile a little as I glance around. I notice an odd detail. "Is that the stage?" The curtain looks comically small. How could they do a show for such a big house on such a small stage?

"I suppose we'll see," Elm says, eyes sparkling.

The curtain on the stage draws back, and I'm even more confused. Instead of a large stage, seven Mentalists stand on a narrow platform.

"Welcome!" says the man standing in the middle. "We hope you enjoy our show this evening. We ask that you not talk during the performance." He winks. "But *ooh*s and *aah*s are permissible. Step inside a new world as we present to you the origins of Magus!"

The lights dim and the crowd hushes. Sweeping music

cascades through the air, and I search for an orchestra or a sound amplifier, but I can't find one.

At once, I'm transported. I'm no longer in the theater, but on a raft in the middle of the ocean, feeling the cool sea spray on my face and inhaling briny air. Sunlight warms my skin, and the call of seagulls drifts on the wind. A large ship looms before me.

"Land ho!" someone calls from the ship's nose.

"Impossible!" cries a passenger. "This is the Bermuda Triangle!"

Stretched out before me is a great mass, shrouded in purple mist. The waves become more tumultuous as we approach, and I instinctively clutch Elm as we rock wildly. The crew of the larger ship bustles about, bracing themselves as the vessel plunges through the mist.

Silence.

Stillness.

The mist clears and I hear birds. I see trees.

The ship bumps against the shoreline, and the awestruck crew disembarks. "What are you waiting for?" a crewman shouts in our direction. "Come on!"

I step from the little raft, and the grit of sand meets my feet. Even though we can't have been in the theater for more than a few minutes, it's like I've been at sea for ages. Trepidation and excitement dance on the air as we venture into unknown territory.

We continue our immersive theater experience, participating with the theater company as we see the exploration of Magus, the first sparks of magic entering the people's veins. I feel it burst through me too. I am entranced, and I almost forget the reality we face. I can pretend for a moment that everything is fresh and new. That most of the land isn't suffocating under a barrier, and everyone can live together.

It's as though I've barely blinked and have lived a hundred

lifetimes all at once. When the show ends, and the splendor of the new Magus fades into the dimly lit theater once more, the audience bursts into cheers and clapping and the cast bows.

"Wow," I say, gaping at Elm.

"Extraordinary talent," he agrees, standing and adding his own appreciative applause to the crowd.

Nikki is also on her feet, and I steal a glance at Blake who is sitting with an awestruck look on his face. He stands slowly and joins in the applause.

"That was amazing!" Nikki's eyes sparkle as we leave the theater.

"Yes," Blake agrees. "That was definitely amazing."

I half expect Elm to gloat and give Blake a hard time about his admission, but of course, he behaves himself. "What did you think, Miss Ava?"

"It was wonderful." My words come out breathless with awe.

I carefully fold my program and place it in my messenger bag. I look up. "Elm and I are going to get something to eat. Do you want to join us?"

Nikki makes a face. "That sounds great, but it's my turn to interview with Ivan today." Ivan has taken turns with each of us to squeeze out as much information as possible about the Benefactors. Now he's on round two, and everyone is getting a little tired of answering the same questions. But it seems like there's more to her hesitation.

"Is everything okay?"

She runs a hand through her curls. "I guess so. It's just . . . well, he offered me a job."

"What?" Blake is suddenly very alert.

Nikki blushes. "I told him about being an Elite student, and I showed him some of the things I can do with object modification. He was impressed. He says they could use someone like me to improve structural integrity around the city."

My emotions are mixed. On the one hand, I'm excited she's

been offered an opportunity that will utilize and appreciate her talents. On the other hand, that sounds like a pretty permanent situation. I sneak a glance at Elm, but he stands, silent. "So, did you accept?"

"I haven't yet. I don't know if it's what I want. But it is tempting."

Who could blame her? A good job in a safe place. She's not wrong for wanting that.

"Anyway, I'll see you all later! I'll be late if I don't go now."

"All right. See you, Nikki. Good luck." I shake off my emotions—no sense worrying now over something that hasn't even been decided. "Blake?"

Blake still seems lost in thought, and he doesn't respond as he watches Nikki disappear down the crowded sidewalk.

"You know, Blake, you could—"

"Nope." He cuts me off and walks in the direction of the hover-cart platform, hands shoved into his pockets. "You go have fun. Thanks for inviting me."

I shake my head as he departs. Why are guys so stubborn sometimes?

Elm's pick for dinner is a small restaurant with outdoor seating that serves local cuisine. The tables are tiny and round, allowing for easy conversation and an intimate atmosphere. Colorful dishes full of fresh seafood and tropical fruits decorate the menu. Each bite of the spicy grilled pineapple on my plate sends fireworks of flavor over my taste buds. This feels so ridiculously normal yet so extraordinary. Were we really living in a cave a few weeks ago?

I savor a sip of cold fruit juice and give a satisfied sigh. "This was a good choice. You should have birthdays more often."

He smiles broadly at my pleasure. "Sammy recommended it."

His reply sours the bite of food I'm currently working on. She hasn't said a word to me since I went to her apartment. I'm afraid my attempt at a better relationship might have only made things worse. "Where is she today? It seems like she'd be all over you on your birthday, of all days." I wince at my spitefulness.

Elm squeezes a lemon over a plate of grilled white fish. "Ah, well, she knew I would be spending the day with you." He shrugs and spears a bite of food. "She says she plans to thoroughly spoil me tomorrow."

His words spike anxiety. She still hates me. And is still after Elm.

"Don't fret, Miss Ava. You've extended the olive branch. Things will come around in due time."

"I hope you're right."

He pauses and observes me with those keen hazel eyes. "My dear, you don't give yourself nearly enough credit for your ability to win people over."

His words leave me flustered, but before I can reply, a group of teenage girls approaches our table, the air at once filling with nervous whispers and giggles. What is all this about?

A girl with sleek, black hair holds out a pen and notebook, and her friends urge her forward. "Sorry to interrupt, Elm, but could we have your autograph?"

Autograph? Seriously?

Elm doesn't take his eyes off of me, but they now sparkle with amusement, the faintest hint of a smile on his lips. He leans closer to me, chin resting on one hand. The girl gasps as the pen floats out of her grasp and puts itself to the paper, scrawling out what I assume is Elm's signature. The pen finishes its work, and the girl clutches it again, looking puzzled at the notebook.

"What does it say?"

Elm blinks and looks away from me to glance at the illegible scribble on the paper. Now it's my turn to look amused. It certainly doesn't resemble handwriting.

"That is my signature, of course. May you treasure it always."

I cover a snort as the girls wander away, confusion on their faces.

"I think you disappointed them," I say, swirling my straw in my drink.

"I've been known to do that on the odd occasion," he says merrily.

"Well, you can't be perfect all the time. But you could easily perfect your signature. If you practiced."

"It's my birthday," he says firmly. "You aren't permitted to hassle me."

"Tomorrow, then," I grin. "For today, I have a present for you."

"Oh?" He watches with interest as I rummage through my bag. "I thought the theater tickets were more than sufficient."

"I think you'll like this too. At least, I hope." I feel heat creep to my cheeks—it seems inadequate in comparison to all he's done for me. I hand him a thin square package wrapped in bright yellow paper. "It's no sunflower field, but . . ."

He takes the package and opens it with care. His eyes widen a moment as he examines the gift. "What is this?"

In a silver frame is a photograph of him—a favorite candid shot I snuck of him with Kaito's camera on an outing last week. His face is alight with laughter, bathed in warm light at golden hour. Carefree. Happy. It's the Elm I got to know so well all those months we spent together. The photo was edited to look like one of his wanted posters with the words:

WANTED:
FOR BEING AWESOME

"I know it's a little cheesy," I say, still feeling the red in my cheeks. "But I hoped to reframe everything. You're not a wanted criminal anymore, and you never should have been." I motion for him to flip the frame over. "Read the back too."

I watch his face soften as he reads the words I've written in permanent ink: *I'm glad you are you.*

"Every time you forget how amazing I think you are, every time you go down that path of wondering what's real, every time words or actions of the past make you question your worth, I want you to look at this and remember. Because you are incredible."

He doesn't say a word, but he leans across the table and surprises me with a kiss that says it all.

24

I SQUINT MY EYES AT THE SILVERY
shapes splashing in and out of the water in the distance. It's
hard to make them out with the sun glinting off the waves.
"What are those?"

"Dolphins," my mom smiles. "A whole pod of them."

Today's outing was her idea. She wanted to show me the
Emerald Overlook—an area of sea cliffs covered in lush green.
While it still feels a little strange, I've been making my best
effort to see my parents when I can.

I gaze in wonder as the creatures frolic in the waves. There
are so many things about the world that I haven't experienced.
What else lies beyond the horizon?

"Ivan told me that nobody gets in or out of Magus
anymore," I comment. Out of the barrier, but still boxed in.

"It's true," my dad replies. "Anyone who tries is stopped
one way or another. Storms. Waves. Some just disappear."

"Ivan thinks it's Magus itself."

"This place does seem to have a life of its own sometimes."
He picks up a pebble and tosses it. Over the roar of the waves,
we never hear it hit the water. "But who could really say?"

"Speaking of Ivan," my mom says, "we met with him
yesterday."

I can't even begin to guess why Ivan would be meeting with

my parents. I brush my hair out of my eyes as the sea breeze whips through it. "What did he want?"

"He wants to know what you need. Well, what your group needs. He said you've been, quote, 'tight-lipped about it,' and he thought you might have been more open with us."

I hug my knees to my chest and gaze toward the horizon. The dolphins have gone. I know Ivan would give us anything requested. I also know it's because he's working up to something, and I'm just not sure what. He sends Marabell every day to prod for requests, but every day I give the answer that I'm giving my parents now. "We're fine."

My dad chuckles. "Figured you would say that. There's one thing we said you could use, though."

"What's that?"

"Learning space. A room to practice and grow in skill."

My curiosity is piqued. "What did Ivan say?"

My mom reaches into her pocket and pulls out a set of keys. She hands them to me. "There's a school close to your apartments. It has a big gym. Ivan says you and your classmates are welcome to use it whenever it's vacant."

My eyes widen. "That's . . . actually perfect! Oh, thank you!" I'm already thinking of the possibilities. A space where we're free to practice. Free to develop White magic and who knows what else. That is exactly what we needed. "Be sure to thank Ivan for us."

"Well," says my dad, "we hoped you could tell him yourself. He's requested a meeting with you this afternoon."

I sigh, standing and brushing the sand from my clothes. "Of course he did," I mutter.

It's harder leaving my parents this time, and that's a good thing. I'm much more comfortable and look forward to being with them. I would have liked to spend the afternoon together with them, but when the leader of a city requests a meeting, you go. Especially when that leader has given you everything you need to survive. The thought of being so indebted to him still fills me with discomfort. We—or at least Elm and I—aren't planning to stay outside the dome for long. There can't be any unnecessary complications to our leaving.

I cross paths with Kaito leaving the compound as I enter. This in and of itself isn't unusual since we all meet with Ivan frequently, but this time he looks a little flummoxed. "Are you alright, Kaito?"

He scratches his head. "Um, yes. Ava, he offered me . . ."

"A job?"

He nods. "An engineering position. A good one."

"Are you going to take it?"

"I told him I have to think it over."

I give his bewildered face a light smile. "If you want to take it, it's okay, you know." Elm would miss his inventing buddy, but I know he'd be happy for him too.

"I know. But there are other things that matter too." His eyes are distant. "My family is still back in the dome. I don't know if I could take a good job and live the high life here while they're all there—most likely against their will." He focuses briefly on me. "Anyway, good luck, Ava."

I feel bad that any of my friends feel like they have to make this hard choice. It seems unfair to ask them to go through more than they already have. My steps feel heavy as I approach Ivan's office. This time, I'm sure to knock. I have no interest in being slammed to the floor by Dawz again.

The door opens, and Ivan motions me inside without a word. Dawz didn't even bother to get up. The dog is probably used to people coming and going several times a day by now. I take a seat opposite Ivan and wait. This feels oddly like some of my uncomfortable meetings with Selene. Ironic, since I know she's the last person Ivan would want to be compared to.

Ivan surveys me from across the desk, a silver clock ticking away seconds on the wall behind him. He twirls a pencil in his fingers. If he's not going to get this meeting started, I will.

"Thank you for the gym keys. It's great to have a place to practice."

He continues fiddling with the pencil. "You're welcome. Since as of yet you've all refused to attend our schools, I wanted to at least give you a place to study independently. You're a talented group of students. Be a shame to let that go to waste."

Is he trying to make me feel guilty? "We're all a little leery of schools at the moment, and I hope you can understand."

"Of course. Selene did a number on you. Which brings me to the reason I called you here."

Here it comes. The proviso. "I'm not sure there's anything else I can tell you. You interrogated me pretty thoroughly last time."

He sets the pencil down. "I'm actually hoping to acquire more current information."

More current information. As in . . .

"You mean sending me back inside the barrier? Like a spy?" If that's what he's getting at, I have no desire for that.

"Not exactly." He stops to throw Dawz a treat. That's the third the dog's had while I've been here. "Word on the street is you got mixed up in Selene's dreams."

I can't mask my surprise. How did he know that? I never told him. Not even all of my classmates are aware. I kept that between my close friends only. The thought that a friend could have let him know this during one of their meetings stings, but I force my face back into a neutral expression. "What about it?"

"I'd like you to do it again. See if we can tap into any new information."

The request hits me like a meteorite. Does he really think I'm going to fall down that hole again? I'm still afraid to go to sleep at night. There's no way I'm going to repeat that mistake. "No." The sound of my loud answer reverberates off the confining office walls.

"We could train you. It won't be so dangerous if you know exactly what you're doing."

I purse my lips together, trying to find calm before I answer. "Isn't the reason I ended up in her memories to begin with because I messed up the dream hopping? Tapping into memories is not something Mentalists are supposed to be able to do."

"True," he concedes. "But if it can be done on accident, it can be done on purpose. We can hone it in and use it to our advantage."

"I'm still dealing with the negative effects of trying it before. What makes you think I'd be willing to do it again?"

"You would be a hero to the people here. If we can keep tabs on Selene, we'll never be caught off guard. All it takes is one loose stone to start the avalanche that crushes us all."

He's obsessed. Always watching to stay one step ahead of what's happening behind the barrier. All to protect what he has, because he knows it's fragile. He knows it could all crumble at any moment. I want a more secure foundation. A future that will last. And I'm never going to open my head to Selene's mind again. Ever. "I can't do that again, Ivan. I won't."

"I see. Well, think about it. You may change your mind. In the meantime, I'd like to offer you a job."

"So then he asks me if I'd like to head up intel operations." I carve furiously at the piece of meat in front of me, ignoring the looks of concern on my friends' faces.

"What did you say, Miss Ava?" Elm hasn't taken a single bite of his own dinner since I began talking about my visit with Ivan.

"I said no, of course."

Elm nods. "I suspected you would. I would have done the same. At least until we've accomplished what we've set out to accomplish."

Blake puts down his drink. "What do you think he's trying to pull by offering everyone jobs?"

"Perhaps he's not trying to pull anything," Elm remarks. "It is possible that he simply wants to help everyone find their place here."

I swallow a bite of food. "I do think that's what he wants. But I also think his reasons for that aren't completely unselfish. If we're all happy here, there's less chance we'll want to go back there. And if we don't go back there, there's less chance of something messing up his utopia."

Nikki raises her eyebrows. "And do we want to mess up his utopia?"

"Of course not. If we can avoid that, that would be ideal. But we also don't plan to just settle in here and pretend there's nothing happening behind the barrier."

"I actually kind of like it here." Nikki looks down at her

plate. "It's happy here. It's free. I don't want to see Selene destroy that."

Is she telling us she's out? I knew there was a possibility we would lose our companions along the way, but losing Nikki causes a knot to twist in my stomach.

She glances up at us. "I'm not bailing on you. I'm just saying, once this is all over, I wouldn't mind calling this place home. I just want to leave it all in one piece if we can, okay?"

If we're lucky, any fighting will take place inside the barrier and Neo Prism will remain untouched. But I do wonder how long it might be before Selene realizes they can get through without taking the barrier down entirely. For all I know, her buggerflies already managed to capture that information. Who knows what they've seen.

I poke around my meal, appetite lost. The rest of our dinner conversation is muted and forced.

25

THE GYM IS STOCKED WITH A CLIMBING
wall, sporting equipment, cushioned mats, and even bleachers
with an upper and lower level. We have plenty of training space.
Today it's just Blake, Elm, and me. I try not to let it bother me
that everyone else had other plans. They should have fun, and
they've been practicing hard with us this past week.

"So are we going to dump balls on our heads again?" Blake
asks wryly.

I give a nervous laugh, remembering thud after thud on my
head after multiple failed attempts at White magic. "Well, if
it's good motivation to get that shield up, yes."

Elm eyes me as I approach an oversized metal basket full
of yellow kickballs in the corner. "Perhaps we could do just a
few this time rather than the full basket?"

"Motivation." I grin and kick a ball in his direction, which
immediately swerves away from him.

My eyes widen, and I turn to Blake.

Blake shakes his head. "Don't look at me. I would've let it
hit him."

I give Elm a smug smile "So you used your Shaper abilities."

"It was merely a fluke. A reflex."

"Uh-huh." He'll embrace it one of these days. I just know it.

The entire basket of kickballs floats to the handrail of the upper bleachers.

"That certainly wasn't me," Elm remarks.

"Obviously not." Blake is derisive. "Let's get going."

Blake seems to be in a foul mood. He's been a little snippy ever since Nikki mentioned Ivan's job offer. Nevertheless, we all bunch together in the pathway of the soon-to-be-falling balls and prepare for our first attempt.

"Let's get the barrier up this time. On three, Blake."

Blake nods, already deep in focus.

"One. Two. Three!"

The basket tumbles and the balls come fast. "Shield!" I cry. *Thumpthumpthump.*

Elm rubs his nose, where he took a direct hit, and Blake laughs.

I shoot him a look and return to our task.

Blake rounds the balls back up with a spell and attempts to get the basket steady again. It falls. He tries again. It falls again.

"Sorry. I guess I don't have the focus to get it balanced today."

"Do we need to stop?"

He shakes his head. "This is too important. Let's try again."

It's not like Blake to be unfocused. He pinches his brows, looking perplexed. I jog to the steps that lead up to the second level bleachers. "I'll get the basket this time. Maybe focusing on getting the balls arranged is making it too hard for you to work on getting the barrier up."

Blake sends the basket back up my way, and I lunge to grab it. It's heavier than I expected, and it yanks me off balance. Before I know it, I'm tumbling right over the railing.

I brace myself for a hard impact, and somewhere in the back of my mind I hear Elm's frantic shout of "Net!"

There's a flash of green light, and instead of the hard crack to the floor I expected, I bounce into a net, albeit a somewhat flimsy one, held between Blake and Elm. I'm uninjured, but I feel like a fish, caught up every which way.

Elm rushes to untangle me. "Are you hurt?"

"No, I'm fine." Realization hits me. "Did you do that together?"

"Yes. Imagine that! We *can* agree on something."

Blake huffs and assists with freeing me from the netting.

"But this is wonderful! It means blending only two magic types between individuals is possible. Think of what we can do!" Excitement builds inside me, and I can hardly contain myself. "Wait! Maybe a Mentalist and an Augmentor can heal a mental illness."

My out-loud thoughts continue to free fall. "If an Augmentor can heal physical injuries and a Mentalist can influence the mind, couldn't the two work together to heal the mind?"

"It sounds like a plausible theory," Elm says thoughtfully.

Blake's brow is furrowed.

"Will you try it?" I grasp Elm's hands. "Please, with Dr. Iris?"

Elm looks alarmed. "Dr. Iris is an accomplished Healer, and I trust her explicitly. But as to my own abilities in that regard . . ."

"There's no Mentalist I would trust with my mind more than you," I insist. "I know you're afraid of hurting me, but we have to try it."

"But I only just now managed to combine magic with Blake— accidentally, I might add."

"He's right, Ava," Blake interjects. "Practicing with balls is one thing, but healing is something that can't be experimented with except by getting others—or in this case, you—involved."

"Precisely," Elm says. "Working with objects is a little different. Much less risk involved. It's not going to be a big loss if something comes out the wrong color or shape. But with a person . . . the consequences there could be far-reaching and unchangeable."

I can hardly believe they're agreeing with each other right now. Elm and I look at each other. I cross my arms. Waiting to see who is the most stubborn.

Elm speaks first. "I know what it's like to be a guinea pig," he says, his jawline defiant. "I won't turn you into one."

"I don't mind being the guinea pig. It has to involve someone anyway, why not me? Taking this risk might help others for years to come. Please, Elm."

Elm takes in a sharp breath and closes his eyes, running his hand through his hair. "I beg you, Miss Ava. Don't make me regret this. Nothing in the world would console me if I hurt you."

"This sounds extremely risky." Dr. Iris looks just as uncomfortable with the suggestion as Elm still is. Blake wouldn't even come with us, wanting no part of what's about to transpire.

Dr. Root seems equally unsure. "Wouldn't it be better to be more experienced at combining magic types before attempting something like this? I've been training Trisha on White magic, but I haven't even thought to attempt what you're speaking of."

"But it has to be tried on someone to know that it works. Just like practicing healing."

Dr. Iris shakes her head. "I think it's wiser to give your issue time to resolve on its own."

"I can't wait for that. We have too much at stake, and I need to have a clear head. I need every part of Selene out of me before I go any further." Add to that the additional fear I can't voice—that it will *never* resolve on its own.

"Well," Elm comments, "we do want to help you, Miss Ava. I think it's easy for us to agree on that."

There is a pause, loaded with weighted options.

"We will try it," says Dr. Iris at last. "But Ava," she levels her eyes at me, "if you feel even the slightest discomfort, you must tell us so we can stop immediately."

"I promise."

Dr. Root sighs. "I suppose I consent, but if it goes wrong, I don't want any scandal pinned on my office."

"If it goes wrong, I will take full responsibility," Dr. Iris vows. Now I'm even more anxious for it all to go well. I don't want anything to create problems for Dr. Iris if it doesn't.

Dr. Iris motions to me and places her hands on my head, and Elm rests a hand on her shoulder. "To verbalize the goal here, we're trying to heal Ava's mind and remove Selene's memories and emotions."

"I'll be focusing on the latter, specifically," Elm nods.

"Okay, then." I feel Dr. Iris's hands shake just slightly. "Let's get started."

Heat builds in my head. Pressure. I'm about to ask them to stop when suddenly it's as though a balloon bursts and then . . .

Clarity.

The fog over my brain for these past few weeks lifts. The disgust at my own powers that I have had to forcibly stuff down all this time is gone. I search my inward thoughts. There is no more disdain toward Mentalists. All that's left is me.

"Miss Ava?"

"It worked. It worked!" I fling my arms around Elm.

He releases a huge sigh and holds me tight. "Thank goodness."

I turn to Dr. Iris and hug her too. "Thank you, thank you!"

She shines with excitement. "Do you know what this means? Think of what can be accomplished? How many lives can be restored?"

"Astounding!" Dr. Root is beaming. "What was it like, Trisha?"

Dr. Iris thinks for a moment. "It was definitely different. It was like feeling my energy combine with Elm's."

"Difficult to explain, certainly," Elm agrees. "I started as I might do if I was trying to change someone's mood, but then focused on Dr. Iris and her healing ability, and at once it was like our magic simply snapped together. Like two waves converging."

"With something like this," I wonder, "would it be possible to undo the effects of Yellow magic controlling those within the barrier?"

Dr. Root's eyes widen and then grow thoughtful. "It might be very possible indeed."

This could be a huge turning point. If this could happen, there would be no need to wonder if anyone was being controlled or not. We could truly help the innocent . . . and decide how to handle the guilty. My parents will be thrilled.

Dr. Root and Dr. Iris are deep in excited conversation about this breakthrough. We need to tell the others.

As expected, we find our group in the downtown courtyard. The spacious brick-paved octagon has been a favorite hangout spot since we arrived in Neo Prism. Light flickers on from the frosted glass spheres surrounding the area. Everyone seems happy, chattering away with one another. Kaito immediately draws Elm into a geeky conversation about the latest tech, which has Blanca rolling her eyes.

Nikki motions for me to come join her on the steps of a covered pavilion. "Ava!"

The first blush of sunset casts everything in a pink glow. A floral scent whisks on the breeze from neatly trimmed bushes nearby. It's like I'm appreciating these things for the first time. Just like coming out from under the barrier.

Nikki takes a second look at my face. "You look calm."

"I am. I'm better than I've been in a while." I recount the news of my healing, and the rest cluster around, eager to hear the good news. Of course, this means some of them are hearing about my foray into Selene's memories for the first time.

"You were going through all that and you didn't tell us?" Blanca's eyes are bright with anger, but to my surprise it diminishes almost as fast as it came. She tosses a hand through her hair as though to shake off the feeling. "You know what, it doesn't matter now. I'm just glad you're ok."

Everyone else echos Blanca's sentiments, expressing happiness for me and optimism about the possibilities.

Gemma raises her voice. "While everyone is here, Sarah and I have some good news to share too." She seems a little anxious about whatever she's going to say. "Want to go first, Sarah?"

"Oh . . . um. I've accepted a job."

My breath catches. I knew it was bound to happen sooner or later. I tell myself this is a good thing and force a smile on my face. "That's great, Sarah! What job?"

"A Healer apprenticeship!" She looks truly excited, her eyes lit with a fire I rarely see in her. "It's all thanks to you, Ava. I never considered Healing, but you helped me see that I could do it. Ivan keyed in on my interest and arranged for me to go through one of the top programs. It's an amazing opportunity!"

"So you're staying in Neo Prism, then?" Brie asks.

"For now, yes. I guess I am. You all know I'm not much of a fighter. And it just feels right being here."

"I'm happy for you, Sarah." And I am, even though it means

leaving her behind in the fight. "What's your news, Gemma?" I ask, even though it's obvious it will be along the same lines.

"I took a job too! I'm going to be a stylist at one of the top salons." Her smile is huge. "It's what I've always dreamed about."

Congratulations ring out, and it's hard to tell if anyone feels as mixed about it as I do. Kaito and Nikki's expressions are muted, and I wonder if they're thinking about the opportunities they were offered.

Nikki stands. "Let's go for a walk," she suggests. "The night is too nice to just sit around."

We walk the downtown streets, admiring the change of the city at night. While the day is a pastel dream, nighttime is a vision of neon. Everything flickers with new life and vibrancy.

We pass a particularly colorful building with dark windows and hear music coming from inside. A loud, heavy beat that brings energy even from the outside of the building. A group about our age just outside the door glances our way. "You guys should go in! It's our peer group night."

"Should we?" Gemma turns with a hopeful look in her eyes. "It might be fun!"

"Not my thing. And definitely not Kaito's," Blanca states. "But we'll go if you do."

"Wait for me!" Brie squeals, already running inside.

"Brie!" Jazz sprints after her, and Gemma takes that as her cue to follow. One by one our students go through the swinging door. When it's down to me, Elm, Blake, and Nikki, Blake shrugs at Nikki and heads inside.

Nikki laughs. "All right. I'll come. Ava?"

"Go ahead. Give me a minute." I look at Elm as Nikki disappears inside. "Do you want to?"

"It wouldn't hurt to unwind a bit, would it?"

"No. It wouldn't. It's just things like this have never been my strong point. I feel awkward."

"Because you don't know how to enjoy yourself or because you're afraid people will see you not being perfect?"

"Maybe both?" I grin.

"I have a secret for you." He leans down to whisper in my ear, "You're going to look perfect to me no matter what you're doing."

I blush. "Okay, but don't leave my side."

"Wouldn't even dream of it."

We plunge into the din, immediately immersed in neon lights and confetti. It's so loud! But it's an exhilarating noise. Laughter. Rhythm.

Off in one corner is a shock of neon color, tattoos, and piercings. All seem to be conversing over high fashion. Gemma has found her people. Blake and Nikki dance side by side, Nikki letting go in full force to the rhythm while Blake moves off beat, but with a huge smile on his face. They inch closer together as they dance. Brie carries on an animated conversation with a group of others about her age, drawing out roars of delighted laughter. Jazz is sitting back with a fizzy drink, looking relaxed for once. I can't find Blanca and Kaito, but I imagine they found some quieter corner to enjoy. Even Sarah is talking to a few people, and as parts of the conversation come to my ears, I realize she knows them. She's made friends here. She looks confident, and I have to concede that taking Ivan's job might really be the best thing for her.

I startle as Elm takes my hand and eases me into a twirl, pulling me out of my thoughts.

"May I have this dance, Miss Ava?"

"Of course." My eyes twinkle at him. "You can have them all."

"I'll hold you to that."

He is elegant, and it's easy to follow his lead. We glide across the dance floor, whirling in the rainbow lights. Alive. Radiant.

In this moment, it's easy to imagine staying here. Easy to picture living in this little utopia without a care in the world. Why shouldn't we stay? We could follow our dreams or find new ones if that's what it takes. Back inside the barrier, there are no guarantees for any of us. I'm starting to understand what my parents were talking about.

The pattern of the lights changes, sparking white across Elm's face. For a moment, I flash back to the image of him the first time I saw him. Gaunt. Pale. Fresh from a nightmare.

I stop dancing.

"Miss Ava?"

"It's not fair," I whisper.

He leans in closer to hear, but I just shake my head, fighting the lump in my throat. He furrows his brow in concern and steers me to the back stairway. It leads out to the roof of the club. The night air is cool, and I take a few slow breaths. Why can't I just enjoy this evening like a normal person?

Elm waits.

"I was thinking that it might not be so bad to stay here," I confess.

"Ah, I see. Well, this has been liberating for the moment, I must admit. I take it you didn't stay on that conclusion?"

"No. Because I just thought about . . . you."

He raises his eyebrows. "You changed your mind on my account? Don't let me be the one who decides your future."

"It's not what you think. I thought about . . . before. The way you were captured and imprisoned. And how you suffered so needlessly. How many more are suffering like that while we are here dancing? I'm ashamed of thinking even for a moment about staying here and turning a blind eye to those inside the barrier."

"It's easy to get swept away." He rests his hand on the small of my back. "I was quite lost in the evening myself. But we know what our goals are. We'll get back on track."

"I don't know how many of our friends will come with us. We already have fewer than when we started."

"It's true."

"I know it's up to them. I can't force anyone."

"I can." Elm grins.

I nudge him. "But you won't."

"I won't," he agrees solemnly.

"So, we just go forward. Even if it's just us." The thought is terrifying, but there are no certainties. We were determined to do this alone in the beginning, so we can't back out now just because it's a possibility once more.

Holding hands, we stare out over the lights of the city.

We let the music fade into the night.

26

MY MOTHER IS STILL BEAMING AS SHE
pauses from clearing the table in their tiny kitchen. The smell
of breakfast lingers in the air. "Completely healed! I'm still in
shock. What a wonderful discovery Ava! Combining only two
magic types. Who would have ever thought?"

"We are so proud of you, Ava." My father's eyes show it.

"It's a start," I say. "Now we need to figure out how to take
out the barrier entirely."

My parents' demeanors alter, and they exchange an
uncomfortable glance. My father clears his throat.

"You have to understand, Ava, that not everyone wants the
barrier taken down. In fact, most of us don't."

I stare at him, refusing to believe what I'm hearing. I don't
miss the "us" in his statement either. "Why would you want it
up? What about the Mentalists *inside* the barrier?" He can't
know what he's saying.

"It's not that we don't want to get them out, but we don't
know what the repercussions would be. We are safe here."

"So you would just let the Benefactors continue their
deception and maintain control?"

"Most of the people who remained there, except young
children who didn't know any better, are there because they
hated us even before the Benefactors took control of their

minds. Why do you think it was so easy for Selene to rise to power? There were so many already willing to join her cause—without the help of Yellow magic."

I try to process what he's telling me. "You think that even if the barrier was gone and the Benefactors defeated, Mentalists would still be attacked?"

My mother speaks. "Sweetie, we admire that you want to try. But we believe there must be a way to get Mentalists out and retain peace here. Then the Benefactors can continue to destroy their own society within the barrier."

"But this is wrong!" I protest. "You're willing to just stand by and let Selene get away with everything she's done? Let her keep controlling people's minds and fostering deception about an entire population?"

My mom rests a gentle hand on my shoulder. "Nobody is saying we agree. We're only saying we must do what it takes to keep our people safe."

Something inside me shatters. The frail hope I had that Magus could be united again crumbles more by the minute. People here have no more desire to stand as one than those inside the barrier. It's just a different set of reasons. I knew we wouldn't have everyone joining our cause, but more than anything I wanted my parents by my side.

I twist away. "I have to go."

"Ava, please . . ."

I'm already at the door. I refuse to look back, knowing the pleading in my mom's face might make me change my mind. I use an agility spell and sprint off. I know this will hurt her—my using Augmentor power to get away—but I can't help it.

The multicolored city is a blur of bodies, and I can only hope people will move out of my way as I speed through. As I approach Elm's place, I experiment with my Mentalist capabilities and throw the suggestion at him hard: *Open the door.*

To my shock, the door actually opens a moment later, an intrigued Elm on the other side.

"It . . . worked?" I pant, breathless from my retreat.

"Well, not fully," Elm apologizes. "I felt the suggestion, but it wasn't strong enough to force me to obey."

"But you did open the door."

"Because it was you, Miss Ava. Obviously."

I collide with him, breathing in the comfort of his scent, wishing again that it could be just us like this for a while. I'm in a constant tug-of-war between a desire for normalcy and a desire to take action. I reach around his neck to draw him closer.

To my surprise, he pulls away. "You might want to hold that thought, darling."

He nudges me further inside to where Blanca, Blake, Kaito, Jazz, Brie, and Nikki are sitting.

I blush and Elm smiles. "Very considerate of you to save us the trouble of coming to get you."

"Why is everyone here?"

"This place is crazy," Blanca says, adding a few other more colorful words.

Jazz gives her a disapproving look, but Brie pipes up, "She's right."

"Everyone's living in lala land," adds Blake. "They don't care what goes on inside the barrier as long as it's not bothering them."

I'm not sure if knowing it's not just my parents who feel that way is a relief or an even greater disappointment. "I've been noticing the same thing. And since you're here, I'm guessing you think differently too."

There are nods and murmurs. Perhaps Elm and I won't be returning to the barrier alone after all. "Then the question is, what are we going to do about it?"

Blanca crosses her arms. "I don't do the brainy stuff. Just tell me what to hit, and I'll hit it."

Nikki is off to the side on an ottoman, staring at her feet as she gently kicks them.

"Nikki?" I think of her job offer. "What about you?"

She sighs. "I know things could be good here. But I just feel like I could never be completely happy knowing what's going on out there. If we can change things, I'm sure I'll have a chance somewhere."

I sit beside her and give her a hug. "We're all the better having you with us."

And so the plotting begins. We share about the progress we've made combining magic types. Thankfully, we've crossed one hurdle. Now that we know who wants to return inside the barrier, we are all the stronger in unity for our goals.

"Combining magic is not going to be easy," I warn. "Elm and I don't even really understand how to properly use our dual-magic types yet."

Elm gazes at the ceiling, his mouth quirked to the side.

"I also get the feeling we shouldn't be open about this," Blake remarks. "It's important everyone keeps it secret."

"Oh." Brie is a little crestfallen. "I'm not good with secrets."

"I'll help you," Jazz assures her.

"You have all of us to talk to about it," Nikki adds. "No need to blab to anyone else."

Kaito reaches across Blanca to grab a chip from a snack bowl on the table. Blanca steals it from him before it reaches his mouth. He sighs and grabs another. "Are you sure we need to be so secretive? Ivan said we're free to do as we want."

"He did say that." Elm is now replenishing the snacks that suddenly everyone has taken interest in. "However, he also said that was only as long as it didn't interfere with life in Neo Prism."

"And I have a feeling he won't take any chances," I say.

"He allowed us into the gym to practice our ideas, because he recognized the benefits to Neo Prism. But if he gets wind that we're training to go back for a full-blown rebellion, I have a feeling he would shut us down. And fast."

Blake nods in agreement.

As the day wears on, we discuss meeting times. Meeting agendas. Strategies and goals. One by one our group dwindles, exits being made with stretches and yawns. Soon only Blake and I remain in Elm's apartment. But we really should be going. We're all exhausted.

But Blake has a look of hard concentration on his face, and his skin reddens slightly.

"Thinking of something?"

"Trying to," he growls. "Except your stupid Mentalist keeps trying to mess with my head!"

Startled, I glance at Elm, who looks smug.

"Took you long enough," he says.

Blake's expression is instantly relieved, obviously cut free from Elm's attempts to control him. "What's that supposed to mean? I've recognized it for a while. Maybe if you were a better teacher—"

"Wait, what?" I look between Elm and Blake with wide eyes.

"I've been training him." Elm waves a hand as if it's nothing. "Helping him build up his resistance to Yellow magic."

I look at Elm, stunned.

"And I've been helping him with his Blue magic," Blake grouses. "Don't know why."

"Really?" Joy fills me. "That's great! But," I hesitate, "what made you change your minds?"

Elm's eyes soften. "Because I know that if something happened to me, Blake, of all people, will try to keep Miss Ava safe."

My heart pinches with a mild mix of emotions, warmth and dread and fear all at once.

"No," I blurt.

They both stare at me.

"I don't want anyone to keep me safe. I can take care of myself. I will take care of myself."

"Everyone needs help sometimes, Ava." Blake gives me a pointed look. "You're not going back to this solo thing, are you?"

"I'm not going to let anyone die playing the white knight for me is all." I can't chance losing them. I won't. "So both of you just forget it." I said I wanted us to be unified. I do. But it has to be for goals that help everyone. Not just me. The thought of losing any of my friends because they were focused on keeping me safe is the worst thing I can think of.

"Miss Ava," Elm says gently. "Would you deprive me of my free will? Shouldn't I decide what I value most?"

"How dare you bring free will into it," I mutter, but a small smile comes to my lips. "Just . . . don't forget what it's all for. Remember the important things."

"I always do," he says, gazing into my eyes in a way that makes my heart stutter.

"Ava," Blake reminds us he's here. "I'll protect anyone I care about, and that includes you."

"All right, all right," I huff. "Well, ditto, then. We'll all look after each other, okay?"

Blake and Elm nod rather triumphantly in agreement, and we say our goodnights.

27

WITH OUR DESIRE TO EXPEDITE HELPING those behind the barrier, we have found a new spark. The training goes better than ever. The gym comes to life with the sounds of my classmates hard at work—and having fun. We enjoy being together, and there is a new closeness with one another. White magic comes easier, and we are finding new combinations as we go.

"Ava! Come see this!" Brie runs to me with excitement bursting from her features. "I made something! Well, *we* made something. Come see!"

I follow Brie back to Elm, who holds a plush squirrel nearly as big as he is. It sparkles with glitter, and its fur is splashed in a patchwork of bright colors.

I laugh. "That's amazing! How on earth did you manage perfect unity to make something like that?" I'm sure Elm probably let Brie choose everything, down to the last detail.

Elm winks. "What can I say? Brie has magnificent taste."

Brie dives in to squish the giant squirrel to herself. "So, what do we call what happened? Green magic?"

"Makes sense to me." I can't stop smiling at her enthusiasm and their success. "Combining the imaginative power of Mentalist magic with the physical object manipulation of Shaper magic: Green magic."

"Come see some Purple magic, then!" Blanca shouts from nearby with Kaito in the bleachers.

"This is way, way cool." Blanca holds her arm out. "Watch."

Kaito holds one of the balls against Blanca's arm. The two of them focus. There is a bright flash of purple, and suddenly Blanca's arm looks as though it was painted to match the ball."

I reach out to touch her arm, and just as I thought, the surface is textured and rubbery. "Wow. It is Purple magic! Combining Augmentor body capabilities with Shaper object modification."

Blanca rolls her eyes. "Why do I feel like you're writing a textbook in your head?"

I shoot her a grin. "More like a research paper. Now we need some . . . Orange magic?" I sneak a glance at Elm.

He taps me lightly on the head. "We already have a wonderful example of that. No need to explore further for the moment."

As much as I do want to explore more of what Yellow and Red magic might achieve, I haven't been able to talk Elm into trying it with me. Or any other Augmentors. "Maybe I could ask Samantha?" I tip my head toward where she stands in a corner of the gym, observing. Elm finally convinced her to start hanging out with us again, though she still won't come near me.

"You know as much as I do that Sammy would reject that request."

"I know. I wasn't being serious." For now, it will just have to be enough that we know Orange magic worked once.

"Are we ever planning to share any of this information?" Nikki asks uncertainly.

"Eventually. I don't think it's right to keep it hidden. But of course we won't announce anything to Ivan until everything is over."

None of us is entirely sure what "over" entails yet, but with each new success, that moment feels closer.

Tomorrow.

We've set our date. In the early hours of morning tomorrow, we'll sneak back to the inside of the barrier. And there, we'll head into battle. It seems so strange to use that word, but I don't know what else to call it. We have a plan of attack. What else is it if not a battle? The Benefactors have proven time and time again that they have no interest in peaceful discourse. Hopefully this will settle this once and for all.

We've come such a long way. Everyone is using White magic as though it hasn't been a long-time mystery. And we get better by the day. But is it enough?

I lay my hand against the cool windowpane of my apartment, watching drops of rain roll down. The streetlamps reflect off wet surfaces, and puddles turn the world outside into a spectacle of silver glitter. The gentle sound of the drizzle is inviting. Maybe I'll go for a walk. I take an umbrella and step into the unusually silent hallway.

Normally, walking these halls brings the sounds of laughter and social gatherings—we've never really been a quiet bunch. But tonight is different. Tonight I can sense the reality hanging over everyone's heads. The knowledge that everything is about to change again.

I pass Elm's apartment and hover my fist over the door, preparing to knock, but stop myself. He may be lost in his own thoughts right now. I want to see him, but I don't want to intrude. He'll come to me if he wants me.

I step into the night, the chill of the evening air invigorating my senses. The drops pelting my umbrella sound like warfare, but the spray of misty wind and the smell of the rain invigorate me. Few people are out in the storm, and they're too preoccupied with the deluge to notice me.

As I walk, the trees in the distance catch my eye—dark, towering silhouettes with giant, boat-shaped leaves. It's not quite like the forests I'm used to, but right now it still beckons to me. I always did like heading for the trees when I needed to think, and something pulls me there. I let my feet and my heart lead the way, telling myself I won't go too far off the beaten path.

I stop short, seeing the shadow of a tall figure in a small clearing ahead of me. I'd recognize the shape of him anywhere. But what is Elm doing out here in the middle of the rain?

He looks almost like he's encased in some kind of bubble. The rain torrents around him but doesn't touch him. Eyes closed, his face looks serene, glowing in the light of the full moon turned blue by the storm raging overhead. My heart leaps, and I rush to him, drawn like starlight to the darkness.

"So you *have* been practicing," I say jubilantly, having seen the drops manipulated away from him. He must have been doing such things a lot in order to maintain that kind of control, well beyond working with Blake.

He opens his eyes slowly and smiles. "Now you know the terrible truth."

"I think it's amazing!" I beam back at him. "Why didn't you tell me?"

"Pride, I suppose, Miss Ava. But I knew it was important to you that I learn to control my Shaper abilities, so here we are. I practice every day."

"Can I join you?" I ask tentatively.

He takes my hand gently and pulls me close. The noise of rain on my umbrella stops. He's warm, and his fragrance blends with the wind and rain, and the effect is intoxicating. I drop the umbrella and bury my face in his shirt, wrapping my arms around him as though he's my only lifeline to the world. His arms encase me with security and strength. How long has it been since I've really had him to myself like this?

I look up at him, meeting his sparkling eyes, and rise to my tiptoes to greet his lips. He kisses me fiercely, the raindrops dancing around us. I reciprocate with equal passion, my senses heightening and my heart ablaze.

I feel him smile against my lips, and suddenly the rain comes crashing down over me.

"Hey," I squeal. "Not fair!"

In his unbridled laughter, he slips on the slick ground, taking me with him and losing his control until we are both giggling in the mud. Even without Elm's spell, the chill of the rain can't touch me now. Not when I'm with him. He is my golden sunshine. My blue sky.

"I love you, Miss Ava," he says. "So very much."

The words roll over me, and there isn't a trace of doubt he means it. "Me too," I say, my voice choked with emotion.

He grins and raises his eyebrows. "You love you too? Wonderful. Self-love is so important."

"No! You know what I mean. I—"

His lips steal me away again before I can finish.

My alarm barely releases one screeching beep before I shut it off. It's 2:30 a.m., half an hour before we are to meet at the gym to set out. Not that I really needed the alarm—I'm wide awake.

As quietly as I can manage, I slip into the hall. I pause at Elm's door, wondering if he already left. We agreed we needed to stagger movement so we didn't draw too much attention by leaving all at once.

The gym is dark, which was expected. We agreed: no lights

allowed, except a small penlight we each would carry. Gym lights in the middle of the night might as well be a banner that says Rebellion. I cringe as the door squeaks, the sound amplified by my nerves.

"Ava?" Blake whispers once I'm inside. He sounds a little spooked; we're all feeling that way.

"Yes. Who else is here?" I strain to make out faces in the dark.

"Everyone except Brie, Jazz, and Elm."

Relax, Ava. Elm is fine. He'll be here.

On cue, the door opens and Elm arrives. "Miss Ava?"

"I'm here."

"Wonderful. I saw Brie and Jazz not far behind me. They'll be here shortly."

He sidles up beside me and I take note of his clothing. "Back in your fancy attire, I see."

He tips his top hat. "Well, I always say, if you're going to do something, do it right."

"Can you please stop talking?" Blake says anxiously. "Kind of need to be on alert here."

We wait. Everyone has stopped breathing. I wish we still had Elm's invisibility devices. Although, perhaps in a city full of Mentalists it wouldn't do us much good. My fingers automatically glide over my locket, and it's strange to think I haven't used it once since being here.

I inhale as the door opens once more. Exhale as Jazz and Brie step in.

"That's everyone, then?" I whisper.

"That's everyone," Nikki chimes. "Let's go."

The lights turn on.

Confused, indignant shouts fill the room.

"Turn it off!" Blanca yells. "What idiot turned on the lights?"

"Me."

Ivan's voice comes from the doorway on the other side of the gym. We've been betrayed.

28

MY THOUGHTS WHIRL. *DID* SOMEONE
betray us? Or was someone followed. Blanca charges for the
door that leads into the school, but her way is blocked by a
group of people in golden uniforms. Ivan's soldiers.

"I don't suggest trying to leave," Ivan says grimly. "As you
can see, you're a little outnumbered."

And then I see her there at the back of the group, head
hanging down.

"Samantha?" My voice cracks.

"Sammy, what is this?" Elm demands.

She looks up at Elm, tears in her eyes. "I couldn't let them
take you away from me again. I just couldn't. I'm sorry."

Hands grab us from all sides. Nobody fights. What's the
point? We're not trained for combat the way Ivan's soldiers
are, and there are so many of them.

I glare at Ivan as two soldiers usher me out.

"Sorry it had to be this way, Ava. But I just couldn't be the
stone that starts the avalanche."

Prison in Neo Prism is just like prison everywhere else—
Hopeless. Drab. Confining. In stark contrast to the glittering
rainbow buildings decked out in artful architecture, the place
they take us to now is a cement, rectangular building, made for
one utilitarian purpose: a holding facility. The soldiers corral us
roughly into the compound, slamming the heavy doors behind
us. The *clunk* of the latch seems like it is sealing our doom.

A guard approaches with a large bin. "Personal effects here,
please. That includes your pendants and any other jewelry."

I clutch my locket, which has become so important to me as
both a gift from Elm and a memento of my discovery of truth.
Will I ever get it back once I surrender it? Letting go of this feels
impossible.

The guard nudges the bin forcefully at me. "In."

With heavy reluctance, I remove the locket and my pendant
from my neck and drop them into the bin alongside my
classmates' pedants. I feel instantly naked without them.

We are taken to divided rooms and forced to change into
gray jumpsuits. I flashback to the time I first met Elm when he
wore something similar. Oh Elm . . . how is he feeling now?

They drag us back to the main area of the compound. "Hold
your wrists out," the guard commands.

I comply, knowing refusal will get me nowhere. The guard
produces a pair of red stone cuffs. I think I know exactly what
those do thanks to my experience with Veronica. I shiver.

"What are these?" Blake asks as a guard locks him into a pair
of blue cuffs. "Why do we need to be shackled if we're already
going to be behind bars?"

"So you can't use your magic to try anything funny. This will absorb any spell you try . . . and make you sorry for trying."

Now that we're all in our prison attire and solidly cuffed, they walk us through the maze of cells. Prisoners leer at us. One man cackles madly as we pass through, and I can't help but wonder how long he's been here. We turn a corner and enter an empty cellblock. I'm grateful at least that we'll be separated from the other prisoners. The guard ushers us through, unlocking the bars to a large cell and motioning us inside. Then he leaves, though who knows for how long.

"What do you think that guard meant by saying these would make us sorry for trying a spell?" Nikki rotates her wrists, examining the cuffs with a frown.

"Well, one way to find out." Blake's face pinches with concentration for a moment, and there is a crackling sound and a jolt of blue light from the cuffs. He yelps and falls to the floor.

"Are you alright?" My impulse to heal him is strong. But if I try it, I'll just end up curled on the floor with him. I let my arms drop, fists clenched.

Blake sits up, face pinched. "I'm okay. But don't anyone try it."

"If I ever see that traitorous Yellow snake again, I'm gonna kick her—"

"Save it," Nikki cuts Blanca off. "There's no point."

Blanca looks like she wants to keep raging, but she kicks one of the bars instead.

Elm stares into the distance. I wonder if he's thinking about the last time he was kept prisoner. I want to go to him, but maybe he just needs a moment to himself. I do a quick visual check over everyone else. Nikki sits on the floor, looking like the world is about to end. Kaito stands a ways off from Blanca, looking like he wants to say something to her but knowing better than to cross her anger right now. Brie and Jazz are together in one corner, silent and expressionless. Other than our broken spirits, everyone looks okay.

Ivan walks through the corridor a moment later, Dawz padding along at his side. Disdain billows inside me at the sight of Neo Prism's leader. I know he's just doing what he thinks is going to protect his city, but I still can't control the heat of anger rushing through me.

"Why, Ivan?"

He raises his eyebrows. "You know exactly why."

"You said you keep no prisoners. People can come and go as they please."

"I believe I said that's the way I'd like it. But that doesn't mean I can ignore threats."

"We weren't going to involve you at all. We would have gone back inside the barrier to fight Selene and left you out of it completely."

"And by doing that you would have put us at risk." He peers at me through the bars. "If you got back in, don't you think the Benefactors would have questions about how? We don't know how many Mentalists they've got on their side. How hard do you think it would be for them to extract information? It would be only a matter of time before you led them straight to us."

"Maybe you're right," I concede. There is logic to what he's saying. "But how long do you think you can keep this up? If it's not us, it will be someone else. Someone is going to go in or out of that barrier one of these days, and this whole thing you've built will come crashing down. You know it will happen eventually."

A vein pulses at the side of Ivan's head, and Dawz growls. "It won't happen so long as we're vigilant. And we have been."

Elm has been watching and now speaks. "The only way to end this is to end it from the inside once and for all. You must realize this is the only reasonable course."

Ivan smirks. "Think you know everything just because you bested Selene once? Think again. You'll have plenty of time for that while you cool down here."

"And how long do you intend to keep us imprisoned?" Elm asks.

"You'll have trials, of course. And then we'll decide what to do with you. I intended to give you all a good home here, and I know some of your group wanted to accept it. Would've been better off if you had."

He exits without another word.

I wake shivering on my cot. I gave my blanket to Brie earlier on, assuring her that I was fine. I'm not, but I feel a lot of responsibility for her being here. I can deal with a little cold.

I hear footsteps, and light shines into our cell.

"Locke," says the prison guard—a burly Shaper. "Get up. You have visitors."

I can't think of anyone who would visit me here except for my parents, and I'm not sure how to face them. Still, I get up wearily from the cot and follow the guard.

The guard takes me to a glass-walled room with lights that seem too bright. My parents are seated, waiting. They both look exhausted. My dad's graying ginger hair is unkempt, and Mom holds her face in her hands.

"I'll give you some privacy, but I won't be far." The guard hooks my shackles to a long table with benches, then leaves me alone with my parents in this room where the lights hurt my eyes.

"Oh, Ava . . ." my mom chokes.

My dad's eyes are sorrowful and tired. "What happened? They said you were planning a rebellion?"

Irritation prickles at me. "A rebellion against Selene. The

same rebellion we've been part of from the start. This isn't anything new."

"But if all the students were training to fight, why didn't you try to coordinate something with Ivan?" my mother asks.

"Because Ivan wasn't interested in coordinating anything. Just like you and Dad aren't interested in coordinating anything." I don't want to be annoyed with them. But I'm so tired of it all. "I'm sick of it, Mom. I'm sick of people wanting to use me. Sick of having to hide. Sick of trying to make some little corner of normalcy work, all the while just waiting for it all to fall apart. I want to end it. *We all* want to end it."

"Ivan said he offered you a job," my dad says slowly. "A good job. You could have been happy. Things are secure here. Instead you decided to do something that would jeopardize this community and endanger your friends? Why, Ava?"

"It's not going to stay safe here, Dad! No matter what you think, it's all going to come crashing down in the end. You rebelled against the Benefactors once. I thought you would understand."

"That was different," my dad replies. "That was survival. We just wanted a life where Mentalists could live freely, and we found that here."

"Without me."

They look as though I slapped them. My mother speaks first. "We never intended to be apart from you more than a short time. And now that we're finally together . . . this." She swallows.

"Look, Ava, we talked to Ivan."

I stare at my dad. I don't trust anything Ivan says or does now. But I wait for him to continue.

"He's willing to ignore this. If you are willing to take your places in society here and take those jobs he offered, he'll let this slide. You just have to agree his terms. You would be on a probationary period, with some surveillance to start. But with good behavior—"

I stop him. "We didn't do anything wrong, Dad. And we don't belong here. We never belonged here. Now we just want to go back . . . home."

My mother utters a small sound. While it doesn't feel right to call the area inside the barrier home, Neo Prism certainly isn't either. Not after this.

"Maybe it's not what you want, but what about the others?" Mom asks softly. "You've all been through so much turmoil. Perhaps some of your friends would appreciate the chance of a normal life."

"That's up to them," I say abruptly. "And they've known that from the beginning. Some of them have already left. But what I want hasn't changed. I want to help the people of Magus. All of them."

We sit in silence. This isn't at all how I thought my parents would be. How could we want such different futures?

At last the door opens and the guard returns. "Time's up. Let's go."

The guard removes my shackles from the table, and I stand as straight as I can manage. I give my parents what I mean to be a hard look, but my resolve shatters when I see the heartbreak and grief in their expressions. So instead, I face the door and follow the guard, not knowing when I might see them again.

We've been here over a week now. Spirits are glum. Ivan continues to offer the same deal—agree not to trouble the waters, and it will be like nothing ever happened. So far, nobody has taken his deal. Everyone is wearing down. None of us expected to end up imprisoned, especially not on this side of the barrier.

Elm breaks my heart most of all. He's already spent most of his life a prisoner, and he's shackled once again. "Elm, I'm so sorry. This was supposed to turn out a lot better," I say over and over again.

His reply is always the same. "Never apologize, Miss Ava. You have given me more happiness than I dreamed possible. I knew there were risks with what we were doing."

This breaks my heart even more.

The door to the cellblock swings open, and the wait staff enters with our meals. I'm still not used to eating with these cumbersome shackles. I've come to accept that nothing, not even mealtimes, will be easy anymore.

The guards fall into conversation as we eat, laughing and telling stories. Elm glances their way, then back to me.

"Miss Ava," he says, voice low, "watch my spoon."

I stifle my gasp of surprise as his spoon lifts just slightly off the table, then lands softly back in place.

"How is that possible?" I whisper.

"These power-absorbing shackles are only made to absorb one magic type. They weren't designed for dual magic-users."

"So, that means I could use Yellow magic, you think?"

"I wouldn't doubt it."

My mind at once begins weighing the possibilities. "I could manipulate the guard . . ." I stop. People are more familiar with Yellow magic here. If I do something to tip anyone off, it will ruin our chances. I bite my lip. "On second thought, maybe it would be too risky." I wish I had spent more time honing the mind-control aspect of Mentalist power instead of focusing so much on illusions and flitting around in Selene's dreams.

"Your abilities are still somewhat unpredictable, yes. But, Miss Ava, we can train here."

I mull it over.

"If you're uncomfortable with that idea," Elm gives the guards another glance, "I wager we could use Green magic. If we're able to create what we need, Kaito and I could make more invisibility devices."

My heart leaps. We could all disappear right out from under the guards' noses. It would be easy to do when they take us out for exercise. And if we were invisible, we'd stand a chance at getting back inside the barrier. Maybe all isn't lost.

The next few days Elm explains the components of his invisibility devices to me, down to the last detail. We have to be careful to mask what we're doing, disguising Elm's intricate sketches as an art game or his low instructions as idle conversation.

"The hexagon-shaped panel inside needs to be highly reflective," Elm murmurs, as I pretend to cry with my face in my hands. The guards usually pay less attention to us if someone seems distraught. Whether this is due to their guilt or discomfort is anyone's guess.

The one thing we haven't addressed yet is how we're going to get yellow stones. Each device will need one. We aren't sure if that's something we could create. Some stones interact so differently with magic that we don't know if it is possible to make one work like it ought to. It might end up as no more than a pretty piece of glass. If only we could get access to Elm's personal effects, since he had several on him. And my locket. Elm could utilize his Shaper abilities if we're close enough to where they're being kept, but that might require a little extra persuasion.

"Now, tell me what you know about Charlie."

Elm has been quizzing me on each of the day-shift guards, helping me to observe their traits. If I'm going to use Mentalist abilities on them, it helps to play on their own tendencies and personalities. Giving them a little nudge in a direction they already lean toward is easier than making them do something they would never do. I think of what I know about this particular guard. "He's tough, and it doesn't seem to be an act. He has a strong sense of justice." He may not be the easiest guard to manipulate.

"We'll have to find out how to crack that tough shell."

"Why does it have to be Charlie? What about Elena or Max?" They both seem a little more vulnerable, at least compared to Charlie.

"Because Elena and Max both believe we deserve to be here. Charlie seems less sure. Perhaps we could use that strong sense of justice to our advantage. Can you think of anything that might convince him to let us into that room?"

"He has a daughter," Nikki chimes in beside us, putting an arm around me as though consoling me. We've all gotten good at acting lately.

"Brie is the youngest one here. Could we convince him if it were something to help her?" I give an exaggerated sniffle.

"We could say your locket is Brie's," Nikki suggests. "Maybe she got it from her dead mother or something."

Elm looks at her, bemused. "Now there's something. Poor homesick, lonely Brie." He gives an exaggerated sigh. "Desperately in need of this particular item of comfort." He darts a glance her direction. "It might work."

"Ridley," Charlie's voice rings out, causing all of us to jump. "Visitor."

"Who is it?" Elm asks, though I'm sure he already knows the answer. His weary face tells me as much.

"Samantha."

"No, thank you."

Samantha has been by to see Elm every day. Sometimes multiple times a day. He refuses each time. But what did she expect? She betrayed us all. I'm a little surprised at Elm's coldness, though, considering he was so quick to defend her before. But her antics changed everything.

Charlie shrugs. "I'll tell her again. You know she's just going to keep coming back."

"I'm aware. But I stand by what I said. I will not see her."

The next few days are spent priming Charlie, planting doubts in his mind. We've clued in the others so that everyone helps.

"Hey, Charlie!" Blanca shouts one day. "Can you tell us what we're here for?"

Charlie raises his bushy red eyebrows in surprise from his place in the corner of the cellblock. "Organizing a rebellion."

"Against Selene. Last I heard, your boy Ivan's kind of doing the same thing."

Charlie doesn't respond, so Blanca keeps pushing. "What law did we break?"

"Disturbing the peace."

"But we didn't disturb anyone, did we?"

Charlie looks uncomfortable now. He crosses his arms and shifts his feet. "Anything that could bring the Benefactors down on us is a disturbance of the peace."

Blanca shrugs. "Whatever you say. Sounds like rot to me, but I guess you're just the muscle."

A vein throbs in Charlie's forehead, and I worry Blanca may have taken things too far. "Listen, Valencia, I'm not here to yap. Unless you got something worth my time, I suggest you can it."

Blanca backs down, but her face is smug.

The next day, during our reading time, the conversation doesn't fare much better for Charlie.

Kaito pours over a law book. "It's funny," he says loudly. "I can't find any law against students practicing magic together."

"What are Neo Prism's laws about securing legal representation?" Nikki inquires.

Charlie leaves without a word as Elena takes over the shift. "Fifteen more minutes of books," she warns. "I want to hear less talking, or you'll get no next time."

We're all relieved when we see Charlie take over for Max this morning. We have seen less of him the last few days. We worried we may have gotten under his skin too much and driven him away.

The cell door opens, and he gestures us out. "Yard time. No funny business."

Elm and I hang back as the others head out for exercise. We both have to be together for this to work. As we near the hallway where our belongings are kept, Elm clears his throat. "Charlie, may I ask you something?"

"What." Charlie's face is hard, leaving no room for misunderstanding. He's not here to play. Maybe he suspects that we've been needling at him with a purpose. Hopefully, he's just trying to avoid any more reasons to question our imprisonment here.

"I wondered if perhaps you might do us a favor," Elm asks politely as I work on soothing Charlie. Taking his suspicions away. *Elm is just a twenty-year-old kid. Nothing threatening. Silly to be locked up in the first place. Just kids who got into something bigger than they are.*

"What kind of favor?" Good. He's at least being receptive to listening instead of just pushing us off to the exercise yard.

"Well, the youngest in our group has been feeling especially depressed recently. Her mother's birthday is soon, you see."

"And?"

"Her mother, sadly, passed away a few years ago. The last thing she left to her little daughter was a locket, which is currently in the holding room. I wondered if it might be possible to get it for her? I know it would bring her a great deal of comfort."

I send thoughts to Charlie, imagining them floating by a string from my head to his. *Just a little girl. Like your daughter. Alone in this place. Just a simple piece of jewelry. No harm from it.*

He doesn't answer right away, and there is conflict on his face. I push harder. *Such a small thing. Why not let the little girl's life be just a little brighter. She probably had no idea what she was getting into. Just wanted to be with her friends. Probably thought it was a game.*

At last, Charlie gives a sigh. "Let's be quick about it. Show me where it is."

Hopefully Charlie doesn't have any way to recognize they're my belongings he and Elm are rifling through. I doubt he paid much attention to who came in with what when we were brought here. I hold my breath as a few pea-sized stones float my way from the bin Elm's belongings are stored in. I'm careful not to do anything that might cause Charlie to look my way. If he sees those floating stones, we're lost.

"Ah, here it is." Elm produces the locket with a bright smile. "Thank you, Charlie. This will surely put her at ease."

"Wait." Charlie's deep voice makes me start. He holds out

his hand. "I need to check it and make sure there's nothing that could be used as a weapon." I hold my breath. If he opens the locket and sees that stone, he might not let us keep it. Even though, as far as he knows, we wouldn't be able to use it, I can't see them letting prisoners have any type of stone on them.

"Of course." Elm hands the item back and gives me a pointed stare. "I believe it has a picture of her mother."

What? No it doesn't. Oh. Oh! I scramble to get the illusion in place before Charlie opens the locket. What am I doing? In my panic, I realize I'm focusing on the image of my own mother—I have no idea what Brie's mom looks like. Drat. I hope Charlie doesn't know my mom. Was he on shift the day my parents visited?

He opens the locket and raises an eyebrow as he looks more closely. "They don't look alike at all."

"She takes after her father," Elm says.

Charlie nods and closes the locket, then runs the chain through his fingers and examines every bit of its surface. My illusion seems to have done the trick. Once satisfied, Charlie hands the locket back to Elm. "Hope this helps her feel better. Get out there and exercise."

29

NOW THAT WE'VE SECURED THE stones, the hard part is finding moments for Elm and me to create what is needed without the guards noticing. They pay less attention to us during mealtimes, so we do a lot of our work then. I have Elm's diagrams memorized backward and forward, so he simply tells me what part we need, and we work on creating it. We're getting faster at combining our magic, and the pieces are coming easier.

Our current guard, Max, raps on the bars, and Kaito fumbles to shove pieces out of his line of sight.

"Ridley, visitor for you."

"Samantha, I presume?"

"Want me to tell her to get lost again?"

"Perhaps not so harshly, but yes."

Even I'm starting to feel a little bad for Samantha. "Maybe you should talk to her, Elm. If nothing else, just to reiterate that she betrayed your trust and it's going to take time."

Elm shakes his head. "Miss Ava, I appreciate the sentiment. But we put our lives in her hands—you against your better judgment. I gave my word that her character was unquestionable. Her actions are also a reflection on my inane foolishness."

"Nobody is blaming you for this, Elm."

"Even so . . . I simply can't face her right now. I was never naïve enough to assume being imprisoned again was out of the realm of possibility . . . but I never imagined it would happen because of my childhood friend."

"Well, when you put it that way . . ."

Elm whispers the name of another piece to me, and we set back to work.

Making the invisibility devices in secret is slow going, and they're certainly not as beautiful as the ones Elm crafted previously, but they're here. Now we just have to wait for the right moment. Using them in a locked cell won't do us a lot of good. But the exercise yard could be promising. It's more spacious, and we could scatter in different directions. I'm not sure how difficult going over the fence will be, but it is our best option.

"Ridley," Charlie says. "You already know what I'm gonna say."

"Please tell Samantha to go home."

"You sure? She's really annoying. I think you oughta—"

"No, I'm sorry."

Charlie nods and exits the block.

A few moments later, steps near us again, but this time they are lighter.

"Elm, please look at me."

Elm and I both jerk our heads up to see Samantha clinging to the bars of the cell, tears running down her face.

"Where is the guard?" Elm asks sternly.

Samantha bites her lip. "He's . . . unavailable at the moment."

"Did you mind control him?"

"What choice did I have? You won't talk to me!"

"I should have suspected as much." Elm's voice is cold. "Charlie's been pushing me to speak with you. That probably didn't take much convincing."

All our group is watching their exchange with hard eyes. If Samantha is looking for sympathy, she's not going to find it among the people she led to prison.

Samantha looks at the floor and twists her dress in her hands. "Listen, I was wrong. I made a terrible mistake."

Elm eyes her. "That's an understatement."

"Elm, please, I'm trying to fix this. We don't have much time." Our eyes widen as Samantha holds up a large set of keys. We watch, stunned, as she starts jamming them into the lock one by one, searching for the correct key.

"Did you steal those?" Elm's terseness is lessened.

"Yes," her reply is brisk. "You all have to be ready to go as soon as I find the right one. I'm pretty sure at least one of these go to your cuffs too."

There is a satisfying click, and the cell is open. Samantha grabs a startled Jazz, as he's nearest to her, and sets to work looking for the key to our cuffs.

"Do you have the devices?" I turn to Elm quickly.

He pulls them from his pocket. "We were only able to make four, plus your locket."

But there are eight of us. I think for a moment. "Anything we're touching is invisible too, right?"

"Yes."

I motion to my back. "Hop on!"

"You can't be serious." Blake is staring at us, likely noting the difference in our height.

I give a smug smile. "You seem to keep forgetting I'm an Augmentor. Carrying another person is child's play. And we have to augment our speed to escape."

"So you, Jazz, and Blanca are going to carry me, Elm, Kaito, and Nikki?"

"Hey." Brie puts her hands on her hips. "I can carry someone too. Easily." Since we have an extra device with everyone paired up, she won't need to, but I don't doubt she could.

"If you've got a better plan, Blake, I'd love to hear it. Otherwise, let's get going."

"Any luck, Samantha?" I watch her fumbling with the key ring, her brows pinched in anxiety.

"I'm down to the last three keys." She nervously inserts another. "It has to be—" There is a click, and Jazz's cuffs fall off. She gets to everyone else as fast as she can.

My wrists breathe with relief as they are freed. It's been so long! We all stretch and revel for a moment in the unrestricted movements of our arms.

I begin a strengthening spell, now that the cuffs are off, while Elm hands devices to the Augmentors.

"Can I come with you?" Samantha's voice is like a tiny bird.

"I say that's a big, fat no," Blanca snaps, giving Samantha a heated look.

"Please," she begs. "I promise there won't be any more trouble from me. There's nothing left for me here. Not if Elm goes. Even if he hates me."

"I don't hate you, Samantha. I'm just incredibly disappointed."

Her face falls at his use of *Samantha*, and she shrinks.

"Well, she did get us the keys," I admit grudgingly.

"A small token of amends," Elm concedes. "Thank you for that much."

"Not to interrupt, but decide quickly. We kind of need to move fast here." Nikki gives an anxious glance at the cellblock door."

I glance at Elm. "Fine, Samantha," I relent. "Come with

us. But even a hint of trouble and you're out." She nods. "Can you carry her, Brie?"

"Of course I can!"

We sweep through the prison, Elm on my back, Nikki flying solo, Kaito with Blanca, Brie with Samantha, and Blake with Jazz. A few of the other prisoners we pass glance up as they hear the sound of our footsteps, but they have no idea what's going on. We stop by the holding area with all of our belongings to retrieve our pendants and other possessions. Then we make a mad dash for the doors and out into the sunlight.

Right about now, Charlie is probably coming to and wondering where all his prisoners are. Would anyone say something about phantom footsteps or an odd breeze when we passed? If so, would that be enough for him to put two and two together? I push myself to pick up my pace.

As we enter the more populated area of the city, my nerves go on high alert. This is different from being inside the barrier. Nobody knew how to deal with Yellow magic there. Most people were totally unequipped for it. Here, there are Mentalists everywhere, and even the Shapers and Augmentors have an understanding of Yellow magic. How safe are we with the invisibility devices?

"Elm, what chance is there of us being noticed by a Mentalist?"

"It's small. Just because someone is a Mentalist doesn't mean they're going to immediately see through an illusion. If you recall, even Jace took a while before he discovered we were invisible."

"But he did figure it out. And you said Samantha can see through just about any illusion." I glance back at her, clinging to Brie.

"Samantha is particularly skilled at seeing through illusions, yes. But most Mentalists aren't going to notice anything unless they're specifically looking for something unusual. That's what makes invisibility particularly tricky—there's nothing visual to tip anyone off, as long as we're careful."

I'm starting to feel a little tired, and I'm sure my other Augmentor companions are as well. But we can't risk taking the hover carts, so we're going to have to run all the way back to the barrier. Once we're well outside of the city, we can slow our pace, but it's still going to be a long trip. And what about resting? The moment we put the others down, they'll be visible again. Would Ivan be desperate enough to chase us down out in the middle of nowhere? I'm sure he'll know we're trying to get back inside the barrier. Drat. Just thinking about it is exhausting.

"Can we stop for a minute? We need a plan." I motion everyone over to a shaded area near the hover-cart platform.

From the looks of it, everyone needs a quick break. Brie sits down, and Samantha wobbles precariously on her back. "Don't drop me!" she cries.

"Keep your voice down," Nikki hisses. "You want to get us all caught *again*?"

It's not likely any conversation would be audible amongst the busy chatter and everyday noise of the city, but there's no need to tempt fate. Especially when a hover cart stops nearby and someone gets off. Marabell. I hold my breath. She glances around, looking frazzled. Then stops. She looks in our direction and narrows her eyes. I swear she's looking right at us . . . but how could she be? We are stone still.

She pulls a communication device out of her pocket, quickly inputting to make contact. "Yes, Ivan? Do you mind if I take the hoverhawk out? I want to scout the area. With those newcomers, I just feel like we'd better be sure there aren't others." There is a long pause, and then, "Yes, the big one! It's more fun to drive. Those little ones are too flimsy. They're too nerve-wracking."

Has she seen us? Does this conversation have anything to do with our escape? Maybe we shouldn't stick around to find out.

I start to motion to the others when Marabell stares me down with a hard look and makes a forceful *stop* motion with her hand while she is still talking. She definitely sees us.

"Let's run!" Blanca says, preparing to dash.

"Wait," I say. "Just wait." For whatever reason, I trust Marabell. If she wanted to turn us in to Ivan, she could have said something to him already.

"Much obliged, Ivan." She hangs up the phone and marches over to us. "Now, don't y'all be running off unless you really want to travel like that the whole way to the barrier."

"I thought you said we wouldn't be seen unless people were looking for something suspicious." Nikki shoots Elm an accusing look.

Marabell laughs. "Well, there you go. I'm *always* looking for something suspicious. If you'll follow me to the base, the hoverhawk should fit everyone, and I can get y'all to the barrier."

"But why would you want to help us? Aren't you on Ivan's side?"

"Ivan's a good man and he means well. But I miss the way he used to be. He's downright obsessed with Selene lately, always looking over his shoulder. I want that to end." She grins. "Besides, it's boring around here. You bunch shook this place up and made it more interesting than it's been in a while."

The hoverhawk is an aircraft powered with Shaper magic and a giant propeller. I have never seen one up close, and it's much larger than I expected. It looks like it could easily hold sixteen or so.

"You know how to fly this, right?" Jazz asks nervously.

Marabell winks at him. "Backward and forward. Inside and outside. I'm one of Ivan's top air scouts. Get in."

Once we're all safely on board, everyone separates. "Thank you for the ride," Elm says with a bow.

I smile. "Perks of having an Augmentor on your side."

"Buckle up," Marabell calls out. "I won't take off until all y'all are strapped in safe."

Nobody wants to prolong our exit, so we all promptly sit down and secure our seat belts. Once Marabell is satisfied, the propeller spins into action. The sound is deafening, and I cover my ears.

"It'll be a little better once we're in the air!" Maribelle shouts.

I certainly hope so.

My stomach does a few summersaults as we lift. Floating this high off the ground is a little nerve-wracking, to use Marabell's term, but I calm down as I watch us leave Neo Prism behind. Another place we can no longer call home . . . at least for now.

Nikki stares out the window with a forlorn expression on her face. I wonder if she's thinking about all the opportunities she is leaving behind. And I wonder if we'll ever see Sarah and Gemma again. Does Nikki wish she were with them?

The chatter as we travel is minimal. I suspect everyone is feeling the weight of uncertainty once more. It's an unwelcome pest that always seems to find its way in and chew through any illusion of security we have. We're returning to the place we fled from just weeks ago, and who knows what awaits us there. What kind of safety or shelter will we find, if any? We can't go back to the cave. Prism obviously is out of the question. Finding refuge at any of our homes isn't likely. We're on the run again. My head starts to throb, and Elm must see the discomfort on my face because he places an arm around me. I melt into his soothing touch. Someday, somehow, this will end.

30

"I'LL HAVE TO STOP ABOUT A MILE OUT. This thing goes haywire once we get close to the barrier."

I give Marabell a grateful smile. "That's fine. That's so much closer than we would have been on our own."

The barrier comes into view, and it's such a strange sight from the air. A massive, flickering dome. From here, the area surrounding it seems singed. Plants don't grow within several yards of the barrier. It's like a poison.

We hover around until Marabell finds a suitable clearing to land. Anxiety hammers me as we approach the ground. This is it.

My ears ring as the hoverhawk propeller stops spinning.

Marabell turns to us as we all unbuckle. "Do y'all know what you're gonna do now?"

The eyes all turn to me and Elm, who tilts his head at me.

"Not really," I admit honestly. "We had a plan before, but I don't think it can be rushed."

"So, what are we supposed to do, then?" Jazz wants to know.

"I don't know. But I'm not going to go at it alone. Doing that has just led to trouble time and time again. Those decisions I was making on my own impacted everyone, and that wasn't right. From now on, we'll decide together and take it a step at a time."

Elm's eyes twinkle approvingly. "At last."

Marabell approaches with two oversized backpacks. "Water and snacks. It's not a lot, but hopefully it's enough until you can find something more." She gives a quick smile, but is looking nervous. "Hate to force y'all out, but I have to get back before questions arise. I'm sorry that I can't be of more help."

Elm graciously takes a backpack and hands the other to me.

"You've done more than enough, Marabell. Thank you," I say. "Can I ask just one more thing?"

"Certainly."

"When you go back, could you find Dr. Iris and Dr. Thompson and tell them what happened? They will want to know. I don't know if they'll want to return to inside the barrier." I falter for a moment, thinking of the repercussions Dr. Iris would face for defying Selene and assisting us, but I think they should at least be aware that we left.

"Can do." Marabell pauses, then she digs into the satchel at her side and produces a black disc, no bigger than a grape. She holds it out to me. "I shouldn't do this, but keep this on the bottom of your shoe, just in case. It's a tracking device Ivan had made so we could locate soldiers, if he ever sent them into the barrier. This way, Dr. Iris can find you if she wants."

When I press the device against the sole of my shoe, tiny hooks shoot out and latch the device securely in place. Knowing Dr. Iris could find us again brings a sense of comfort.

"Thank you again, Marabell," Elm adds his appreciation.

"Good luck, to you. To all y'all. I hope we meet again. I sincerely mean it." She gives us a quick wave and makes haste back to the hoverhawk.

Elm gives the invisibility devices a quick charge, and we resume our earlier arrangements as Augmentor carriers.

"Maybe one of the first things we do once we're inside the

barrier," Kaito says from Blanca's back, "is make a few more invisibility devices."

"Not a bad idea," Elm agrees. "Now that we can all use our magic again, the going should be easier."

We travel the extra mile to the barrier's edge, each step closer filling me with a strong sense of foreboding. The barrier seems to appear in front of us far too soon.

"Samantha, you seem to have this down to a science," Elm says to her, and her expression perks at being addressed by him. "Would you do the honors?"

From her perch on Brie's back, she taps her staff on the barrier, sending a power surge through. We dart forward, back to the place we never wanted to return to but always knew we would.

It's like I can feel the life being sucked out of me as we pass through. Claustrophobic heaviness smothers me on all sides. I buckle suddenly under Elm's weight.

"Miss Ava?" I sense him preparing to jump off my back.

"Don't!" I panic. "You need to stay invisible. Don't move." I take a moment to steady myself, adjusting to the sensations of the barrier. I reach out and grasp his hand to maintain the needed connection for invisibility. "Okay, now."

Elm carefully lowers himself to the ground while holding my hand, and everyone else follows suit.

"Wow," Nikki says, slightly out of breath. "This is a change."

"You're telling me!" Brie groans, readjusting to keep contact with Samantha as she climbs down. "Did it always feel like this?"

"I'm not sure if it's gotten worse or if we're just not used to it now. Maybe both." That was one thing Neo Prism had going for it. It was freeing in many ways. But this only strengthens my resolve to eliminate the barrier for good.

Blanca sits down, Kaito still holding her hand. The rest of the Augmentors follow, too tired to keep standing.

At once we set to task creating more pieces for the devices. The work goes much quicker now, especially since Elm can make pieces on his own. I work with Kaito. Unfortunately, nobody can harmonize with Samantha enough to use her Yellow magic. The discord between her and everyone else is still too strong. But we'll need every single one of us for our originally formulated plan, and I'm not sure how to resolve that.

The hours wear on, and we manage to create two more devices. I give them to Kaito, so he can accomplish things freely, and Samantha, so she won't have to spend more time than necessary with Brie, although Brie seems to be holding her own.

"Ava?"

I start and realize I nodded off in the middle of working with Kaito. "Sorry." I stare at the half-completed device in my hand and blink, my eyes bleary. "What piece were we working on again?"

"I think it best if we call it a night, Miss Ava."

"What, are you going to sleep by my side?" I ask with a tired laugh.

"It's dark," Elm replies. "A few hours fully visible isn't likely to hurt anything."

"But what if there are buggerflies? I'm not taking chances."

Samantha stands and holds out her invisibility device to Elm. "Take it and rest. If they see me, oh well."

Elm takes the device and thanks her quietly.

"If they see you, it makes us all vulnerable," Nikki says with a yawn. "Nice try though."

"Then I'll stay awake and use my abilities to deter anyone who might be in the area," she says stubbornly.

Everyone shares meaningful glances. The implied questions are clear: Can we trust her abilities? Can we trust her character? Is this just another plan to betray us?

She waits, standing awkwardly. Even in the dim light of the moon I can see her eyes misting over.

"Please?" Her voice cracks. "I'm just trying to . . ."

My heart fractures, watching her. "Samantha," I say kindly, "we're all tired. If you want to keep watch for a while, that would be wonderful." I stand and stare her straight on. "Can we trust you?"

"Yes," she pronounces firmly. "I'm going to put everything I can into keeping everyone safe."

I believe her. I don't know if everyone else does, but I do.

"Good enough for me, I guess." Blanca immediately stretches out on the ground and falls asleep. Others begin to settle in.

Elm places his hand on her shoulder. "Thank you, again, Sammy." She sniffles and places her hand on his for a moment, then removes it just as quickly. "You get sleep."

"I'll relieve you in a few hours."

"Thank you."

Content with our current situation, I let the exhaustion take me.

31

I WAKE TO SEE ELM SITTING A WAYS
off. Samantha is asleep nearby with an invisibility device
clutched in her hand. I go sit down beside him and take note
of the invisibility device he just completed.

"You've been busy."

He gives a tired smile. "If I was going to be awake keeping
watch anyway, I might as well do something. I regrettably
could not do any more as it was impossible to maintain our
protection and create objects at the same time. A dual magic-
user might be able to maintain two spells at once, but three
seems to be out of the question."

He looks completely drained. "Should I wake Samantha up
to take over again?"

"No, I think not. She's had a hard time. Most of it brought
upon herself, of course, but even so . . . However, I do think
she's authentically trying."

"I think so too."

We sit for a moment, gazing at the faint glow of the sky.

"Miss Ava, would you like to try the protective illusion?"

"Me? No, no, I can't."

"At some point you have to trust yourself." His eyes meet
mine. "I trust you."

Panic rises in my chest and my breath feels short. "This

is too important. This isn't something as simple as messing up and getting the wrong color. If I do something wrong, somebody could die or be captured or—"

He stops me. "You've proven your abilities in many instances. I have confidence you can do this. Try for an hour, perhaps?"

I don't want to do it. But I can't use my inexperience as an excuse forever. I'll never know what I'm capable of if I don't stretch myself. "Okay. For one hour. Go take a nap."

"Best of luck, Miss Ava. You can do this. Wake me in an hour."

I take a long, slow breath and then focus on projecting illusion: *There's nothing interesting here. You don't feel like going this way. It's unremarkable.*

I let the suggestion radiate out from me, focusing on maintaining those thoughts. The idea is that anyone who gets too close will be inspired to go elsewhere. Is it working? How am I supposed to know?

And then I notice the birds. Tiny sparrows swoop and dive, weaving in and out of the early morning light through the trees to snatch insects, but only on the outskirts of our little group. There are just as many bugs in our area as anywhere else, but the birds aren't interested in them. I laugh inwardly as a little green caterpillar inches away. Even the bugs themselves within our space appear to be making their exit.

A thrill goes through me. It's working! I can do this.

The hour passes faster than I thought it would, but I am exhausted. It takes a lot out of me to project suggestions constantly.

The sky glows brighter now, and the others are beginning to stir. Elm looks so calm that I almost don't want to wake him, but I'm not sure how much longer I can hold out. I give him a gentle nudge, and his eyes flutter open.

"See?" He gives me a sleepy grin. "We're still alive. Well done."

"Thanks for believing in me."

He tips an imaginary hat. "My pleasure."

Samantha is awake now. She sits up and hugs her knees to her chest. She doesn't look around at anyone. There's a part of me that wants to stay mad at her, but a greater part that simply can't. I imagine she's tortured herself enough. Looking at her, it's hard to believe she's the oldest. She seems so much like a child.

I go over to her. "Good morning, Samantha. I want to say thanks. It was really nice of you to let everyone rest, especially when you had to be pretty tired yourself."

"You're welcome," she mutters, then buries her face in her knees. I leave her to her own thoughts.

The first order of business is to get the remaining devices made. Samantha continues to send out protective illusions. After spending the last hour exercising my Mentalist brain, I have a greater appreciation for the effort it takes.

"This Green magic is really working well," Nikki observes. "Things are faster, even compared to just last night."

"It helps that we know exactly what we're doing now." Kaito squints as he places a tiny pin into the device he's working on to hold a gear in place. "Practice makes perfect."

My breath catches as I spot a flutter of crimson in the trees. "Buggerfly!" I point. Samantha's spell has absolutely no effect on it, and it drifts closer to our area.

"On it," Blake says. The butterfly short-circuits and tumbles from the air.

"Thanks, Blake. Would you mind keeping an eye out for more of those?" I scan the treetops for more telltale signs that we're being watched.

"I'll take care of it." Blake scans the area. "They won't get within a hundred feet of us if I can help it."

The remaining invisibility devices are finished soon after. Everyone activates theirs, and Samantha releases a long breath, now that she can finally stop her mental projections. Almost immediately the birds return to the area, and a few begin swooping down.

"Hey, stop it!" Samantha swats away a sparrow that targets her hair.

"They're not more robots, right?" Brie asks anxiously while dodging another sparrow.

Blanca shocks us all by reaching out and grabbing one straight out of the air. The tiny creature's eyes are round with fear. Blanca examines it carefully. "No, just a dumb bird." She releases it, and it takes flight madly toward the security of the trees.

Knowing it's a real bird eases my worry only slightly. I can't help but think about what Ivan said about animals behaving oddly. Unless there was some kind of backfire from Samantha's spell, we haven't given the birds any reason to attack us. Another bridge to cross. But for now . . .

"We need to figure out some kind of solution for where to stay. Our food is nearly depleted, and we can't stay exposed in the open. Nor do we know how long it will be before we can implement our plans." Plus we're all out of practice, and the tension with Samantha adds a layer of complication.

Brie and Jazz share a glance. "Brie and I were talking last night. We were thinking that maybe we could stay with our parents."

"Involving anyone else seems rather hazardous, don't you think?" Elm says. "We have no idea who might be on our side."

"I know they'll want to see us," Brie says, yearning in her eyes. My mind flickers to my parents in Neo Prism. I'm sure the whole group is missing family. But with the barrier up, everyone is being controlled to some level. And even without the barrier, I'm sure Selene has her adherents.

"What do your parents think of the Benefactors?" I ask.

"They didn't like them all that much," Jazz says. "They think people should have more responsibility and freedom instead of leadership specifying everything."

"Well, that could be promising," Elm says. "But then why did they send you to Prism? There are other schools not so directly under the Benefactor's thumbs."

"Prism was the best of the best," Brie replies as Jazz nods. "Regardless of how they felt about the Benefactors, they wanted us to have a good education."

"And it didn't help that Brie got a scholarship there." Jazz gives her an exaggerated glare.

Brie just grins.

"And what if they don't want us?" Blanca asks. "Then they'd turn us all over to the Benefactors, and we'd be a lot worse off getting captured by them than we were at Neo Prism."

True. We may have been incarcerated in Neo Prism, but at least we weren't in any mortal peril there, or at risk of being used to power mind-control devices. A chill runs down my spine at the thought. "It's definitely taking a big chance. But I'm also not sure what our options are. We need a place to go, and we don't know of any friends we can count on here. This may be our best choice for now."

Everyone agrees. We'll head to Jazz and Brie's house and hope for the best.

As we peer inside the windows of the little white farmhouse, we see a woman with a ponytail of braids huddled by a man who could be an older version of Jazz. The latter is hunched over a boxy metal object, examining it and shaking his head.

"What is he working on?" I ask.

"It's that stupid grain mill again," Brie mutters. "He bought it off someone who claimed it would work miracles, but I think he got swindled. It's never worked right."

"I see," Elm murmurs thoughtfully.

I glance around the group. "Any ideas on how we get in?"

Blanca argues that we could simply break the door down, and Samantha points out all the flaws with that plan. Brie says the back door is usually unlocked, so we could just stroll in, but Jazz says that's a bad idea. Kaito has an elaborate strategy, which he tries to illustrate for us in the dirt. Nikki says that's too complicated. My head spins as I listen to the discord. How do you persuade anyone to let a bunch of outlaws into their home?

Elm, who has been silently watching the arguments this whole time, stops us. "That's quite enough. I'll take it from here."

"Why you?" Blake asks.

Elm lifts a brow. "Which stunning individual is Magus's most wanted? Hmm, let me think." He gestures toward himself with a flourish. "I didn't earn such a spectacular title without merit."

"But you won't hurt them, right?" Jazz has a difficult time allowing anyone else at the helm when his family is involved.

Brie quickly comes to Elm's defense. "Of course he won't hurt them. You should know he's not like that." I'm grateful at least one person here trusts him like I do.

"Let's hear your idea, Elm."

"Thank you, Miss Ava." With all eyes on him, Elm removes his top hat and rolls it down his arm, clearly loving every minute of his captive audience. There is a great puff of cobalt smoke from the hat, and when it clears, I blink a few times to be sure I'm not seeing things.

"You're wearing blue! I never thought I would see that." His typical attire has been replaced with an electric blue tailcoat with silver embroidered details along the lapels and cuffs and dark blue pants.

Even more startling, I look down and see that he and I match. My dress is the same shade of blue with similar silver embroidery along the hem of the skirt and down the button-up front of the bodice.

Elm is staring at me, looking stunned.

"What's wrong?"

"Nothing. I'm becoming very fond of blue." He takes his eyes from me and addresses the group. "Do we look 'Violet City' enough?"

Nikki nods her head. "Definitely. You look great."

"What are you going to do?" Poor Jazz looks sick with worry.

Elm winks. "Watch and see."

Suddenly the faces of our friends shift to confusion, and they look back and forth between Elm and me. "You look different," Kaito says.

I study Elm's face, but every detail is the same Elm I've always known. "You look the same to me."

"Because you, Miss Ava, always seem to see right through me." He smiles. "But to everyone else, I've applied the slightest illusion to our faces, just in case their parents recognize us from the posters. Maintaining such an illusion for extended amounts of time is draining, and faces are hard to get right, so minimal is best."

"Good idea." It's easy to imagine the difficulty of projecting an illusion on a face when expressions are so dynamic. I make a mental note of the limitations in case I try his technique in the future.

"What are your parents' names?" Elm asks Jazz.

"Gavin and Skye." Jazz gives his parents a nervous glance through the window. "How are you going to get them to let you inside? I doubt many people are welcoming strangers in right now."

"You seem to be forgetting a key detail." Elm smiles wryly. "I am a Mentalist."

Just like that the door swings open, and a voice inside calls out, "Come in!"

Jazz's face says he's not comfortable with this idea in the slightest. "You can't just control them the whole time."

"Of course not. In fact, I don't think it will even need to happen twice." Elm holds his arm out to me. "Please join me, Miss Ava. Follow my lead. Everyone else, sit tight."

I hook my arm with his, heart fluttering. This feels dangerous, but I trust him. We enter the house, and Elm greets Gavin and Skye as though they're old friends. He gives each of them a vigorous handshake. "Ah, Gavin and Skye! Thank you for inviting us here. We at Skuttleton's Ship-Shape Shapers pride ourselves on our repair skills and appreciate this chance to earn your business."

I hold back a laugh at his invented business name. And I guess I'm a Shaper now. Hopefully I won't be expected to demonstrate that.

"I'm Henry Skuttleton and this is my apprentice Anabelliana Louisa Pendragon."

How on earth does he expect me to remember that name? "Please call me Ana," I state, giving Elm a look and noting the playful gleam in his eyes.

"Where is the device you need us to examine?"

Gavin leads us to the table with the grain mill and explains what it's meant to do and what it's not doing. "It was supposed to all be automatic with Shaper magic, but I can only get it to work manually, and even then, just barely."

Elm's eyes light up, and for a moment, I'm sure he's no

longer acting. "I do believe I can fix that. Pay close attention, Anabelliana." I know he means more than just playing the part of the apprentice; he's teaching me Mentalist skills.

As he examines the device, I realize he's also examining Gavin and Skye. He asks them about their interests. Their convictions. The things that matter to them. He tells jokes and laughs with them. He sympathizes with them. What might come off as small talk to most people is actually his way of persuasion. And he's doing this just by being himself—no mind control necessary. I can see the visible change in Skye and Gavin as they warm to Elm and become more relaxed in his company.

"There now," Elm says at last. "Give that a try."

Gavin uses his abilities to activate the grain mill, which hums to life and sends a wide smile to Skye's and Gavin's faces.

"That's wonderful!" exclaims Skye. "How much do we owe you?"

"Free of charge." Elm's voice is soft and thoughtful, and I sense he's preparing to move to the next phase of his plan.

"No, we insist," Gavin says, reaching into his pocket.

Elm holds up his hand. "No, *I* insist. You see, we know your son and daughter."

Gavin and Skye freeze at once, scrutinizing our faces.

Skye gasps. "Elm Ridley."

It seems Elm has dropped his ruse, and I brace myself in case we need to make a quick exit. But Gavin and Skye remain calm and listen. All the seeds of trust Elm planted, combined with the skepticism they already felt toward the Benefactors, must have done the job. By the time the conversation is over, Skye and Gavin are ready to see their children and welcome us all into their home.

"You're amazing," I tell Elm as we watch Brie and Jazz's happy reunion.

Elm instantly snaps back into his usual yellow-accented garb. He twirls his cane and smiles. "I know."

32

"WE'LL NEED THREE TEAMS, EACH WITH
a Mentalist—Elm, Samantha, or me. Who will team up with
Samantha?"

"Not me," Blanca says instantly.

Jazz looks at Samantha as though she's a rabid badger and
removes all eye contact. Elm watches Samantha with a pitying
look on his face. She shrinks down and clutches her skirt in
her fists. Maybe this should have been done privately.

"I can be on her team," Brie offers. Brie could get along
with almost anyone.

"Great. Thanks, Brie. Now we need a Shaper."

Blanca crosses her arms. "Not Kaito."

I already anticipated that. "I figured the two of you work
well together. It makes sense you'll be on the same team."

Nikki clears her throat. "I just don't think I could get it
together enough to make it work, sorry."

"Fair enough. Blake?"

He runs his hand through his hair. "I'll give it my best, Ava."

"Perfect. So, the teams are Blake, Samantha, and Brie.
Elm, Blanca, and Kaito. Nikki, Jazz, and me. Now that we
have that settled, let's practice getting those shields in place."

Elm's team gets their shield up the fastest. It's not hard

for them to find unity, which holds true for my group as well. Samantha's group is another story . . .

Brie jumps backward, squealing as a spark of magic singes her hand.

Jazz starts over to her, but Brie waves him away.

"Keep working with your own group. Our team is going to find a way to make this work. It just might take more time."

Samantha lifts her head. "You know, I'm not going to betray anyone again. I learned my lesson."

Blake raises his eyebrows at her. "Easier said than done. You didn't spend the last few weeks in a prison cell with shackles on your wrists."

She opens her mouth to retort but abruptly stops.

Brie says gently, "Samantha knows she messed up. How can she make things better if we won't let her have a chance?"

"She just burned your hand," Jazz grumbles.

"*We* burned my hand," Brie corrects. "The haywire magic was a group effort. It's something we all messed up."

"If I might make a suggestion." Elm speaks up. "Perhaps sharing a memory–"

Jazz's eyes widen in panic.

Elm shakes his head. "No, no. Not literally sharing a memory."

"Most of our memories of us together are pretty bad," Blake observes wryly.

"Ah. Fair point. Perhaps that wasn't the best suggestion . . ."

"What's your favorite food, Samantha?" Brie suddenly asks.

"Yellow curry," Samantha says quietly.

"Oh. I've never had it. Because, well, it's yellow," Brie says.

"Red curry is good, though," Blake offers. "Is it similar?"

Samantha looks at him in surprise. "Yes and no."

The youngest of us has done it. Everyone is relaxing. I'm not sure if talking about food is enough of a common ground, but at least it's some sort of foundation.

"Favorite color?" Brie asks.

"Yellow."

Brie gives a wide grin. "Me too, actually. I could never say that before. But it's so bright and cheerful. It made me so happy to see it in Neo Prism."

Jazz stares at her. "I never knew that."

"Because you're a worrywart. If I told you my favorite color was yellow, you would have thought I was headed straight to prison."

Elm watches them, amused. "Well, he would have been right, apparently."

We all burst into laughter. Brie continues to ask her questions, and everyone joins in. There's something outrageously normal and wholesome about sitting down and exchanging favorites. I guess we never took the time to find out the simplest things about each other.

Night comes and with it pleasure of what we've accomplished.

"Miss Ava," Elm gestures toward the porch swing, "come sit with me for a moment?"

I join him.

"Do you think Sammy's group will be able to get it together enough for this to work?"

I swallow. "I'm not sure, honestly. There are a lot of negative feelings still. After what happened, it's understandable."

"They say that nothing brings people together like a common enemy."

I purse my lips. "Selene is about as common as they come. If that's not enough, what is?"

He stretches and places his hands behind his head. "Well," he remarks to the deep indigo sky, "they could fight against us, for starters. Some kind of training exercise. If the stakes aren't so high, they may be able to reconcile goals for a short time."

I sit up. "It's a good idea."

"So, here's how this game will go." Elm stands in the upper loft of the barn early the next morning. Samantha's team is looking on curiously. The others are elsewhere.

"You three will be against Miss Ava and me; however, the catch is, if you want to use magic, you can only use combined magic types."

"Think of it like an aptitude test," I say. "Or Zap Blaster. This is training." I give Blake a wide grin. "Besides, if you don't want to fight me, I know you really wouldn't mind taking a few shots at Elm."

"You've got me there."

"Wonderful. I look forward to besting you." Elm gives a dramatic bow.

Blake rolls his eyes. "So how are we determining who wins?"

Elm produces a large yellow handkerchief with a flourish. It floats to the top of the rafters and drapes across one of the wooden beams.

I applaud. "Nice Shaper work!"

Elm grins, accepting the compliment. He continues his instruction. "Your goal is to get that handkerchief. Our goal is to keep you from getting it."

Blake squints up at the sun coming through the barn windows. "That doesn't seem too hard."

Samantha quirks her head to the side. "You obviously don't know Elm."

"One more thing," Elm adds, a mischievous sparkle in his eye. "Miss Ava and I may use whatever spells we like."

"That's not fair!" Brie objects.

"The goal is to teach you three to work together. And the Benefactors certainly won't concern themselves with fairness." Elm rubs his hands together. "Now then, are we ready?"

Blake, Brie, and Samantha all look a bit uncertain, but they nod and mumble their assent.

"Wonderful. We begin . . . now."

"Blake, just float the handkerchief down," Brie urges him.

I shake my head. "Only combined spells, remember."

"Oh."

The three stare for several moments at the handkerchief. They seem to be at a loss. I didn't think it would be this hard for them to come up with something.

"Well, this isn't proving difficult at all for Miss Ava and me."

"Shut up," Blake says.

"If you and Samantha could use Green magic," Brie muses, "could you create something simple to get it down?"

Blake considers. "That's not a bad idea. We need like a long claw or something. How about it, Samantha?"

"Okay. Let's try."

Green magic seems to involve a Mentalist thinking up an item as though creating it for an illusion, and the Shaper then bringing it into actual form. Whenever Elm and I have created something together, we took the time to talk through it to make sure we were on the same page. Samantha and Blake aren't having any such discussion, but their faces are heavy with concentration.

At once, a plastic lobster with overly long claws materializes and falls to the straw-covered floor. We all stare at it for a moment until Elm bursts into laughter. Brie giggles.

"What is that?" Blake asks, aghast.

Samantha throws up her hands. "You said claws. I don't know what you wanted."

Brie makes a pinching motion with her hands. "He means a grabbing claw. I used to have one when I was little. It had a handle you squeezed to open it and a claw on the end to grab with."

"Okay, let's try again. Stop laughing, Elm."

Elm clears his throat. "Sorry, Sammy." But his grin is huge.

They make another attempt, and this time a functional grabbing tool materializes. My heart leaps. "Great job!" I clamp my hands over my mouth, remembering that I'm supposed to be working against them for this game. Blake gives an appreciative smile anyway.

Samantha frowns a little. "I think it's too short."

"I could modify it," Blake says.

"No, you can't," Samantha reminds him. "Combined magic only."

"Argh."

"Can you make another?" asks Brie. "This one was good. Just do it again but bigger."

Their second attempt is much better, and it looks as though it will do the job . . . which makes me feel bad for what I'm going to do next. Blake grabs the claw and runs beneath the handkerchief, reaching the claw upward. I sprint forward and grab the claw, snapping it in two.

"Aw, come on, Ava!"

"Sorry, Blake. Just doing my job."

"Well, maybe we can make another one out of a stronger material. Should we try a metal one, Samantha?"

She doesn't look happy about it, but she agrees. "Okay."

But then Blake starts walking in circles around a bale of hay.

Brie looks on, confused. "Blake, what are you doing?"

"It's Elm," Samantha mutters.

"Oh."

"He's not going to be able to get out of that spell on his own." She glances at Brie. "Orange magic?"

Brie looks alarmed. "Oh, no. I'm not okay trying that yet. I'm afraid we'll hurt him."

Blake continues around the hay bale, now in a sprint. He slips slightly on the slick straw on the ground.

"Elm," I give a pleading look, "we shouldn't force them to do anything dangerous. I know the Benefactors wouldn't care, but still."

"He's coming out of it anyway," Elm says. "Watch."

Blake's steps slow, and when he stops, he looks at Elm with annoyance.

"You've gotten much better at that, I must say," Elm remarks approvingly.

I gape at Elm. Did he just compliment Blake? Blake, in spite of himself, looks pleased. Or at least, less perturbed.

"Can we try Purple magic?" Brie holds something in her hand. "I think if we could combine one of us with this . . . maybe that person could climb the rafters?"

I'm curious to see if they can achieve this. It would involve Blake and Brie, and I wonder if I should intervene so they do something that relies on Samantha, since that's where the discord lies.

Blake and Samantha examine what Brie holds in her hand, and I lean in for a closer look as well. A hand rake?

Blake takes it from Brie and heaves it into one of the barn's wooden support beams. "It's worth a shot," he agrees. "If my hands could have the properties of this rake, I probably could climb up the wall and to the rafters."

They focus their magic together, and Blake's hands turn metallic and silver. His fingers stretch thin and curl slightly at the ends. He attempts to flex his fingers, but they won't move.

As I stare at Blake's transformed hands, I can't help but imagine them sticking that way forever, and the thought makes me uneasy. "You're sure this is temporary, right?"

"Too late if it isn't." Blake shrugs. He jumps about a foot up and slaps his hands against the barn wall, giving it a test run. They hook in with no trouble, and he alternates hands to climb up the side. "It's working!" It takes him some effort to get his hands loose from the wood so he can place them higher up, but he manages, even though he seems to be taking some of the wall with him. All the Shapers will have to help repair it later.

As Blake makes his way up, I consider how I might stop him. I don't want to let them get the handkerchief this quickly, but I also don't want to cause injury. Anything that might make him fall is out of the question. Maybe I should just suggest Elm move the handkerchief again.

As Blake gets closer to the handkerchief, I see the inevitable turning point where he'll have to move from vertical to horizontal in his climb. Will his hook hands really be able to hold his weight while moving across those rafters? They don't look very stable as it is. In fact . . .

"Blake, stop!" I call. "I think that wood is rotting."

"I'm almost there. I'm fi—"

His words are cut off by a dreaded crack as his hooks come loose, taking a large chunk of wood with them. Brie and I scream as Blake plummets toward the ground, but then suddenly he's flying. I refocus and realize his shirt is being tugged upward to slow his fall. Elm is in a strange daze and comes to as Blake lands safely on the ground.

But Elm has a shocked expression on his face. "Sammy?"

Samantha stands, almost gasping for air.

"Does someone want to explain what just happened?" Brie is looking wildly around. I'm wondering the same thing.

"I broke the rules," Samantha confesses. "I'm sorry. I didn't know what else to do, so I took control of Elm and had him use his Shaper abilities on Blake's shirt."

I gape at her. "That was ingenious." How did she think of that so quickly? And how was she able to take control of Elm like that?

"Elm, I'm so sorry. I just reacted."

Elm holds up his hand. "Not to worry, Sammy. You did the

right thing. And"—he quirks a smile—"it was a good reminder not to let my guard down. I wasn't anticipating a Mentalist attack, so it was no trouble for you to control me."

"But you still caught onto it." I think of the moment he seemed to regain control.

"Yes, but it still shouldn't have happened to begin with. Though in this case, my inattention was much to Blake's benefit."

Blake has dusted himself off and approaches Samantha. "Thanks. You could have just let me fall."

She gives a small shrug. "Why would I want that? We're a team."

I almost can't believe what I'm hearing. She is really trying. Maybe she's becoming the Sammy Elm knew all those years ago.

"Well, thank you." Blake looks at his hands, still silver and covered in bits of crumbling wood. "How do we make this go away?"

"Oh, sorry!" Brie exclaims. "I was so focused on keeping the spell intact so you wouldn't fall."

Blake's hands look almost as though they are soaking up the metal as Brie releases her part of the spell. He brushes the bark away, his hands now back to normal.

Samantha gives Elm a tentative look. "Can we try again?"

"No," I answer before Elm can. "I think that's enough for today. Let's not risk anyone else getting hurt. You keep practicing more, and we'll do it again another day."

Samantha looks disappointed. Elm was right, she really is trying to make this work.

We all head out of the barn, and Blake comes alongside Samantha.

"Thanks again," he says, and the grateful smile he gives is genuine.

Maybe we can be a united front. There is more hope now, and it feels good.

33

WORD OF SAMANTHA RESCUING BLAKE
spreads around our little group in no time, and it becomes a
turning point. Everyone is much kinder to Samantha, and she
appears more comfortable with us now.

"Who would have imagined putting Blake in peril was all we
needed?" Elm muses. "I should have tried that much sooner."

I make a face at him. "Someday, you'll be forced to
acknowledge that Blake isn't such a bad guy."

"Oh, I'm already aware. But he doesn't have to know that."

A thought crosses my mind. "If it came down to it, do you
think you would be able to use combined magic with Blake?"

"Why would I need to? I can already use Blue and Yellow
on my own."

"You never know. If we're expecting mutual cooperation from
everyone else, we should be held to the same standard, right?"

"Hmm. I suppose so. Right as usual, Miss Ava."

"So you're going to be nicer to him?"

"Let's not get ahead of ourselves."

I sigh, although he has that mischievous twinkle in his eye.
Elm may be stubborn about admitting it, but I do think he's
coming around to appreciating Blake . . . or at least tolerating
him. He was genuinely impressed yesterday when Blake pulled
out of his mind-control spell. I'm determined to get those two on

civil terms, although getting Blake to truly align with Elm might be even more difficult. Oh well.

Brie calls out excitedly from where their team is practicing. "We made a shield! We used White magic!"

Brie's excitement bubbles out of her. "Watch!" She looks to her teammates.

Samantha nods and says, "One, two, three!"

A flash of bright light, and the three of them are surrounded in a dome of White magic. They exchange triumphant smiles. Elm applauds.

"That's fantastic!" Now that this team is working, we can move forward. The thought is both thrilling and terrifying. But if we're ready, then there's nothing left to do. Every day we wait is another day lost.

"Elm?" I hear Nikki say sharply as she peers out one of the windows in the loft.

Blanca joins her and utters something much coarser.

"What's going on?" I begin, climbing the ladder to the loft to see for myself.

"Benefactors," Blanca growls.

No. This can't be happening.

Elm takes charge. "Invisible. Now."

We all turn our devices on, and I look out the window. Sure enough, a group of five individuals in black Benefactor uniforms are striding to the house.

"What are they doing?" Brie speaks in a soft, shrill voice. "They're not going to hurt my parents, are they?"

"I don't think so." I try to sound confident and reassuring, but the Benefactors usually don't make house calls for any good reason.

One of the Benefactors raps sharply on the door, and it opens up a moment later to a surprised Skye.

"Can we come in?" the Benefactor asks. Though it's clear that it's not really a question.

I notice the barest flash of concern in Skye's expression before she switches on a bright smile. "Well, of course! Can I get you anything? Fresh limeade? Tea?"

She ushers the Benefactors inside and the inability to hear or see anything is maddening. How are we supposed to know if they need help? I wouldn't put anything past the Benefactors at this point.

"Everyone stay put." I scramble down the loft and out the back door of the barn. Elm calls after me, but I don't have a moment to waste. I slow my speed to a more careful pace once I'm in view of the house, taking care not to disturb anything that could tip the Benefactors off. I tread lightly up the front porch steps to peer into the kitchen window. Skye appears to be inviting the Benefactors to sit, but they decline. I can't hear a thing.

At once, Skye looks at the window. She squints her eyes, and then a flash of surprise crosses her face. She can't possibly see me, can she? Is my device not working? She says something to the Benefactors, and then she comes to the window. What is she doing? Have we been wrong to trust her? I brace myself to run and warn the others it's time to retreat.

Skye looks me straight in the eye—she definitely sees me—and tips her head just slightly toward the Benefactors.

Listen, she mouths.

She cracks the window open just slightly. "There! That's so much better. This room stuffs up so quickly I don't want anyone uncomfortable." It's cold out here, and Skye has a fire in the hearth. Hopefully this won't strike the Benefactors as odd. They stand around the kitchen table, looking stern-faced. However, they don't show any indication that they've seen me. How can Skye?

"To what do I owe the pleasure of having Benefactors in my home?"

The Benefactor who appears to be the highest ranking of the group scans the room like a predator. "We're checking in on all the parents of the students who were kidnapped. How are you holding up?" Her words sound kind, but her expression doesn't match. She's looking for signs of potential trouble. Signs of treason.

"We're doing as well as could be expected. We lost both of our children. And who knows where they are now or what's happening to them."

"And they've made no contact with you at all?"

"I wish they had. Then we'd know they were still alive."

"If you don't mind, we'd like to have a look around."

"Well, of course. But why? You don't think my husband and I are in danger, do you?"

The Benefactor notices a crumb on the kitchen table and flicks it off carelessly. "It's possible. We think Elm may have targeted the parents of another one of the kidnapped students."

My heart stutters. Whose parents? What happened to them that would enable Benefactors to say Elm was responsible?

"Oh dear, who was it?" Skye echoes my thoughts. "We did know some of the parents from the school, but we haven't been very social since the children disappeared."

"They're alright, for now." The Benefactor walks over to the very window I'm staring into and looks vacantly outside, her hands clasped behind her back. I stand as still as I can. "As it happens, these parents are Benefactors. But they haven't been fighting for the cause as enthusiastically lately, which leads us to suspect their minds have been tampered with."

Benefactors. Blake's parents? Is it possible that they're coming around to the truth? The fact that they're drawing suspicion has me worried. They're probably not even aware that the Benefactors have noticed a change in their behavior.

Skye folds her arms, and I can see now that she's feeling some annoyance. "Don't you suppose their odd behavior could be grief? If their child disappeared the way mine did, I imagine that would be mighty distracting."

"Yes, I suppose it would be." The Benefactor at last turns away from the window, though I stay frozen in my position. "I'm sorry about this, but we'll need to search the house." She's obviously not sorry at all. I get the feeling nothing would delight her more than to discover something here. And she might do that, I realize. We have all of our things in Jazz's and Brie's rooms. *No, no, no.*

"Of course you're welcome to search." Skye's voice becomes confidential. "It's just that my husband is napping upstairs. Could I go get him up so he isn't startled?"

Where *has* Gavin been this whole time?

"We'll go up with you," the Benefactor says. "But first we'll start with this room."

Three Benefactors with blue buttons on their uniforms come forward and immediately start levitating objects, casting them aside with carelessness that angers me. The high-ranking Benefactor and the other Red Benefactor pace around the room, giving directions on anything they want moved or strewn about.

Skye just stands there. Her jaw sets, her posture grows rigid as the Benefactors tear apart her beautiful home. But this is what we've all been taught to do. Stand down. Don't make a fuss. Let the Benefactors do whatever they want, and don't ask questions.

In the midst of my indignation, movement catches my attention out of the corner of my eye. Glancing up I see objects floating out of the second-floor window—our belongings. They float down around the house, away from the windows, and underneath the porch where they are obscured by tall, dry grass. Gavin isn't napping after all. Thank goodness for that.

Later, when the Benefactors are satisfied, they come back downstairs with both Gavin and Skye. The two of them look small and defeated, standing in the center of the upturned room. I don't have any delusions that the Benefactors will set things back in order, and I know Skye and Gavin won't say anything. Best to just get the Benefactors out as soon as possible.

"Well," says the leader, "everything appears to be in order." *Completely out of order thanks to you.*

She gives Gavin and Skye a hard smile. "Consider yourselves fortunate. You're under our eye of protection." More like observation.

"Yes. Thank you for that." Gavin manages a nod.

The Benefactor looks out the window again and pauses, eyes narrowed. "Actually, we'd better check out that barn too."

Drat.

"It's just the animals there," Skye says calmly. "Do we really need to disturb them? The chickens won't lay if they get too worked up, and we're always short on eggs during winter."

You don't need to check. I concentrate with everything I have. *These people are farmers. Of course they'll have a barn. It's been a long day. You're tired. You can leave them be.*

The Benefactor eventually sighs. "Yes, I suppose there's no need to disturb the chickens. But you'll tell us if anything odd comes up, won't you?"

"Yes, of course. If there's anything we can do to help bring our babies back, we'll do it."

The Benefactor takes one more look around, and the look of pride on her face sends a hot wave through me. She actually enjoys disrupting people's lives. "Good day," she says. She and her crew make a brisk exit.

I maintain my stillness as they cross the field, holding my breath as they walk past the barn. *Just animals.* I continue to push the suggestion. *Hear them? Nothing but animals.* Only when they are completely out of sight do I trust getting to the barn to tell everyone the coast is clear. For now.

34

EVERYONE STANDS IN THE DOORWAY,
appalled at the disaster the Benefactors left behind. There isn't
an inch that hasn't been upturned.

"We'll assist in cleaning up immediately," Elm says. "I'm
sorry this happened on our account."

"Don't be." Skye brushes him off. "It could have been a
lot worse."

"Does this mean they're going to return?" Jazz pauses as
he returns dishes to their cupboards. "If they feel like they're
close, they won't stay away."

Gavin frowns at a spot where a picture was carelessly
torn from the wall and sets about using a spell to repair the
damage. "I have a feeling they'll be here again before too long.
We're on their radar now, even if they didn't find anything."

I have to say something. "Blake," I adjust a house plant, "I
think they're suspicious of your parents."

"What?" Blake's head jerks up.

"They said parents of a kidnapped student, who happen to
be Benefactors, have been acting strangely. As far as I know,
your parents are the only Benefactors in this group."

He stiffens. "We have to do something fast. If they're under
any suspicion . . ."

I know he's right. Our time of planning and preparing

wears thinner by the minute. Blake's parents are at increasing risk. Gavin and Skye are endangered every second we spend here. And there's no telling what the Benefactors are doing or have done to the parents of anyone else in the group. If the Benefactors grow more desperate for information, they may begin interrogating. Maybe even torturing.

Blanca moves a couch back into place, lifting it as though it were a feather. "I'm not going to let them hurt my dad," she states. "We need to stop this. And fast."

I turn to Elm. "We can't keep putting other people at risk for our mission. The sooner we find where all the Mentalists are, the sooner we can free them and take down the barrier."

"I agree," he says.

"I just don't feel right about sending all you out there." Skye swoops around the room, setting objects back in place and repairing damage. "I don't think you have to worry about anything right away. Just hold on. We could find others who would support you and build up a better team."

Gavin raises his eyebrows. "Are we organizing a revolution now?"

"I don't know, Gav!" Skye throws her hands up. "But we're sitting here talking about letting our children go up against true evil."

The room falls silent. Skye tries again. "I wish you would take time and think this through. We might find a way to help you. But you have to give us time."

"I'm not waiting." Blanca paces back and forth in Jazz's room like a rabid fox. Skye and Gavin went to bed some time ago. The rest of us are gathered together to figure out our next steps. "Waiting will get us nowhere," Blanca continues. "My father lives all alone, and he's not strong. They'll hurt him."

"I believe the Benefactors will keep their heads down if they don't have a good reason to investigate your father," Elm says.

She gives a hoarse laugh. "They turned you into a human battery, Elm. They don't need a reason to be cruel. They just do what they want."

Kaito speaks up. "Right now, they want to be on the community's good side. If word gets around that they're harassing citizens—especially citizens who supposedly just had their children taken by a wanted criminal—that's not going to look good."

"And," Nikki adds, "because of the devices we destroyed, there might be doubt creeping into some people's minds. So they wouldn't want to fan those flames."

Blanca's breathing slows, and she seems placated. For now.

I speak up. "Blanca's not totally wrong, though. They may not have a good reason yet, but it won't take them long to fabricate one. If they suspect any of our parents have been in communication with us, things could get bad fast."

Elm nods. "We need to enact our strategy now and trust that it's enough."

"As in, *now,* now?" Blake clarifies.

"Well, obviously not this very instant. But soon would be best."

"I'm ready to leave whenever everyone else is," Brie announces.

"Brie, your parents have been generous to us. They don't want you and Jazz involved in this at all. We must consider their wishes."

"No!" Brie protests. "We're part of the group. We planned all this with three teams. We're part of those teams!"

"Besides that, what are we supposed to do?" Jazz puts in.

"We'd still be putting my parents in danger if we stay here. Are we just going to hang around being invisible forever? Well, not even forever. Once the invisibility devices go dead, we won't have a way to recharge them. And then what? We lie in wait until the Benefactors show up?"

"He's got a point," Blake says.

"I don't like deceiving Gavin and Skye after they took us in," I say slowly. It feels wrong to sneak their children into something as dangerous as this.

Brie crosses her arms. "I'm going with you guys no matter what. You can't stop me."

At breakfast the next morning, the visit from the Benefactors still hangs over everyone's heads.

"We're leaving in three days," I say.

Skye pauses with a fork halfway to her mouth. "Three days? Well, you can still change your mind and take more time."

"Or you'll try to change it for us," Brie mutters.

"Enough," Skye reprimands. "A group of youngsters comes to my house for safekeeping, and I'm supposed to send them to their doom without saying anything? I won't hear another word about it, missy."

Brie's mouth sets in an angry line, but she goes back to her breakfast in silence.

Later on, Skye walks in just as I'm preparing to start on a basket of clean laundry.

"Let me help you with that."

She floats a shirt into the air, and I watch with fascination as it seemingly folds itself and then lands neatly on the couch.

"You know, Ava, it would probably do you good to stay here and train a little with Samantha."

Samantha? "And why is that?" I smooth out another shirt, trying to fold it as neatly as Skye just did, but my fingers fumble.

"I asked her to help me learn how to see through illusions. She's extremely capable and very good at it."

"So that's how you were able to see me the other day." I glance at her as I pull out a bright cerulean sock and search for its companion.

"Yes. She's taught me well. I was on guard with the Benefactors here, and I noticed something off about the light patterns. So I focused a little more and there you were."

I pause. "I guess we can't really rely on our invisibility devices to keep us safe. It doesn't seem like it takes much to see through some illusions." Marabell saw us too. How easy would it be for the Benefactors?

"Well, I'm not sure how easy it really is," Skye remarks. "I was already on high alert. I already knew you had invisibility devices and was ready for signs of any one of you in case I needed to shoo you away. Being aware makes it much easier." She takes the sock from my hand. "Let me."

She examines the sock for a moment, then focuses on the basket of clothing. After a moment, the sock's mate floats out, and she pairs the two together.

"How did you do that?"

"Shaper trick," she says with a wink. "Sometimes these objects just call to us."

"Thank you." Skye is so kind and has been like a mother to all of us these past few days. I wish we could have met her under different circumstances.

"You must miss your mama."

I start at her sudden comment. "Yes," I say slowly, "I do. I just got my parents back, and now I've lost them again. I don't even know when I'll see them next."

"Maybe the best thing for you would be to go back to Neo Prism. I'm sure they would be reasonable. Maybe we could all go, and Gav and I would talk to them. We could all start over."

"Maybe." It's a nice thought, but there's no guarantee they would trust us at all.

She looks at me. "Your parents are probably worried sick about you, Ava. It's a horrible feeling and an awful way to live day to day." She knows it firsthand.

I swallow. We just vanished again without warning. They weren't happy about me being in prison, but at least they knew where I was. And I didn't even get to leave them on good terms. A heaviness settles on my heart.

"Just think about it, honey," Skye suggests. "There just has to be a better way."

We finish up with the laundry. "I'll think about it," I tell her. But my choice is already made.

35

THROUGHOUT THE DAY, ELM AND I PULL our friends aside at different points, asking them to meet in Jazz's room tonight after Gavin and Skye go to sleep.

Once everyone is gathered, Blanca says, "We're leaving in three days? What do we need to do to prepare?"

"We're not leaving in three days," I say. "We're leaving tonight."

Everyone looks surprised.

"Tonight?" Jazz asks. "How? Why?"

"Your parents aren't going to let you and Brie leave. And I have a feeling if we wait, they aren't going to let us leave either. Telling them we're leaving later throws them off so we can get away easier."

"We won't be able to rely on the invisibility devices," Samantha says. "I've been teaching Skye about illusions, and she caught on really fast, as you know."

"I could always assist in making sure they don't notice," Elm says, "or perhaps keeping them behind so we can make our exit."

I look at him gratefully. "I know you don't like to use your power that way, but this is important. If there were another way . . ."

"I understand, Miss Ava."

"If there's anybody who doesn't want to do this—"

"Oh, will you stop with that already!" Blanca swats at me. "Don't you think by this point if we're with you, we're with you?"

I make a face at her. "I just want to be sure. People can change their minds."

Elm gives a sideways grin. "Since there are no defections, let's get our things together as quickly as we can. As soon as we are all ready, we'll go."

It takes less than 30 minutes for everyone to get ready. In the dim kitchen night-light, nobody looks as confident as they did a little while ago. Our mission is much more intimidating when directly confronted with the reality of it. By morning's light, we'll be storming into the Benefactor's base.

Elm holds up his hand, motioning everyone into silence. He closes his eyes for a few moments, and then says, "All right. Skye and Gavin should be sleeping easy now. They're both under the illusion that the house is quiet and we're all sound asleep."

I'm sorry, Gavin. Skye. Thank you for being so good to us. I don't know what we would have done if they hadn't been willing to take us in. I hope someday I'll be able to repay them.

Everyone moves quickly out the door, invisibility devices on in case we encounter anyone else along our way. Even knowing their vulnerabilities, they're still better than nothing. We need whatever extra protection we can get at this point.

Jazz and Brie pause in the doorway, looking back into their home. Jazz puts an arm around Brie, and they continue on.

The moon casts a blue light over the fields, and a chilled

wind stirs the trees. I take a deep breath, catching the musty scent of hay, grain, and dirt, which has become somehow comforting over the past few days. I suddenly feel totally unprepared.

As soon as I feel I'm about to unravel, Elm's strong hand grips mine. Just over a year ago, I had almost nobody in my life I cared about, and the ones I did care for didn't matter to me anymore. Now, I'm cocooned in the love of Augmentors, Shapers, and Mentalists supporting one another and being willing to fight to bring that same unity to all of Magus. My eyes unexpectedly flow with tears, which Elm gently wipes away.

I clear my throat, and everyone turns my way. "You're each so important to me. Be careful, okay?"

Elm squeezes, then releases my hand, and I give him a tremulous smile. "Elm, Samantha—lead the way."

36

MORNING SHEDS A PINK LIGHT OVER
the large field outside the base. I squint my eyes in the
distance for a better look. The area looks totally innocuous.
Plain industrial buildings. There's not even a fence or
anything keeping it in—or keeping anyone out. My guess is
the Benefactors didn't want to draw any sort of attention to the
area. If I were just passing through, I probably wouldn't give
this place a second glance.

"This is where you think they're keeping them?" I ask.

Samantha nods. "Based on what I've seen and heard, it
seems like the most obvious place. I've seen lots of Benefactors
going in and out, and I can't be sure, but I saw them bringing
in something that looked like Yellow stones. I don't know why
else they would be here."

"Apart from that," Elm adds, "there are no other obvious
places where they could be secluding so many people. Unless
it doesn't take as much energy to power the barrier as we
assumed."

Kaito shakes his head. "That's doubtful. Keeping
a barrier over a large portion of land mass, plus powering
all the mind-control devices? That has to require numerous
Mentalists."

"Well, that settles it, then." I try to steady my nerves. It doesn't help. I still feel like I might explode at any moment. This is as confident as I'm going to get. "Let's go. We'll get as far as we can while invisible. Save the shields for when we need them."

We move at a brisk pace, staying in our designated groups so that we're ready for action. I haven't seen any Benefactors yet. Is this really the right place? It doesn't seem like they would leave it so open and unprotected, even if they are trying to maintain a low profile.

"Everyone keep your guard up," Elm says quickly. "I suspect there will be hidden security measures."

"Haven't you and Samantha been here before?" Blanca asks.

"Yes, but when Sammy and I were here, we observed from a distance."

My heart pounds faster as we get nearer to our goal. It can't be this easy . . .

At once, the air fills with shattering sounds. My locket breaks right off of my neck. There are gasps and cries of alarm as all the invisibility devices break.

"Get down," Elm orders. Everyone goes belly-down in the dirt, not that it does us much good. Now we're fully visible. Fully exposed. There isn't anything to shield or conceal us.

"What happened?" Blake asks, voice muffled.

Brie covers her head. "Were we fired at or something?"

Kaito holds a decimated device in an outstretched hand. "They broke on their own. All at once."

I suddenly recall something similar happening to my watch in the forest. At the time I wondered if it was damaged when I fell, but then realized if it could have been the unintentional surge in magic. Is that what this is? "It might be the intensity of Yellow magic. If Mentalists are being used to generate magic here, it's possible all of that energy is causing instability. Anything mechanical might not be able to handle it."

Elm regards his own busted device. "At any rate, be

prepared to throw your shields up at any given moment. We have no protection now."

"We have to keep moving forward." I stand and dust myself off, thrusting my broken locket into my pocket for safekeeping. "If they see us, they see us."

We're only a few hundred yards from the compound. And now, I see them coming. Benefactors, flooding out of the corners and crevices of the compound. There are more of them than I expected. And they're drawing weapons.

37

"SHIELDS UP!" I CRY, JUST AS A BARRAGE
of both red and blue light races toward us. Electric beams of
concentrated Red and Blue magic.

White flashes surround me, and with relief I see that all three
groups are encompassed in a glowing shield. Every instinct
within me says to use our protection and flee. But that isn't
what we came for. "Move forward!"

The beams ricochet off of our shields as we continue on. I
wince at every hit, wondering what could happen if the magic
doesn't hold. And it won't hold. Not forever.

The shield goes out on Brie, Samantha, and Blake's group
first. Jazz notices the beams heading for his sister, which takes
out our shield as well as his focus shifts to her. A red beam
grazes my arm, and I scream as the pain sears me. This feels
just like Veronica's body tearing spell. I dodge another beam as
the blood drips from my wound.

"Miss Ava!" Elm exclaims, and with that his group's shield
disappears.

"Get it together!" Blanca shouts. "Get those shields back up!"

Just then she gets hit by a blue beam, which wraps around
her boot and begins pulling her toward the weapon's wielder.

"No!" she screams and kicks her boot off, falling hard to
the ground.

I begin to heal my arm but have to cut the spell short in order to roll out of the way of more beams. They don't seem designed to kill, which means Selene wants to take us alive. I can only imagine what she'll do to us.

Kaito, Blanca, and Elm get their shield up again. This seems to encourage everyone else, and within moments the two other shields are up too. We continue forward. I notice the Benefactors have to stop periodically to charge their weapons with magic. We need to take a more defensive approach at some point, or they're just going to keep laying into us until they wear us down. There's at least thirty of them compared to our tiny group of nine, so it wouldn't take much for them to overwhelm us.

"Let's get close enough to engage them," I say.

"We have to put down our shields for that," Jazz protests.

"The shields will come down at some point anyway," says Nikki. "And when they do, we'll still have to fight."

There's no other option.

This time the shield for Elm's group goes down first, and Elm immediately takes on a fierce and powerful stance. A cluster of Benefactors falls to the ground, writhing in their own imagined pain. Blanca lays a roundhouse kick into one Benefactor and uppercuts another. I have a feeling she's been waiting a long time to do that. Kaito uses his magic to pull weapons out of two Benefactor's hands. He throws one to Blanca, and she whoops and fires at another Benefactor, who prepares to attack her.

I hear a scream and whirl around to see Samantha's hand on her cheek where a red beam sliced into it. Blake is helping Brie to her feet and attempting to protect her from further attacks. Our shield goes down as Jazz again fixates on the danger his sister is in.

"Shield! Focus!" Nikki cries out in panic as a blue beam attempts to drag her by her sleeve. She rips the sleeve off to free herself. I try to concentrate on getting the shield back up again, but it's no use. We're all too caught up in everything going on.

Samantha lets out a wild shriek, and a dark cloud appears around the group of Benefactors. But the beams stop coming toward us. The Benefactors must not be able to see through the cloud, caught up in the Mentalist trick. But Samantha's illusion is uncontrolled, flickering in and out. She looks like she's hyperventilating. She's not going to be able to hold the spell for long.

"Hang in there, Sammy!" Elm calls.

"I hate this, Elm!" She collapses to the ground, tears creating red streaks down her cheek. She shouldn't be here. She's not the fighting type, and she's going to end up dead.

The weight hits me. We *all* could die. This was such a terrible idea. The idea of a revolution sounds good on paper . . . but when you're actually in the middle of it? No more starry-eyed dreamers, just wood for the fire.

Blake and Brie each link their arms with Samantha's, and she looks at them with teary surprise.

"You have to get up," Brie says. "We need you."

"Come on, Samantha." Blake helps her to her feet. "We're with you. Let's get that shield back in place."

Samantha's illusion disappears, but it gave us all enough time to get our shields up again. We need to find the devices shielding the compound as soon as possible—and destroy them. If they're using White magic, all we need is one to take the whole thing down. I scan the area as the beams fire again.

"Whichever group sees a device first, attack it. That's priority number one!"

Then I see it—a red orb off to the left of the compound. That has to be one of the devices used to create their barrier. "Everyone gather up!"

Our three groups huddle as close as we can with our three

shields surrounding us. The beams continue to rain down. "Look off to the left. See the red orb?"

"We shouldn't need to destroy all three devices if they're using White magic. If we can take out one, their barrier will be down, and we'll be able to get in."

"True, Miss Ava," Elm concurs.

"We should delegate." Kaito nods. "Otherwise we'll be getting in each other's way. Who's doing what?"

"Since Jazz and I both use Red magic, maybe our group should be the one to destroy the device. We can do it in half the time."

"The other teams are our backup. When we lower our shield so we can attack the orb, do what you can to keep the Benefactors from firing on us."

"Promise me one thing," Elm says. "This must end. Whatever else may happen, destroy that device. No matter what." While his words are meant for everyone, he looks straight into my eyes. Rescuing these Mentalists is important to everyone, but especially important to Elm. The way that he looks at me tells me in no uncertain terms that he is ready to die for this.

The thought is too hard for me to dwell on, so I simply reassure him. "No matter what."

"You know what that means, right?" Blake tells our group of three. "Don't focus on any of our teams—let us take care of you. Your group is the one that has to make it through."

We won't lose anyone. We can't. "Right, Blake." But do any of us really understand what this means? The deeper question comes to the surface. *Are you ready to give up everything for this? Are you ready to give up your life?*

"Ready when you are, Miss Ava."

"Okay. Just keep those shields strong."

We barrel full speed ahead toward the devices. As long as we have our shields, the Benefactors can't touch us, and it's easy to feel invincible. But knowing we have to go unshielded when it's time to attack the device isn't comforting. Hopefully our combined efforts will be enough to keep everyone safe.

We're almost close enough. Some of the Benefactors are now charging toward us, discarding their weapons. Attacking us in close combat won't do them any good either. They still won't be able to get through our barrier.

In a flash, Elm's group loses their shield.

I stop, the rest of my group stopping with me. "What happened?"

"Keep going!" Blanca shouts. "Don't worry about us!"

But it's impossible not to worry. All of the fire from the Benefactors redirects to focus on our unprotected friends.

"We have to keep going, Ava!" Nikki's voice is pitched with worry.

No matter what.

That's what we agreed to.

I can't.

My resolve falters. I try not to look back, but it's impossible to resist. My friends are back there, and I can't just abandon them. We can block the fire until they get their shield back up. We can wait.

And then it happens. A red beam flies straight toward Elm. The world moves in slow motion as it goes straight through his chest.

No.

No.

This can't be happening.

I scream, and our shield goes down at once, knocking Jazz and Nikki to the ground with the sudden change of momentum.

"Ava!" Nikki's cry barely registers. "We have to get to that device! Remember what Elm wanted!"

Elm's words echo: *No matter what.* But this was the one *what* I really wasn't prepared for. I can't do it. I'm not strong enough for that.

I race toward Elm as the crimson gushes from his wound. He gasps, clutching his chest, as he falls to the ground. A beam hits my leg, but I keep moving, numb to the pain.

"Jazz!" I scream, trying to find the words. "Please!" I can't heal Elm alone.

But as I turn back to beg Jazz to hurry, I see him on the ground too.

"Jazz!" Brie shouts for her brother just as a blue beam wraps around her and yanks her toward the base. Another grabs Samantha, and her cries haunt my ears as she shrieks for Elm, clawing at the ground as she's dragged away.

Elm isn't moving. His face is pale. I thrust my hands onto his wound and try to concentrate through the chaos around me. He feels colder than he should. My body shakes, and I can hardly see through my tears. I can't make my magic respond. I choke in air, trying to breathe. At last the healing spell begins, but the red stream does not still.

"Elm, please. Don't leave me."

If he doesn't respond soon, I'm going to have to make a choice. My friends are hurt. Being captured. I have to save the ones who are left if Elm is . . . if he . . .

There is a flutter of a white doctor's coat beside me. Dr. Iris? I look up, wiping my tears away with my sleeve so I can make out the face.

"Dr. Root?" My voice is shrill with surprise and then desperation. "Oh, Dr. Root, save him! Please!"

She sets to work at once. "Ava, I need you to help too. Every second counts here. His body is in shock from the pain. I need you to focus on that part. I will work on the wound."

"Okay. Thank you." My voice sounds small and helpless. I force myself to get a grip. He's going to be fine. He has to be.

My mind is reeling. "Why are you here? How did—"

"No conversation. Not now."

I close my mouth and focus on my healing spell, imagining the nerve endings and sensory receptors. Flowing renewing energy to them. I lean my cheek down near Elm's mouth, and I feel the faintest breath. We weren't too late. Not yet.

I continue to work alongside Dr. Root, shots still firing around us. I look up and see Dr. Iris at work on Jazz, who is starting to sit up. A new flow of tears begins in gratitude.

Suddenly, I'm aware of an even bigger surprise. There are people. Lots of them. Some of them in yellow clothing. This doesn't make any sense.

"Ava Locke."

I turn my head toward the voice. "Ivan?" To my surprise, he's smiling.

"You're gutsy, I'll give you that."

"No," I say. "I was stupid."

"More like desperate. And I'm sorry we put you in that position. We're here now."

"But how did you know where to find us?" I realize the answer as soon as the question is out of my mouth. "Marabell's tracker?" The device is still attached firmly to my shoe.

Ivan nods. "She gave the tracking access to Dr. Iris. As soon as she saw where you were headed, she came to us for help."

The whir of weapons firing around us has stopped. A dome of white light covers the area, and I see a line of Mentalists, Augmentors, and Shapers, arms outstretched, holding the magic strong. I look at them in awe. I didn't realize that multiple people could work together like that to form such a vast area of protection.

"We're safe for now." Ivan kneels down beside me, eying Elm. "Took a bad hit. But Dr. Root will get him in top shape." With relief working over me like antiseptic, my mind moves to other issues. "Those blue beams can grab onto objects and some of us were caught. We have to get them before something happens to them."

"Already on it," Ivan says. "Let my soldiers do their work. Now, if you'll excuse me." He rises and steps away, barking orders. The Benefactors won't know what to do with so many Mentalists. I would enjoy seeing that under different circumstances.

The color is returning to Elm's cheeks now, and no new blood is flowing. His breathing is becoming stronger.

"I think we're out of the woods." Dr. Root stands and pulls a wipe out of her medical bag to clean the blood from her hands. She gives one to me as well. "I trust you can take it from here, but if not, I'll be back. I'm going to do a quick sweep to make sure there are no more urgent injuries, and then I'll check to ensure Elm is doing well."

"Thank you so much." With the new help and knowing that Elm will recover, I can put energy into healing him more easily.

"Sarah!" Dr. Root calls as she hurries away. "Ava's leg, please!"

Sarah?

She appears beside me with a confident smile and looks like a whole new person in her short training coat. The Healer mentorship has done her wonders. "Let me help, Ava."

"Thank you," I manage. "Sarah, it's so good to see you." I'm so proud of her. She works quickly, healing my leg in no time at all.

"I have to go and help the others," she says, giving me a squeeze of encouragement. "Hang in there, Ava." She hurries away to find out where she's needed next.

"Ava!" Before I can turn, I am crushed in a gigantic hug.

"Ava! My sweet Ava."

"Mom?" I hold onto her tightly in disbelief and joy. I didn't realize how much I needed her until now. How much I needed both my mom and dad. My mother's arms are warm, and her perfume is soft and familiar. Even with everything going on around us, with a battle raging, I feel secure. I don't know what's going to happen next, but I know that I am truly loved.

A moment later my father joins us. This emotional reunion is the one we should have had the first time. The precious moment is short lived as Ivan returns.

He nods at my parents but addresses me. "We will destroy that device the way you all wanted. But in order to do that, we have to take this shield down. Are you ready?"

My parents release me, and I stand with resolve. "Let me do it. I want to be the one. If you can get me there, I'll destroy it." After everything I put my friends through, I want to be the one to take the first step in ending this.

"Allow me to join you?"

"Elm!" I fling my arms around his neck, kissing him with relief.

I hear my mom laugh. "I told you, Lucas."

Blushing, I peek at my father. He has a slight smile. "You and I are going to have a conversation, young man."

"With pleasure, Mr. Locke." Elm grins. My father winks at me.

I turn back to Elm. "I'm so glad you're alright. For a moment I thought . . ." I choke up. His hand caresses my face, and I take a deep breath. "How do you feel?"

He glances down at his bloodstained shirt. "Better than I look." And with that, a soft blue glow surrounds the fabric of his clothing and the stains disappear, the torn cloth magically mending.

"You're getting better and better at that," I say triumphantly. "I knew you would."

Ivan announces, "We just got word that Selene is on her way. It's time to move."

For good measure, I give Elm another round of healing. I want to be certain he's at his best. He's already given me so much.

"Ava!" Brie approaches, flanked by two of Ivan's soldiers. I am delighted to see her. "One of those crazy blue beams got me and was taking me away, but they saved me! People from Neo Prism are here! Did you see?"

"Yes. It's like a miracle! We're going to be okay." I give her the brightest smile I can muster. We still have a big task ahead of us, and I have no idea of the status of the rest of our group. "Do you know if everyone else made it?"

"They were getting Samantha. I think everyone else is doing alright. Dr. Iris healed Jazz, and now he's helping her with other injuries." She adds proudly, "Jazz is going to be one heck of a Healer."

Ivan's voice cuts through the air. "Let's *move*. Now!"

We advance on the Benefactors and the device, shielded by the White magic produced by Ivan's soldiers. But the moment will come when the shield will fall in order to attack. Once that moment arrives, every second is critical.

"We'll get you both in as close as we can. The rest is up to you."

"Thank you, Ivan," Elm says, and I start charging up my strengthening spell. A hundred yards away from the device, the shield comes down, and I sprint ahead, Elm right at my side. Soldiers fly into action around us to keep us safe and stave off attacks. Soon we're right in range of the device. I smash the orb's surface with all my strength, sending it shattering into thousands of shards.

The force field around the compound flickers away, and cheers erupt behind us.

"Well done, Miss Ava. Though, I do wish you had saved a piece for me," Elm teases.

"Sorry," I pant. "It's all yours next time."

"I'd far prefer there be no next time."

"Oh, I agree."

I catch a red blur, and at once I'm slammed viciously to the ground. I gasp.

Selene has pinned me down by the shoulders, her eyes wild with rage. "Always meddling. You never could keep your nose out of things."

I can hardly focus but manage a strengthening spell to force my way free, but she's stronger. She pushes downward, and the pressure sends sparks before my eyes. My shoulder bones threaten to break.

But then she stops. Stands. Spins and steps away from me and lies on the ground. Elm is concentrating on her with a look of revulsion.

I get to my feet and stand next to him, placing a hand on his arm. "Don't overexert yourself, Elm. You still have some recovering to do."

"I can exert myself for *this*, Miss Ava." His voice is hard.

Soldiers appear and seize Selene, dragging her to her feet. She stands like a doll, and I have to admit it's really unsettling to see her this way.

"Do you feel confident that you have her completely secure?" Elm asks them. "Because I'd like her to be aware of what's coming next."

38

IT'S APPARENT THE MOMENT ELM
releases Selene from his power. She at once begins struggling against those holding her. I forgot the extent of her strength. She gets an arm free and delivers a blow to one of the soldiers and knees another. She almost breaks loose, but more soldiers flock to us and are able to restrain her.

Suddenly Benefactors are advancing in a swarm. Elm directs his focus to them, and at least a quarter of the group freezes. Taking Elm's lead, other Mentalists join in and halt the Benefactors. I focus on one Benefactor trying to sneak in on our right. *Stop running. It's over.* He slows to a walk, looking confused, and I push my suggestion stronger. *STOP.*

He does, and satisfaction wells within me. I may not have been able to freeze a whole group like the others, but I'm making progress.

Selene stares around stunned, realizing no more help is coming her way. She's at the mercy of her captors. The atmosphere becomes heavy with an eerie quiet. Everyone eyes Selene under the overcast sky, the chill in the wind more pronounced.

Selene lets out a bitter chuckle. "So . . . Mentalists enter our borders and immediately begin taking over the minds of our people." She tilts her head as she gives Elm a cruel smile. "Tell me, how does it feel to prove me right?"

Elm laughs, and the sound echoes through the air. "It's really quite amusing. Your fear is your downfall. In your desire to stomp out anything to do with Yellow magic—except for anything that benefits you, of course—you've made your people vulnerable and weak against the very magic you're fighting against."

Selene's face contorts as Elm indicates her frozen lackeys. "Look at them. Useless. You could have taught them ways to defend themselves, but instead they don't have the slightest idea how to buffer our power. Did you even know, Selene, that Yellow magic can be defended against?"

Selene's voice is steely, but her eyes are fearful. "There would be no need to defend against it if it didn't exist at all."

"Then wipe us *all* out," Elm dares. "You don't get to pick and choose, using some Yellow magic to your advantage and stomping out the rest. It's all or nothing."

"Insipid hypocrite." Ivan's scoffing voice joins in.

"Me?" Selene's eyes flash at him. "Look at how you've been holed up, Ivan. Letting your people rot while you stay sheltered in your utopia. You're no better."

So, Selene *is* aware of some of what goes on outside the barrier. With how close of a watch Ivan kept on Selene, it only makes sense she would be doing the same.

Ivan brings his face down to Selene's eye level. "I never tried to commit genocide. I'm not innocent, but at least in my utopia, everyone is allowed. I'm not like you."

"Tell yourself that if it lets you sleep at night."

Ivan looks as though he wants to throttle her, but instead he straightens. "You will be taken back to Neo Prism and tried for your crimes. I suspect the punishment will be . . . harsh."

Selene raises her voice. "Look around you. Look at this.

Do you really think a power that does this can be good? Can it really be anything but evil?"

I think about the times Yellow magic has been used to create beauty. To entertain and to dazzle. To take people's minds off of the things that seem too hard to bear. The way it can be used to lift others up. "Just minutes ago Elm was almost killed by Red magic," I say. "Friends were dragged away with Blue magic. Every power can be used for good or evil, not just Yellow."

"The Mentalists will never be good. It's not who they are at the core." The contortion of Selene's face tells me she believes every word she's saying.

There are angry murmurs around us. But with the barrier up around so much of Magus still, Selene's words could very well be taking root and already spreading doubt.

I notice Elm watching me out of the corner of my eye. He gives me a slight nod. I brace myself for what I'm about to do, knowing it's necessary.

"Enough of this." I step in front of Selene. "Let us in the building."

"No."

Gutsy of her when she's being restrained on the ground, outnumbered. In spite of everything, I still feel conflicted at seeing her this way. This woman who was my pillar for so many years. Memories echo through me, and I feel a taste of her pain again.

"Let us in the building," I say, "or I'll *make* you." The words send a sick feeling to my stomach, but I keep my expression firm.

Selene releases a sharp laugh. "Make me? And just how, little Ava, will you do that?"

"You know what I mean. I might not be able to do it myself, but I'll have plenty of help."

I see the realization hit her. The thing she's most afraid

of—being controlled. To drive the point home, I focus, willing with all that I am. If nothing else, those connections to her memories make this easier. But we are both awake, and she is aware of what I'm doing. Her arm shoots up, erratically and strained, but nevertheless, it moves.

She stares in horror at her arm, raised against her will. "All right," she snaps. "I'll let you in. Stay out of my mind. Get out right now!"

I return her arm to her, not that it's of any use. She's still being restrained physically. I wish we had some of those magic absorbing cuffs, but even if she did try to use her power, it wouldn't do her any good. She's flanked on all sides, and she must know someone would seize control of her mind the instant she made a break for it.

We march to the heavy metal doors of the building, a strange lot of students and citizens of Neo Prism. A group of Benefactor guards have halted, eyes narrowed, but Selene waves them on. They pause.

"Are you incapable of following orders? Let us pass."

Still hesitating, they reluctantly move aside and let us continue on. We may have to worry about them later, but now we're too close to our goal for me to care.

"Take us to the other Mentalists, Selene," Elm says.

"Where are you keeping them?" I demand.

"What makes you think there are Mentalists here?"

"Don't play dumb," Ivan snarls. "We're getting what we came for one way or another."

Her shoulders slump just slightly. "We continue down this hall and then to the right."

"Guards up, everyone." Ivan narrows his eyes at Selene. "In case, like usual, she's lying."

We turn the corner and find another set of heavy automatic doors, this time with a keypad outside.

"Tell me the code," I say, my hand already hovering over the pad.

"Even with the code, it won't open for you. I have to do it." I turn. "Let her go so she can enter the code."

"Should you try anything," Elm says in a silky voice as the soldiers release Selene. "I'll be happily standing by to make you my puppet. Believe me, I think it's high time you had a chance to see what that feels like."

Are her hands shaking? Is she at last feeling the weight of her choices and recognizing that she's at the mercy of those she hurt?

She pauses again. "When we go in, it shouldn't be all of us at once. For their safety, and so they won't be afraid."

Ivan scoffs. "Nice try."

"I know when I've met my match, Ivan. I'm telling you the absolute truth."

Strangely, I believe her. She's genuinely scared of what might be done to her. I think she's trying to make it clear she's not responsible if something goes wrong.

"I think she's telling the truth." I glance at Elm. "Elm and I will go with her." Elm motions everybody to stand by. "No more stalling, Selene. Get us into that room."

Selene quickly punches a code into the keypad, and a blue light scans her handprint. The door opens, and Elm and I follow her through.

Behind the door is . . . another door? We stand in a tiny breezeway. This door is just a standard door. No security pad. Not heavy metal. A normal, white door with a pretty silver handle. What is this?

I spin around to the *whoosh* of the security doors closing behind us. I realize nobody else will be able to come in after us if needed. Were we tricked?

"I'm observing your every move, Selene," Elm warns grimly.

She motions to the doorway. "Well? Go on. This is what you wanted so desperately."

Elm and I pause outside the white door. I'm afraid of what we might find inside. Horrors. Weakened prisoners. Moans of pain. Tortured, lifeless bodies. I shiver. Elm's face looks a shade paler. I'm not sure I'm ready to see the gruesome ways these Mentalists have been held captive, but we're here for their release.

"Shall we do it together?" Elm asks, sounding less confident than usual.

I place my hand on the doorknob, and Elm places his hand over mine. I hold my breath as we turn the knob and swing the door open slowly.

My eyes blink in confusion at the sight before me. This is none of the things I expected. I wasn't prepared for this.

Children.

Hundreds upon hundreds of happy, healthy children.

Acknowledgments

HERE WE ARE AT THE END OF ANOTHER chapter in Elm and Ava's story! It has been truly heartwarming to see all the love for these characters, and I'm so happy to continue sharing them with you.

A big focus of this story is the strength that comes from being united. Teamwork is so important! On that note, it's so hard to even know where to begin my thank-yous because there are so many people working together to make this happen.

So many thanks go out to my Enclave family: To Steve Laube for being a publishing genius and blessing us all with your knowledge. My fantastic editor Lisa for untangling those sticky spots and always doing so with such compassion. Trissina for juggling a million and one balls and somehow managing not to drop any of them (You are amazing!). Jamie for such beautiful typesetting work and behind-the-scenes magic (and the skills to create incredible maps from my terrible, vague sketches!). Thank you all for putting countless hours into these books and for having so much faith in your authors.

To Jonathan, Steve, and Lisa at Oasis, thank you for everything you are doing to help Enclave grow and for allowing *Radiant* to shine as an audiobook! To Charmagne at Oasis, thank you for your great enthusiasm and your kindness. I love to see your excitement. Emilie, thank you for another stunning cover design. Your creative mind is brilliant, and I'm grateful you can take my choppy ideas and craft them into perfection. Megan, Katie, and Sarah—proofreaders and copy editor extraordinaire! Thank you so much not only for your work in polishing up the text, but also for your kindness. I'm so glad we met!

Thank you to my sweet husband Chris for continuing to support me through this journey and for being excited with me through every stage. I love you! Thank you to my precious children for sacrificing some mommy time for "book stuff." Books are fun, but you're still the best things I've ever made.

Many, many thanks to my parents, who show more support than any daughter could ask for. Your excitement for my publishing career makes me smile. You've made so many sacrifices to support me, including that trek to Realm Makers! I love you so much. Thanks to my in-laws for helping with the kiddos so I could get my edits done. It really takes a village.

Thanks to my purple-shirt crew Chantel, Sara, and Hannah for being my cheerleading squad (and especially Hannah for not killing me over the cliffhanger. You know you need me alive for book three!). To author friends Candice Yamnitz and Jennifer Burrows for sympathizing with me and providing so much support. Thanks to Jessica Guernsey for chatting about the series with me and making me laugh! Thank you to my street team members for being absolute rockstars.

Thank you to my fellow Enclave authors for being so supportive and welcoming. Especially Sara Ella, Cathy McCrumb, Morgan Busse, and Jasmine Fischer. You have been so encouraging and true examples of kindness. I'm happy to work alongside such amazing talent!

Thank you to each person who loves this series and shares it with everyone they know! To name a few, Jane Maree (Your Elm reel still makes me smile!), Drew Taylor, Eva Muhlenkamp, Carla Verdoni (at the best dentist's office ever!), Erin Phillips,

Victoria Lynn, Callie McLay . . . I could keep naming for pages and pages, and I would still probably forget someone. Just know that if you have ever told a friend about the Color Theory series, I'm so grateful. THANK YOU! To each person reading these pages, it's such a pleasure to craft these stories for you, and I'm so honored you picked up this book.

Last but certainly not least, this year has been full of many new adventures and challenges for me, and at times, it was a struggle to get the work done. I'm grateful for my Savior who understands my trials and my heart who bore more than I will ever have to, just because He loves me.

On to the next adventure!

About the Author

ASHLEY BUSTAMANTE (AUTHOR OF *A Lamb and a Llama*) has been creating stories from almost the moment she could write. She never considered writing as a profession when she was young because it was just something that was always there.

Ashley strives to create stories with positive messages that encourage others to come together.

She enjoys participating in the writing community and hopes to nurture other writers in the way she was nurtured by so many throughout her youth.

When not running through lines of dialogue in her mind, Ashley enjoys taking photographs and spending time with her husband, three children, and any furry, feathered, or scaly creature she can find. She is happy to connect with other writers and readers at ashleybustamante.com.

  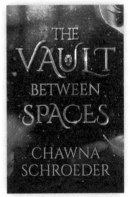